MW00876849

THOMAS FINCHAM

A KILLER'S STORM

A JO PULLINGER NOVEL

A Killer's Storm © Thomas Fincham 2023

ALL RIGHTS RESERVED, including the right to reproduce this work or portions thereof, in any form.

This is a work of fiction. Names, characters, places and incidents either are products of the author's imagination or are used fictitiously. Any resemblance to actual events or locales or persons, living or dead, is entirely coincidental.

Visit the author's website:

www.finchambooks.com
Contact:
contact@finchambooks.com

Jo Pullinger Series

A Killer's Heart

A Killer's Mind

A Killer's Soul

A Killer's Shadow

Contents

PROLOGUE

The hunter pursued his prey through the night. He drove along familiar streets, following a distant set of taillights. Sometimes, he lost sight of them around a bend. The hunter didn't worry. He knew whose car it was. He knew where they were going.

His headlights were turned off to hide his presence. It was lucky that the course was mostly downhill. It meant he could coast along without accelerating much. Without making any extra noise.

His three passengers whispered amongst themselves.

"Do you think we can get him?"

"He'll probably have a gun with him."

"We'll just have to be quick. We can't fail. This is our fate, right?"

The hunter took a tight curve. There was ice on the road, and he began to lose traction. He was afraid. Not of sliding off the road, but of alerting his prey. He tapped the gas pedal twice. The old engine groaned. The tires spun, biting down through the powdery snow and the sheen of ice below it.

With a lurch, the car straightened out and continued on its way.

"Do you think they heard us?" someone asked.

The hunter shook his head. The taillights ahead of them continued receding into the distance, headed down a residential road. They had no reason to suspect they were being followed.

The car pulled into the driveway of a house. It was set far apart from its neighbors, separated from them by dense strands of trees. The driveway was long, but the car had parked right in the mouth of it, close to the road.

Inside, the two passengers were impatient. The hunter could already see their silhouettes coming together, kissing. Their hands running tentatively over one another. Even if he turned on his high beams, the hunter doubted they would pay much attention.

Perhaps that was a foolish idea, though. After all, one of the people in the car had extensive training and was capable of defending himself.

The hunter drove past the house. He stopped three driveways down. He and his three passengers got out, lingering in the frosty moonlight.

"Everything up to this point has been just talk," he said. "This is where we jump to the next level. This is where everything we've been talking about becomes real. The point of no return. If anyone wants to back out, this is your last chance."

He looked at his fellow disciples. Nothing but stoic gazes were returned to him. He felt confident.

"Then let's do it," he said. "Act fast. Strike decisively. No room for fear or doubt."

He headed down the road on foot, and his people followed.

The man and woman in the car were still making out. They were being much less shy now. The man's face was buried in the woman's neck, and her eyes were closed. That was good.

They would need to deal with the man first. The hunter ripped open the passenger door. As the man turned, yelling out with surprise, the hunter slammed a fist into his face. The blow landed on his right eye with crushing force, and it started to swell and bruise instantly.

The man's head rolled back as if fading into unconsciousness. But there was enough life left in him to struggle a bit as the hunter dragged him out onto the ground. The man kicked and punched halfheartedly.

The woman screamed only once. Then she shut up. She looked around at her attackers and submitted herself to them, letting them tie her wrists together with rope. Everything was going according to plan.

"He's waking up," a disciple warned.

The hunter kicked the man in the side of the head. His feeble stirrings ceased, and he fell limp, fully knocked out.

One of the other disciples crouched beside him, reaching into his pocket. "Let's hope he didn't leave it behind. I want to see it with my own eyes and know we got the right guy."

His face scrunched up with concentration as he searched the man's pockets. Then he smiled as he pulled something out. It looked like a black leather wallet at first, and then the disciple flipped it open.

Inside was a golden shield. An eagle with spreading wings jutted out of the top.

It was an FBI agent's shield.

The hunter grinned. "Now we've done it. Father's going to be pleased."

ONE

A Day Before

"There's a thin line between relaxation and boredom," Agent Ian McKinley said with a sigh.

Jo Pullinger looked over at him. He was languishing in his chair. His thin arms were hanging off to either side, almost touching the floor. Both feet were up on his desk, crossed at the ankles. He was fidgeting, causing his dual monitors to wobble back and forth.

"You're at work," Jo said. "You're not supposed to be relaxing. Being bored, on the other hand... well, that's what we get paid to be."

"On a good day," McKinley added. "On a bad day, we get paid to be shot at. Hmm... I was thinking. Maybe I should start making another rubber band ball. What do you think?"

Jo smiled as she flipped through the file in front of her. It was a case she had already wrapped up. A man, going by the alias "Graff," had gone on a strange crime spree. It involved everything from bomb threats to an attempted kidnapping of Jo's own nephew.

Graff had even killed his own father. He had murdered a young woman from a running club he was part of. And he had done it all to get Jo's attention. There was no way she would ever let herself feel responsible for the creep's actions, but she'd be lying if she said the whole thing didn't disturb her.

She looked down at a photo of Graff. He was admittedly handsome, but there was something wrong with his eyes. Something inhuman.

What was it about me that could attract a man like that? she thought.

"Still looking at that case file?" McKinley pelted her with a paper-clip. "That's old news."

"Old news? We just arrested this guy a week ago," Jo replied.

McKinley shrugged. "A lot can happen in a week."

"Not this week. We've spent the whole thing doing paperwork."

"Yeah. And there was that time I microwaved my frozen burrito too long, and it exploded. Remember that?"

Jo sighed. "How could I forget."

She stared down at Graff's photo again, her mind wandering through a dark mental landscape.

"Hey." McKinley brought his feet down with a thud. He snapped his fingers. "Graff's been taken care of. You can move on now. On to the next case."

"You're right," Jo agreed. "Just let me know when one comes in."

"I'll do that, don't worry." McKinley opened his drawer and pulled out a canister of rubber bands. "Guess I should get started."

A ding issued from under the pile of papers on Jo's desk. She slid Graff's file away and shifted other pages around until she found her phone. A new photo had arrived from her brother Sam. It showed him and the family on a beach. Kim, his wife, was a beautiful African American woman with amazing cooking skills. And then there was Chrissy, their young daughter and the light of Jo's life.

Baby Jackson was cradled in his mother's arms. She was holding him tight, close to her heart. She had nearly lost her son when Graff broke into the family's house. It would be difficult for her to ever let him go again.

"A new picture from the clan?" McKinley asked.

Jo nodded. "I'd give anything to be there with them right now."

McKinley waved a hand. "You've got a nice Seattle winter to look forward to. What's not to love about nonstop rain?"

He chuckled to himself. He had a few rubber bands in his hands, and he was balling them up tight. When they were mashed together, he took more rubber bands and started wrapping them around the wad he had formed.

His fingers slipped. One of the rubber bands pinged away, bouncing off the broad chest of an imposing man who was walking toward the two agents.

"Ian," boomed Robert Grantham, the Special Agent in Charge at the Seattle field office. "You're making another one of those balls?"

"No, sir!" McKinley shoved the canister back into his desk. "I mean, yes, sir. Jo's niece, uh, asked for one. For Christmas."

"Is that true, Pullinger?" asked Grantham.

"Not at all, sir," she replied. "McKinley's just bored out of his mind. Maybe you could give him meter-maid duty to keep him occupied."

"Very funny," McKinley groaned.

Grantham rubbed his chin. "It would be funny to see him in one of those vests. But I actually have a job for you two. Follow me to my office, and I'll give you the details."

TWO

They followed Grantham. He led them toward his office at first, but he suddenly veered off. Into the break room.

"Either of you need a coffee?" he asked, filling a cup from one of the dispensers. He pushed down on a button, allowing the dark, steaming liquid to bubble out.

McKinley grabbed a cup and was right behind him. As Grantham was stirring cream into his coffee, McKinley took several large sips from his own, then quickly got a refill.

"Isn't that hot?" Grantham asked. "You must have blisters on your tongue now, McKinley."

"You get used to it after a while, sir," McKinley replied.

Grantham looked vaguely disturbed. He noticed a box of donuts and put a raspberry-filled one on a plate. "You know, you have to prove that you're fit and healthy to become an FBI field agent. So, naturally, we stock our break rooms with plenty of pastries. Who wants one? Come on, don't make me pig out all on my own."

He grinned at both his agents. They shook their heads politely.

"Ah, come on," he goaded. "McKinley, you're like a beanpole. If you want to get more action, you should beef up. Pullinger, are you still on that health kick? Still running and all that? Then you can just burn your donut off later. Come on," he repeated.

Jo narrowed her eyes. "Sir... is everything okay?"

"Yes, of course, it is," he replied with a grunt. "We finally got that Graff guy, and now I'm able to sleep a full six hours each night instead of five. And the urge to drink myself into oblivion has disappeared."

"I didn't realize the case affected you so much," Jo said.

"There's probably a lot you don't know, Pullinger. That's by design. It helps you focus on what matters. I've got my wife to look after me. I will tell you this, though." Grantham let out a sigh. It was the closest thing to a complaint Jo had ever heard from her boss. "I am going to miss you two."

Jo looked at McKinley. He stared back at her, his eyes wide with alarm.

"Sir," he protested. "Miss us? What does that mean?"

Grantham picked up his donut and coffee. "Come with me, and I'll tell you."

This time he took them straight to his office. They all sat down. McKinley had his coffee half finished before Grantham could even open his mouth.

"While you two have been slacking off out here, making paper airplanes and rubber band balls and whatever else, I've been on the phone with a colleague. A man named Alton Pierce. Either of you know who that is?"

Jo shook her head. McKinley had the answer.

"He's the SAC at the Boise office," he said.

Grantham nodded. "Good guy, Alton. Very good agent. Not a lot of crime in Idaho, as I'm sure you're both aware. It ranks in the top ten safest states. Alton's had one hell of a career, and transferring to Boise was as close as he'll get to retirement, I think. But that's beside the point. Alton's got a slight problem over there. Care to guess?"

"Are you stalling, sir?" Jo asked.

"Just take a stab, Pullinger. I want to check your instincts."

"Well..." She searched her mind for anything she might have heard about the Boise office. She came up empty. "Maybe they're dealing with a higher-profile crime than they're used to. They need some more experienced agents to come over and lend a hand."

"That was going to be my guess, too," McKinley added.

"You're both very close to being right. It was a hard call for Alton to make. A few of his top agents were caught performing certain extracurricular activities. It's an ongoing situation, so he couldn't give me all the details. But it's something to do with drug trafficking. His agents are in deep trouble. And now there are gaps in the ranks, and I'm sending you to fill them."

THREE

"I don't want to go to Boise, sir," McKinley said. "I like it here."

"My family's here in Seattle," Jo added. "That's the main reason I picked this post in the first place."

"Relax, you two." Grantham took a bite out of his donut, looking at them like they were crazy. "You're not being transferred. It's a temporary thing. Alton already has his replacements picked out, but one of them needs to wrap up the case she's working on. You two will work in Boise until that happens. More for a morale boost than anything. You probably won't even have a caseload. Should be less than a week."

McKinley breathed a sigh of relief, though his leg was still bouncing a mile a minute. Probably from the constant caffeine intake, Jo thought.

"Sir," said McKinley, "you said you were going to miss us."

Grantham spread his hands. "And I am! Seeing your faces is the highlight of every morning here."

McKinley rolled his eyes.

Jo laughed. "Sir, just tell us when we leave."

"Hmm." He checked his watch. "Right now. As soon as possible."

McKinley jumped to his feet, rushing toward the door. Jo grabbed him by the sleeve and pulled him straight back into his chair.

"We have some questions first, sir," Jo said. "I don't think waiting a few more minutes is going to do much damage."

"Not at all," said Grantham. "Ask away."

"Why us?" Jo asked. "There's a second field office in Idaho, isn't there?"

"In Pocatello," Grantham confirmed.

McKinley got on board with Jo's line of questioning. "Pocatello's a small place. Less than a tenth of the population of Seattle. Not much going on there. Not to mention it's way closer to Boise than we are. I'm sure they could spare an agent or two for a week."

Grantham shrugged. "They could. Alton originally just called me for advice. Grabbing someone from Pocatello was his initial idea, but I nixed it. Why kill one bird with a stone when you can kill two?"

McKinley smirked. "I knew it. You're completely sick of us. We just cause too much trouble."

Grantham let out a huff like an angry grizzly bear. "You wanted more field experience, McKinley. It's not much, but it's something. And Jo... as much as the Graff case hit me, I know it hit you a thousand times harder. We FBI agents like to pretend that we're machines, incapable of getting tired and worn out. But it isn't true. You need a break. This is a nice, easy assignment. One more surprise for you. You know, I talked about killing two birds, but..."

He held up three fingers.

"Three birds?" McKinley exclaimed. "That's asking a lot of your throwing skills, sir. No offense."

"Don't be a smartass," their boss grumped. "One of Alton's picks has agreed to the transfer. You're going to drive him to Boise. Yes, I said *drive*, not fly. I understand it's inefficient and time-consuming... which is the point. A nice little road trip to let you both decompress."

He shoved the rest of his donut into his mouth, chasing it with a gulp of coffee.

"Three days," he said, keeping the same three fingers up. "That's how long you have to reach Boise. Maximum. It's better if you get there in two, of course. There will be a car waiting for you outside, so no need to worry about that. I suggest you get moving. And make sure to stock up on road trip snacks."

FOUR

Jo and McKinley walked back toward their desks. McKinley was clearly in a state of shock. He didn't even go back to the break room for more coffee.

"Does he really think all we do is make paper airplanes all day?" McKinley shook his head.

His eyes took on a glazed appearance. Idly, his hands wandered to a stack of forms on his desk. He grabbed the top sheet and almost began to fold it before realizing what he was doing.

"Hey, I'm good at making them," he grumbled. "When you're good at something, you should never stop doing it."

"I didn't say anything." Jo sat down and checked her emails. "Nothing about the agent we're supposed to be transferring. Maybe they're going to meet us at the car."

Jo logged off and shut her computer down. McKinley was busy getting his own things in order. Unlike most of the agents around the office, who used desktop computers, his was a laptop. It connected to a dock, which linked it to the monitor and other peripherals. He removed the laptop from the dock and slid it into a backpack.

"I've already got a spare charger in here," he said, patting his bag.

"You've been ready for this," Jo remarked, nodding her approval. "But seriously, where's this agent?"

She looked around. Her eyes landed on a man who was striding toward them.

Edward Swann was a relatively new face around the Seattle office. The first time Jo met him, she'd had a hard time peeling her eyes away. He was very good-looking. But whenever she spotted him now, she couldn't stop a chill from crawling down her back.

His eyes were warm and friendly. But other than that, he looked a lot like Graff. They were about the same height and build and around the same age. And both of them admired Jo Pullinger.

The coincidences had added up to an uncomfortable moment when Jo suspected Swann and Graff were the same man. Even though she knew now that they weren't, part of her mind had a hard time accepting it.

"What are you two chatting about over here?" Swann asked. He had a suit jacket slung over one shoulder and a travel cup in the other hand.

"We're on our way to Boise," Jo told him, still staring at her blank computer screen.

"I know," Swann said.

"We're supposed to be bringing a transfer with us," McKinley added.

"I know that, too, because it's me," Swann replied. "I'm the transfer."

Jo looked over at him now. It all made sense, but she still hadn't seen it coming.

"You're leaving?" she asked.

"Don't act so surprised," Swann said. "Things haven't gone very well for me here. It's partially my own fault. I still feel off-kilter from that whole mess involving you."

"Boise?" Jo said.

He nodded. "Boise."

She smiled. "I think that'll be good for you, Swann. You told me you came here from L.A. looking for a place where you could actually make a difference. Maybe Boise can be that place."

"That's the goal." Swann sighed, casting a wistful look around the office. "Seattle definitely isn't it. I'll kind of miss it here, but not as much as I would have thought."

McKinley patted him on the arm. "Hey, it's never too late to get a fresh start."

"Again," Swann added. "I guess there are no limits to the number of fresh starts a guy can have."

"Just don't have too many and burn through *all* the field offices," Jo told him. "Then you'd have to get a job with the CIA or something."

Swann wrinkled his nose. "You don't have to swear at me on my last day here. By the way, I forgot to turn my keys in for my apartment. So I'll need to do that."

"I should grab some things from my place, too," McKinley said.

"Well, since everyone's doing it," Jo said. "I wasn't planning on a road trip today, so I didn't bring, you know, *anything* with me. Let's all meet back here in half an hour. Then we'll head for Boise."

FIVE

Edward Swann barely knew who he was.

Some people said you could tell a lot about a person by looking at their home. What kind of decorations they had. What kind of books they read. The pictures of their family.

Other people said you could tell much about a person based on their friends.

Swann stood in the doorway of his Seattle apartment and took a good long look. Not at the empty rooms in front of him but at the turmoil inside.

He didn't have anything in his home, to begin with. What few items he brought with him had already been boxed up and sent to the Boise office. Everything else, like the cheap furniture, he'd left by the dumpsters. Scavengers could have it, or the trash collectors. He didn't care.

So, that got rid of one way of telling what kind of person he was.

As far as friends... he didn't have any.

The closest thing he got to a friendship was with Jo. And she could barely look him in the eye.

He didn't even know why he was here, inside his old place. He already had his keys with him. He could have gone straight to the building's office. Dropped them through the mail slot. Walked away and never looked back, not even in memory.

Instead, he shut the door behind him. He didn't walk inside. He stayed on the tiny patch of linoleum where he used to kick off his shoes when he got home from work.

Swann took out his FBI identification folder. He flipped it open. The golden shield was highly polished, reflecting light into his eyes. A glorious sight. It still inspired awe in him. But right now, he felt like a phony. Instead of fulfilling his dream legitimately, he felt like he had somehow tricked the academy into letting him skate through.

What kind of agent are you? he thought.

Jo had saved him from Graff. The guy had been *this* close to jabbing a needle full of a toxic substance into Swann's neck. He didn't see it coming. Worse, he didn't even think it was worth it for Jo to save him. He had caused nothing but problems in his short time in Seattle.

It didn't feel right to carry the FBI shield. But he was still going to give it one more shot. If things went bad in Boise the way they had gone bad in L.A. and Seattle, he'd just have to admit he wasn't meant to be an agent.

And he'd quit forever.

He thought about kissing the shield for good luck. Instead, he just rubbed it a bit and put it away.

"Don't mess this up," he whispered to himself.

He left the apartment and tried to forget everything about it.

***

Miles away, Jo Pullinger was having a much more chaotic time at her own residence.

She went tearing through like a tornado, trying to find everything she needed. She wasn't much of a girly girl, but there was still a surprising amount of junk a woman was required to carry. A brush, a comb. Hair-ties. Hygiene products. She even grabbed a bit of eye makeup. It helped a lot to hide sleep deprivation. A common ailment among field agents.

She also wanted enough clothes to last her at least a week in case she couldn't find a place to wash them. The extra change of clothes would come in handy.

It took much longer than she thought to gather all her stuff up. She had to wonder how someone who spent so little time at home could still manage to turn it into a disorganized mess.

"I'll be back," she told the silent apartment as she stepped out the door. Unlike Swann, she didn't want to forget the place. She liked her bed. The pillowcase was one Kim had given her when she moved out. It still smelled a bit like the detergent she used.

Jo tossed her overloaded bag into the trunk. She jumped into the driver's seat and drove away.

It was time for yet another new adventure.

***

"I guess there's nothing much to worry about," McKinley muttered to himself.

He was staring into his refrigerator. He had been worried there was some food that might go bad during his absence. There wasn't. The only things inside were a bottle of salad dressing, a few non-alcoholic beers, and a box of baking soda. To absorb smells.

The fridge smelled like death when he first moved in. McKinley wasn't a fan of odd smells. He hated them slightly more than the average person.

All in all, there wasn't much to bring. Mostly because he didn't have much. He grabbed three of everything. Three shirts, pairs of pants, pairs of underwear, and socks.

He thought that was more than enough. If he found he needed something else...

"I'm sure they have stores in Boise."

He headed back to the field office. For the first time since his brother died, McKinley felt a true sense of glee.

SIX

"Are we there yet?" groaned Swann from the backseat.

Jo craned her head forward to read the sign that was flashing past above them. "We're about to merge onto 90 East toward Bellevue. Which means we're about one percent of the way getting close."

"It's just too bad we couldn't stop at the pinball museum," McKinley said, watching Seattle fade in the passenger side mirror. "Maybe on the way back."

"I won't be coming back," Swann reminded him. "And I don't think Jo is that big of a dork."

Jo grinned. "You'd be surprised. But I'm more of a skee-ball girl."

"Skee-ball is pretty fun," Swann admitted. "I'm pretty good at it. I can usually sink it in the hundred-point hole about half the time."

"Yeah, right," Jo snorted. She threw her blinker on, merging left. They followed a sharp curve left, right, and left again before straightening out. "If we have time in Boise, I think I'll challenge you."

She glanced in the mirror at Swann. He was smiling.

"We should do that," he said.

McKinley pointed through the windshield. "Guys, check it out! We're about to cross Lake Washington. The most scenic driving in

Seattle. This is the Lacey V. Murrow Memorial Bridge. And if you look ahead... huh."

Jo followed his gaze. She saw nothing but a few fuzzy, distant tree-covered hills. Everything else was hidden by mist.

"Well, if it wasn't such a rotten day," McKinley added, "you could see all the way to the Cascade mountains."

"It's all right," Jo told him. "We'll probably see a lot of cool things on this drive. Idaho has plenty of mountains."

"Not the part where Boise is located," McKinley said. "But let's just find another way to pass the time. You guys ever play the sign game?"

"What's that?" Swann asked.

McKinley twisted around to look at him. "You'll be at a slight disadvantage in the back. But it goes like this. You start with the letter A. You have to find a word on a sign or a building that starts with that letter. And you go all the way to Z."

"I thought everyone knew that game," said Jo.

"Not quite," Swann replied. "Seems like a bad place to start, though. We are on a bridge in the middle of a huge lake."

It got worse.

Almost immediately upon reaching Mercer Island, they drove into a long tunnel where there was even less to look at. When they came out, the sun had finally broken free from its cloud cover. The light stung Jo and McKinley's eyes, making them blink.

"77th Ave! That's an A word," Swann announced.

McKinley blinked again and looked. "Yup. You got that one. Beginner's luck."

***

The car Grantham had provided them drove like a dream. It handled well and was quiet. The only problem was it ran almost too smoothly. Jo kept accidentally accelerating way above the speed limit. Every time she noticed, she cursed and made herself slow back down.

"Hey, if we get pulled over," said McKinley with a grin, "just let me do the talking. I happen to know the Special Agent in Charge at our local FBI office."

The sign game continued into the afternoon. All three proved to be awful at it. After driving past Bellevue, they entered more rural terrain. Soon, they were moving through Snoqualmie Pass and were well into the mountains. Dense pine forest surrounded them, sprawling across the vast foothills.

They had reached the letter F and were at a total standstill for a while.

"Pretty out here," Swann commented. "Not a lot of signs, though."

McKinley nudged Jo. "His competitive side is coming out." He scanned a sign as they were passing it. "Cle Elum? Weird name for a town."

"It's someplace to stop," Swann suggested. "If you want to trade off, Jo."

She shook her head. "I'm good. I don't mind driving out here. It's kind of fun after dealing with Seattle traffic. And we still have a lot of gas."

"Uh-oh." McKinley pointed at another sign. A red one. "Road work ahead."

Jo pointed past it. "And what does that one say? I believe it says, 'Fines double in work zone.' That's an F for Jo, you losers. Is someone keeping score?"

"You never keep score," McKinley said. "It's just for fun. And now we're out of the F rut, so thank you. Let's move on."

The terrain flattened out. They could see much further into the distance now. And there were no G's in sight.

SEVEN

"Okay, got some stuff coming up," McKinley said. He was scrolling through the map on his phone. "Ellensburg is where we have to make the turn onto 82 and start heading south. There are some hotels there if you want to stop for the night."

"No," Jo mumbled, glancing at Swann in the rearview. "I'm good to keep driving. Get as far tonight as we can."

McKinley gave her a stern look. "Remember what Grantham said? This is only about an eight-hour drive, and we have two or three days to make it. We're supposed to be taking our time."

"Well, Grantham isn't the boss," Jo said. "All right, he actually *is* the boss. But this is me relaxing at my own pace."

"At seventy miles an hour?" said McKinley. "We're all hurtling through space at about eighteen miles a *second*. No need to rush."

Jo gave him a sideways glance. Hoping McKinley would catch her meaning. He noticed this time and nodded.

If it was just the two of them, McKinley and Jo, she could have relaxed more. Swann's presence had her on edge. She still didn't know whether she could rely on him as an agent. Whether he would have her back if things went south. She also didn't know whether to trust him as a man.

They were entering some interesting country. She wanted to see as much of it as she could before the sun went down. It was hard to pinpoint when it happened, but the terrain had changed dramatically. No more deep, dark valleys full of pine trees. No more brooding clouds of mist and constant drizzle.

They were in the badlands. It looked more like a desert the further they went. Nothing but rolling hills sparsely dotted with scrub grass. Everything looked yellow and dead.

Then it started snowing. Big, fluffy flakes fell, slowly burying everything.

McKinley checked his weather app. "Didn't see this on the radar. Must be some freak weather. Maybe we should think about stopping soon after all."

But Jo had no problem driving in the snow. If anything, it kept other people off the roads and gave her more space. She did drop her speed a bit, though. Reluctantly.

Her plan was to get to Boise as soon as possible. Get rid of Swann. Spend a few days like Grantham wanted, and then she could actually relax on the drive back to Seattle. Maybe she would even stop at the pinball museum that McKinley wanted to visit. One last hurrah for their "vacation" before it was back to their normal lives.

"Gibson Truck Wash." She pointed toward a business sign in the distance. "There's the G."

EIGHT

Night fell like a hammer. A smothering blanket thrown across the landscape by a vengeful deity. The land was immense and empty. Crisscrossed here and there by the feeble headlights of other motorists who were gone in an instant and forgotten.

On the road, you could pretend to be anyone. Or you could pretend to be no one. Jo let her mind drift somewhere between the two, imagining other lives. Maybe she was a waitress at a lonely highway diner. Or a truck driver piloting one of the big rigs that trundled past.

At times like these, it was easy to see the bright side of those other life paths. But Jo knew she was exactly where she was meant to be.

The snow continued to fall. The storm had started south of them. By the time they approached the Oregon border, there was a good six inches of accumulation. Swann was dozing in the backseat. McKinley had a white-knuckle grip on his door handle. Every time they hit a patch of snow that hadn't been plowed yet, he tensed up.

"Maybe time to stop now?" he suggested.

Jo nodded. "It's not getting much better out here, is it? Look ahead and see if you can find anything."

On his laptop, he pulled up a map and first searched Umatilla and Hermiston, two small towns just over the border. He got the same result at every hotel he called. Because of the storm, a lot of people were looking for rooms. They were fully booked.

"We could always wait at a rest area," Jo said.

McKinley gave her a disgusted look. "No. They have even worse coffee than most motels. I'll keep looking."

He looked further south. He chuckled at a place called Hinkle, then called the one motel in Stanfield.

"No vacancy," he said with a sigh.

"There'll be something," Jo encouraged him.

"The next decently-sized town is Pendleton," he said. "But maybe I'll look here..."

He stopped at a place on the map that barely counted as a blip. It had only one tiny hotel. When the receptionist picked up, he spoke with zero optimism.

"Yeah, we need two rooms. Preferably three. I know, with the storm and everything, it's kind of... you do? That's great. Thanks. We'll be there shortly. Yeah, go ahead and reserve them under 'McKinley.' Thanks again."

He hung up and grinned at Jo. "We've got three rooms at the Lapse Lodge."

"The what-who?" asked Jo.

"The Lapse Lodge. The premier and, well, *only* hotel in the small town of Lapse."

"Weird name for a town."

"Not as weird as Cle Elum."

"Still, it sounds a little creepy. Like we're going to roll up and realize everyone in town has been turned into a wax figure. Maybe stopping in a place called Lapse would count as a *lapse* in good judgment."

"I see what you did there," McKinley said. "It wasn't that funny, but I see what you did. They have three open rooms, and if we keep driving in this, we'll end up buried in a snow bank. So?"

"So we'll stop," Jo said, sighing. "Just tell me how to get there."

***

A man in a ski mask stood at the edge of a snow-covered parking lot. He was watching the hotel. Staring at the glowing window of the lobby. The OPEN sign was on. Below it, the word VACANCY glowed bright red. The word NO beside it was blacked out.

Now and then, the man caught a glimpse of the hotel clerk. Just a hint of her fluffy gray hair passing by.

He thought about his life. The one he used to have. It used to make perfect sense why he'd want to leave it behind. Now it seemed way too late to ever go back.

It was lucky he stood there as long as he did. If he had left even a minute earlier, he would have missed the car.

It was black and sleek. The kind of car you don't see often. And usually only in movies. The people who got out of it looked the same way. They were dressed in slacks and fancy shirts. Their shoes were polished and reflected the moonlight.

They were no ordinary travelers. The man in the ski mask crouched behind a snow bank and watched, trying to figure out who they could be. Some kind of cops, he thought. Maybe even FBI agents.

Why on Earth had they come to Lapse?

They're here for us, the man thought, his heart pounding. He took a deep breath. *Relax. We can use this to our advantage.*

He waited until the three travelers entered the lobby. Then he crept away, eager to let the others know.

NINE

84 South took the agents to the exit for Truman Road. The ramp was in a sorry state, and Jo ended up sliding down it. Not quite out of control, but close enough to it that McKinley let out a little shriek of fear.

"What's that?" Swann mumbled from the back. "What're you yelling about? Nothing's the matter..."

He went back to snoring before they even reached the bottom of the ramp.

They got to the flat road and turned right. Jo regained control. "Here we go. Like nothing ever happened. Are you sure this is the right place?"

"This is definitely the town of Lapse," McKinley replied. But he sounded skeptical.

Other than a farmhouse on the right, there was nothing here. Just endless fields filled with snow. And the occasional stand of trees to break up the monotony.

"Looks like a good place to dash through the snow in a one-horse open sleigh," Jo dryly quipped.

"Just keep going," McKinley told her. "Right around the corner, we should see something."

And so they did. The town of Lapse revealed itself. A collection of five or six roads in a tiny grid pattern. There was a train track on the right. After passing through a small residential area, they spotted a big wooden sign.

Welcome to Lapse – Established 1889.

Beside the sign was a strange life-sized cutout of a hunter in plaid holding a rifle. At first, Jo thought it was a real person. Some kind of weirdo standing there in the cold, holding perfectly still.

It gave her an eerie vibe. So did the rest of the town. It wasn't very late yet, only half past eight, and yet every house was completely dark. Most of them didn't even have porch lights on. The train tracks were filled with snow and looked abandoned. Even the hunter cutout had an odd look on his face. A sort of uncomfortable grimace.

The Lapse Lodge appeared on their left. Jo thought she saw someone standing out at the edge of the lot, but she didn't give it a second glance.

Probably a snowman.

She navigated the treacherous parking lot and slid to a stop.

"Not sure if this is a parking space," she said, "and we probably won't know until the spring thaw."

She and McKinley got out, their shoes sliding in the slush. Jo knocked on one of the back windows, and Swann stirred from his slumber. He got out slowly, stretching his long arms.

"Careful how high you reach. Your fingertips might get frozen," McKinley said. "It must be about ten degrees out here. Brrr!"

"It's a far cry from Los Angeles," Swann agreed, stifling a yawn.

Jo glanced toward the edge of the lot again. The figure she thought she saw was suddenly gone. Maybe it had been nothing at all, a trick of the light across a mound of snow.

She led the way into the lobby. It was warm and dry inside, replete with the smell of cloves. The aroma came from a half dozen spice-scented candles that were arranged across the desk. Unlit but still fragrant.

An elderly woman was sitting in an armchair behind the counter, reading a book. She set it aside and stood up, smiling at her guests.

"Welcome to the Lapse Lodge. You must be the McKinley party. I must say, you don't *look* related."

"We aren't, ma'am," Jo said. "I'm Jo. This is Ian and Edward."

"Ah!" The old woman's eyes lit up. "I happen to be reading a romance novel at the moment. The main character's two love interests are men named Ian and Edward. What are the odds?"

"As long as the main character isn't named Jo, I think I'll still be able to sleep tonight," Jo replied.

The elderly clerk laughed. "My name's Miriam, and I'll be glad to host you three kids. I only have six rooms at my hotel, but they're all empty at the moment. Very strange. Usually, I'm booked up all year, but things are different now..."

Miriam's eyes glazed over.

To smooth through this awkward moment, Jo pulled out her wallet and opened it, looking for a credit card to pay for the rooms.

McKinley cleared his throat. "We'll need a receipt, ma'am. As long as this doesn't exceed our per diem, we'll get a full reimbursement."

Miriam's eyes were focused again. She was staring at the FBI shield inside Jo's wallet. She looked up at Jo, and all the friendly warmth was gone from her.

But she didn't look angry. She looked scared. But it passed quickly. The old woman recovered and gave them another smile.

"Lovely," she said. "I'll make sure to get you a receipt, young man. I'll bet you three are hungry. There isn't any food here, but the diner is close by. And it's open until ten most nights."

TEN

Miriam had given them three rooms right next to one another. For the sake of privacy, Jo would normally have liked to be spaced out. But tonight, she was glad to be tucked in close to the other agents.

She would have liked to have the middle room, but McKinley happened to grab that key. Swann took the room on the end, leaving Jo with the room next to the lobby. It was still a nice, cozy spot.

They went into their rooms to put their things away.

Jo shut the door behind her, cutting off the chilly air. The first thing she did was turn the thermostat up a few degrees. Then she dropped her bag on the floor and made sure her phone and wallet were in her pockets.

This was an ordinary part of life in the FBI. Traveling. Sleeping in strange and sometimes sketchy motels across America. Going wherever cases took you, even if it was somewhere ugly.

Not that Lapse was ugly. On the surface, it seemed like a quaint little town. The type of place you wouldn't mind retiring to.

But that was the surface. Jo had barely scratched it so far, but she already didn't like what she was seeing.

She found a pair of gloves and a knit hat in her bag. She pulled them on and stepped out of her room. McKinley and Swann were already waiting for her.

"Let's eat!" McKinley said gleefully.

"Okay." Jo held out the keys. "You're driving."

McKinley hesitated, his eyes going wide. He had been issued a challenge, and he wasn't one to back down.

"Fine." He grabbed the keys. "I'll drive. Just don't complain to me if I get us all killed. I've never driven in snow before."

"You'll be fine. Look." Swann showed him the map of Lapse on his phone. "The diner's only a quarter mile from here."

"And it's not like there's any traffic," Jo added. "Is it just me, or does this town feel completely dead? And what was the deal with the look on Miriam's face when she saw my FBI shield?"

The two men just shrugged.

"Never mind," she said. "I'm starving. Let's go."

***

The diner turned out to be called just that. *The Diner*. It was in big, neon letters above the front door. It was indeed open until ten, going by the posted hours.

And it seemed to be the social hotspot for the whole town. Most of the tables were full. Not that there were many tables, but it was still a good turnout.

The three agents got some strange looks as they headed for their booth. Not as strange as the look Miriam gave them, though. These were just curious glances. A bunch of people who weren't used to seeing many strangers.

Their waitress was a gorgeous woman in her twenties. "My name's Carmen, and I'll be your waitress. Can I get you anything to drink?"

"Coffee," McKinley said. At a look from Jo, he added, "Decaf, please."

"I'll just have water," said Jo.

"Same for me," Swann added. "A glass of water."

"A nice, tall glass," Carmen replied, her eyes lingering on Swann. She walked away with a certain sway in her hips.

Swann watched her like a hawk.

"Calm down," Jo warned him. "She's just angling for a good tip. She sized you up as the person most likely to give her one."

"Yeah, I'm sure Swann will give her a good tip," McKinley chuckled.

"Don't be a child," Jo said.

"Why? Sometimes it's fun. Hey, look at this." McKinley pointed at a menu item. "This meal is called the 'Lapse in Judgment.' They stole your joke."

"What's in it?" Jo asked.

"A cheeseburger with four patties, an order of fries, and an order of onion rings. With two extra sides of your choice. Think of the leftovers. I could be picking at that thing for a week."

Their drinks arrived, delivered with flair by Carmen.

"So, what brings you three to Lapse?" she asked.

"Just passing through," Swann said. "We're with the FBI."

"Ooh, are you working a case?" Carmen asked.

"Something like that," Swann replied.

"That's so cool! Can I see your badge? We have a ten percent discount for law enforcement people, you know."

"In that case..." Swann pulled out his identification, giving the shield a quick flash.

Carmen looked like she'd just met the pope. She was very attentive for the rest of the meal. Their food arrived quickly and was pretty good. Better than the average diner fare. Less greasy, too.

Swann paid for the three of them. When the check arrived, he tucked his receipt into his pocket with a big smile on his face.

ELEVEN

Jo fell onto her bed and rested her hand on her belly. She was full of pot roast and mashed potatoes. The starch was flooding her bloodstream. Making her sleepy. Dampening her senses. Muffling her sense of alertness.

She left the bedside lamp turned on and stared at the ceiling. Listening to the progression of the night.

The walls of the hotel must have been well-insulated. At one point, she heard a surge of water. A shower turning on. A toilet flushing. But that was all.

She closed her eyes for a bit, drifting through a shallow dream. She never fell fully asleep, and she snapped awake ten minutes later. She'd never had much luck falling asleep in new places. Especially not in places like Lapse, Oregon, where everything felt slightly off.

Jo scooted up into a sitting position, wedging a pillow between her back and the headboard. There was a book in her bag, one she had been meaning to read for a while. She pulled it out now and cracked the spine.

"Oh, that's right," she muttered to herself. "I forgot this book was about a young couple getting stranded in a creepy little town. Maybe I'll just watch TV instead."

She was reaching for the remote when her phone rang, and she grabbed it instead. It was her brother Sam calling.

"Hello," she said brightly, sitting up a little higher. "How's everything going?"

"It's really great, Auntie Jo!" Chrissy's distorted voice cried in the background. "I got to pet a giraffe today."

"I'll interpret that for you," Sam added. "We went to a zoo, and Chrissy got to feed some lettuce to the giraffes. There was also some other weird animal. What was it called again?"

"A zebu," Kim's voice replied. "It's a type of cow."

"Yeah, a zebu!" Chrissy called out. "The horns were all crooked, and it had a big hump on its back. And all this hangy skin, too. It was very weird but cute."

"What was his name again, Chrissy?" Kim asked.

"His name was Rodney!"

"Yup. Rodney." Kim laughed.

"Anyway," Sam said, "the reception here is kind of spotty, so don't be too alarmed if the call drops. How's everything in Seattle? Is the weather terrible?"

"I'm sure it is," said Jo. "But I'm not there. Had to drive to Boise for work. Right now, I'm lying in a hotel room in a town called Lapse."

"Never heard of it."

"Neither had I. But that's where I am. In case I go missing."

"Are there any weird animals there, Auntie Jo?"

"Not so far, Chrissy. But I'll be sure to give you a full rundown the next time I see you. How's that?"

"Perfect!" Chrissy then said something else, but the signal was too weak. Her voice kept breaking up.

"Sounds like I'm losing you," Jo said. "I love you guys. I'll see you back in Seattle soon."

The call dropped. Jo set her phone aside and leaned her head back. Her family was more than a thousand miles away, someplace warm and lovely. And she was sitting in this frozen town.

Usually, she enjoyed these relaxing nights after a day of work. But she just wanted the sun to come up. Another couple hours of driving would see her to Boise. And maybe she would take a different route on the way back, avoiding Lapse entirely.

She rolled over to try and get some sleep. Rather than having yet another nightmare of Graff, she hoped she would instead dream of Rodney the zebu.

TWELVE

Swann took off his shoes as soon as he got into his room. He paced in front of the TV for a while, letting the stiff carpet and hard subfloor massage his feet. They were always sore from all the running he did. He thought he was developing a slight case of plantar fasciitis. His left heel had a sharp pain whenever he took a step.

A week ago, he might have complained. But after almost dying, he welcomed the pain. At least he was feeling something. And that meant he was still breathing.

Besides, he had something else to look forward to.

He sat on the edge of the bed, rubbing the soles of his feet. His mind wandered back to the diner and the pretty waitress, Carmen. She somehow maintained a nice tan, even though it was winter. Her hair was dark brown, and so were her eyes. She had a nice smile. And who could forget how good she looked in a white button-up shirt?

The receipt crinkled in his pocket. He pulled it out, rereading the message she'd written. Her phone number, plus a short note.

Be out by 10:30. Text me.

She drew a smiley face as well.

"Just angling for a tip, huh?" He laughed victoriously, copying the number into his phone. He *had* given Carmen a nice tip, but he always gave good tips whether it was a pretty girl or not. It was just a nice thing to do.

It was 9:45. Still a lot of time to wait. He turned the TV on and tried to find something decent to watch. Somehow, even in the modern area, the TV managed to only have five channels. Two of them were already showing infomercials. One was a very old courthouse drama movie. Another was a trashy reality show which absorbed Swann immediately.

He got so into it that he lost track of time. In the next room, McKinley turned the shower on. That broke Swann out of his trance. He checked the time.

10:29.

"Perfect. Take a nice, long shower, McKinley. I can hide my movements behind the sound of the spray."

Not that he felt he was doing anything wrong. He just didn't want Jo to find out and give him one of those looks.

He made himself wait until 10:35 just to give Carmen plenty of time. Then he sent a text.

It's Agent Swann. Are you out of work now?

She replied quickly. *Yes! Just got everything wrapped up here. Want to meet me somewhere?*

We only have one car between us, Swann typed. *Can you pick me up? I'm at the Lodge.*

Sure! Be there in two minutes.

Swann scrambled out of bed, putting his shoes back on. He grabbed his phone and wallet, along with his FBI identification. Maybe Carmen would want to see it again. When it came to attracting the attention of women, having a badge was almost as good as having a cute puppy with you.

Of course, it helps when you have devastating good looks, Swann thought. He was feeling good about himself again.

THIRTEEN

McKinley was still in the shower when Swann left his room, shutting the door quietly. He jogged across the parking lot, reaching the entrance just in time for an old, yellow car to pull in. Carmen smiled at him through the window.

He hurried around the other side and got in. The car smelled like a mix of old musty seats and perfume. It smelled the same as his high school girlfriend's car. He wasn't about to tell Carmen that, though.

"Hey," she said, touching her hair.

"Hey," Swann replied breathlessly. "Don't want to rush you, but we should drive out of here. You know that woman I was with at the diner?"

"The other agent?" Carmen asked.

Swann nodded. "Well, she's probably the best agent I've ever met. She saved my life not too long ago. But she's kind of got this mother-bear thing going on. And I'd rather not have her storm out here and demand to know where I'm going."

Carmen laughed. She reached out and touched his knee. "Don't worry, Agent. You're safe with me."

She drove back onto the road and turned right. They went past the Welcome sign with the creepy hunter cutout. Carmen looked in the rearview mirror. If she saw anything back there, she didn't tell Swann about it. And he didn't care enough to look. He was too busy admiring her.

"How was work?" he asked.

"Normal," she groaned. "Pretty boring for the most part. But I met you, so it's all good now. What do you like to do for fun?"

"I like running."

"Like, for exercise?"

"Yeah. I actually just ran the Seattle marathon a week ago. Hit a new PR." He cringed to himself. Now, it just sounded like he was bragging.

But Carmen was receptive. "Wow, that's impressive. No wonder you look so athletic. Do you like doing anything else?"

She looked in the mirror again. This time Swann looked as well. He didn't see anything, though. Just darkness.

"I like movies," Swann said. "I'd probably be at the theater every single night if my schedule allowed it."

"That's cool." Carmen nodded. "I have lots of movies at my place. We can pick one out and let it play."

"Works for me. Just as long as I'm back at the hotel by morning. We'll probably be heading out bright and early."

"Not a problem." Carmen turned onto a side road. They drove past widely spread houses. There was no shortage of space out here in the countryside, and everyone had plenty of it to themselves.

"You live down here?" Swann asked.

She nodded. "Got myself a little house. That's the benefit of living in the middle of nowhere. Even working as a waitress, you can afford your own place. It's right up here."

She turned onto a long, sweeping driveway. Swann could barely see the house at the end of it, tucked into the trees. He expected Carmen to drive all the way, but instead, she stopped as soon as her back tires cleared the mouth of the driveway.

She unbuckled her seatbelt and turned toward him. She reached over and unbuckled his belt as well.

Well, this is going just about perfectly, Swann thought.

A second later, he was tasting her lip gloss. He supposed it was meant to be strawberry flavored. He liked strawberries, but this stuff tasted terrible. In his present situation, he didn't care.

He was completely distracted. He should have seen the people coming, but he didn't. There were four of them, loping along the snowy road with a deadly purpose in each step.

One of them yanked the door open. Swann turned and immediately took a punch to the eye. He reared back. For a moment, he lost all sense of time and space. Suddenly, he was out on the ground. Snow trickled into the neck of his jacket.

One of his eyes was swollen shut. He couldn't see well through the other one either because his brain had been completely rattled. The world was a swimming mess.

He could tell someone was looming over him. And it wasn't Carmen. This person didn't smell nearly as good. She smelled like cooking oil and perfume. The other person reeked of dirt and body odor.

They were wearing something over their faces. Swann reached up, trying to push them away.

"He's waking up," a female voice said. Still not Carmen.

Swann took a boot to the side of the head. It was hellish pain, exploding through his skull. But he stayed conscious and somehow had the presence of mind to pretend like he was knocked out.

He felt hands searching through his pockets.

"Let's hope he didn't leave it behind," a man said. "I want to see it with my own eyes and know we got the right guy."

The searching hands found Swann's FBI identification and pulled it out.

"Now we've done it," another voice said. "Father's going to be pleased."

FOURTEEN

Jo had no idea one of her fellow agents was in trouble. She didn't even have an inkling that Swann was anywhere other than where he should be. In his room. In bed. Getting plenty of rest so he'd have enough energy to continue the sign game tomorrow.

Still, she was troubled. Troubled by this eerie town. Troubled by the fact she had to be the one to bring Swann to Boise. She knew Grantham had some master plan. The SAC was secretly a teddy bear. He had deep, fatherly feelings for all his underlings. He would want to give Swann and Jo a chance to make peace.

It made sense. Also, she'd never have to see Swann again once she dropped him off. Unless, by a strange twist of fate, they ended up working the same case in some random town in eastern Washington. That would be something. She just hoped it wouldn't be in summer because it got really hot out there.

These worries ran through her mind as she drifted off to sleep. Naively, she thought this was as bad as it was going to get. At least until she got back to Seattle after her "vacation" and found the next bad guy to chase.

She dreamed of the beach. Waves curling over her bare feet. Sun beating down, making her sweat. Running through the sand with Chrissy.

It was a lot of fun, even if it wasn't real. Dreams usually never made sense. But this one did. It made all the sense in the world.

Then Chrissy started tapping on her leg. Trying to get her Auntie Jo's attention. For some reason, it made a sound like someone knocking on a door.

Eventually, she realized the sound was coming from the real world. Drifting through the layers of sleep, the sound reached her. She woke and sat up straight. As far as hotel beds went, it wasn't bad. The mattress was too firm, though. The blanket was too scratchy. But Jo stared at the door.

She could just see the outline of the door frame. From the other side, moonlight bled faintly through the blinds, along with the lone streetlamp that glowed at the edge of the lot. It was positioned at an angle, shining slantwise, throwing the shadow of *someone* across the window blinds.

Someone was standing outside her door.

Jo's sleepy mind skipped straight past logic, which would have told her it was McKinley or Swann wanting to talk about something. Instead, she decided some mysterious person was here to murder her. Who else would knock on a hotel door this late at night?

How late is it? Jo thought. She squinted at the red numbers of the alarm clock. 12:03 AM.

The knock came again. It was soft and quiet. Like the person outside was trying to make sure no one else heard it.

Jo grabbed her sidearm off the bedside table. She pulled it from the holster and kept it by her hip as she marched over to the door. She cleared her throat. "Who is it?" she called.

The voice that answered was so small and shrill. It could have been mistaken for a gust of wind. "It's Miriam."

The old lady who ran the hotel, Jo remembered. Why was she here? If there was some emergency, why didn't she just dial the room phone? That was standard operating procedure, especially at this hour.

Jo unlocked the door. She left the chain engaged and pulled the door open slightly to look outside. It was just Miriam, barely visible under bundles of winter clothing. No one else with her.

"Can I help you with something?" Jo asked.

Miriam's eyes glowed desperately in the shadows of her hood. "It's very cold out here, Agent Pullinger. Could I please come in?"

There were some things you just did if you were a decent person. Letting an elderly woman in from a bitterly cold night was one of them. Jo opened the door.

She barely had time to step out of the way before Miriam rushed in.

FIFTEEN

Miriam tugged her hood off. She unzipped her coat and hung it on a hook by the door. She finally turned to Jo. "I need to tell you about something. I think it should be safe. You're new in town."

"Right," Jo said, narrowing her eyes.

"You've never been here before in your life," Miriam added, wringing her hands.

"Never," Jo agreed. "Until a few hours ago, I had no idea the town of Lapse existed."

"You're just passing through. In the morning, you're going to drive on. To where exactly?"

"That's none of your concern," Jo replied. "But if you're trying to say you want me to relay some kind of information... I am going to be among fellow FBI agents."

Miriam nodded. "That's good. I wouldn't want to create too much trouble. It's just that Lapse is so cut off, and..."

The old woman suddenly moaned, tugging at her hair. She started looking around. Jo tried to follow her eyes. It seemed like she was studying the bedside table more than anything. The phone, the lamp, and the alarm clock.

"Are you looking for bugs?" Jo asked. "Let me rephrase that. Do you have a reason to suspect this room might be bugged? Is someone listening to us?"

Miriam sighed. "No. Probably not. But you can never be too careful."

"If it would make you feel better, we could go sit in the car we drove here in. I know for a fact it isn't bugged."

"No, no, it's fine..." Miriam stepped over to the bed and fell onto it.

Jo joined her, resting on the corner of the mattress. "Why don't you just tell me what you're worried about? I can help. So can the other agents I'm here with."

Miriam squeezed her eyes shut. It was hard to tell in the dark room, but it looked like a couple of tears came out. "I can't say much. I shouldn't say anything at all, but... if I were you, I'd get out of town as soon as the sun comes up. Get to wherever you're going. And bring the big guns back with you."

There was a thud from somewhere in the hotel. A faint sound, echoing through the walls. Miriam yelped like someone under the bed had just tickled her foot. She jumped to her feet and started spinning left and right. Like she was looking for someone.

"That was probably just Agent McKinley," Jo said quickly. "Maybe he dropped something."

"Sorry, but I have to go," Miriam said.

She put her coat back on and tugged open the door.

Jo was right behind her. She shoved her feet into her shoes and didn't bother with her jacket. She followed Miriam along the front walk.

"You can talk to me," Jo urged. "Whatever's on your mind..."

"This doesn't look right. You following me like this," Miriam whispered. "Just head back to your room, Agent. It's fine. Everything's fine."

Miriam entered the office and shut the door too fast. Jo could have stuck her hand in to block it, but she probably would have lost a finger. She heard the click of a lock and knew she was getting no more out of Miriam tonight.

"If you change your mind," she said through the door, "come and knock again. It doesn't matter what time it is. I'll answer."

Jo went back to her room, knowing she wasn't getting any sleep now.

SIXTEEN

Jo sat on the floor with her back against the end table. The carpet was thin. There was concrete beneath it, cold as ice. The wooden edge of the table dug into her spine. All of this served to keep her awake and alert.

Who needs coffee when you can sit on a hard, frozen floor instead?

She wanted to think. But she couldn't. Her mind just kept echoing Miriam's words back to her. "It's fine. Everything's fine."

Jo waited and listened. Ten minutes passed after Miriam's initial knock. Then twenty, then thirty. Jo hoped she would hear another knock. The old woman coming to her senses. Instead, she only heard the screaming wind. There was some kind of major blizzard hitting Lapse. It just kept getting stronger. The light given off by the lamp kept flickering with every gust.

All in all, it was shaping up to be an unpleasant evening.

Forty minutes passed. At this point, Jo knew Miriam wasn't coming out. If she wanted answers, she'd have to find them herself.

Or better yet, go to someone who could find them more quickly.

She put on her coat and left the room. She had to put her shoulder into the door to get it to move. The wind was blowing against it.

Making it feel like someone was on the other side, trying to keep her trapped.

As soon as she got outside, a stronger blast of wind came. The door was yanked out of her grip. It slammed shut. She jumped back reflexively, turning to face the onslaught. It was near whiteout conditions. She couldn't see more than ten feet across the parking lot.

But it wasn't even snowing. Not yet. This was just all the pre-existing powder, picked up by the wind.

Jo looked into the sky and saw a never-ending expanse of grayish clouds. They looked mean and angry. She sighed, not feeling confident about being able to drive out of town in the morning.

She went to McKinley's door. The blinds were shut on his window, but she could see light coming through. The TV was on. Maybe he was still awake.

She gave the door a soft knock. No answer. She knocked a little harder.

He answered the door this time. Jo had never seen McKinley look quite so disheveled. He was wearing a faded FBI Academy t-shirt and a pair of flannel pajama pants. His hair was sticking up in a million different directions.

"Huh?" was all he said, rubbing his eyes. He blinked a couple of times. "Crap, it's *cold* out there."

"So maybe you should let me in," Jo suggested.

He stepped aside. Jo entered and let him shut the door. She unzipped her coat and let it fall to the floor.

"Is everything all right?" McKinley asked.

"I thought you might still be awake." Jo pointed at the TV.

"Oh. It helps me sleep when I'm in new places. I turn the volume low enough that I can hear voices but not tell what they're saying. It really works."

"Huh. Maybe I'll give that a shot one of these sleepless nights. But first..."

She told him everything that Miriam had said.

By the time she finished, McKinley was already on his laptop and connecting through his VPN to the database at the Seattle field office.

"Lapse, Oregon," he said. "Let's see if anything weird has been going on here. Hmmm... Wow."

Jo bent down, staring at the screen. "What am I looking at?"

"You're looking at a statistical anomaly," McKinley said. "Look at all these missing person reports in the past year. Six people, all young. All in their early twenties."

"That is strange," Jo agreed. "A town this small..."

"...you wouldn't expect to see any missing people. Just one here and there over the years. Not half a dozen within a twelve-month period. Let me look further back."

He scrolled through the FBI file on Lapse. He had to go back nine years to find anything else of note, a murder that had already been solved. And three years before that, another missing person. Her body was found after nine months. Killed by her ex-husband.

"A woman in her forties this time," said McKinley. "That's the kind of thing you expect to see. Someone makes a mistake one day, or they make someone mad, and suddenly they're gone."

"Not like the newer disappearances," said Jo. "Those definitely form a very weird pattern."

She pulled out her phone and took a picture of McKinley's screen. The names of six young people who had gone missing from Lapse. It reeked of foul play.

"Could this be what Miriam wanted to talk about?" McKinley asked.

"There's nothing else on file. Except... what's that?"

She pointed to a brief entry from seven years in the past.

"Looks like a retired agent is living here in Lapse," said McKinley. "Guy named Kurt Black. I don't think I've ever met him."

Jo shook her head. "Doesn't ring a bell for me, either. He might be retired, but I'm sure he still has his finger on the pulse. Might be a good source of information. Maybe we can talk to him tomorrow. If there's time."

"We can look into it more once we get to Boise." McKinley shut his laptop. "What do we do until then?"

"We try to get some sleep. Whatever's going on here, it's not going to get any worse before morning, is it?"

"Is that a rhetorical question?" he asked. "Or do you want me to answer it and jinx us further?"

SEVENTEEN

The night caught up to Jo as she was walking back to her room. She suddenly felt thirty pounds heavier. She could barely keep her eyes open.

Only half awake, she stumbled inside. Through sheer reflex, she locked the door. Then she dragged a chair over and wedged it under the handle.

She didn't know what she was afraid of. But her instincts were telling her she should be afraid anyway. Even though she was too tired to *feel* afraid, some part of her subconscious kicked in anyway.

When she woke up early the next morning, she looked over at the chair under the door.

"Very good," she yawned. "Except, I left the window unlocked. Nice try, Tired Jo."

She got a text from McKinley. *Breakfast at the diner?*

She replied. *You know another place to eat in this town? Meet you outside in 15.*

Great! I'll let Swann know.

After a quick shower, Jo got dressed and stepped outside. The weather had calmed down, but there was still no hint of sun. The sky was one big gray mass.

McKinley was standing nearby, bouncing up and down to stay warm. He looked at his watch. "It's been eighteen minutes, Jo. You're three minutes late. I've been freezing out here for three whole minutes!"

Jo waved a hand. "I'll buy you a coffee. How do you think I feel with all this wet hair? Is Swann up?"

McKinley shrugged. "I texted him. He didn't answer, but I figured he'd be out here."

"Well, he's not." Jo checked the time. "It's already half past seven. We need to be on the road before it starts snowing."

"About that... I checked the weather, and Lapse is supposed to get hit hard. Some kind of severe weather alert."

Jo's skin crawled. "Let's get Swann out of bed and hit it. We can get something to eat on the way."

They approached the door to Swann's room. The curtain was drawn tight. No gap at all to peek through, though Jo tried. She knocked hard on the door.

"Rise and shine," she called. "It's time to blow this joint."

She waited a moment but heard nothing.

"Swann?" she tried again.

She looked at McKinley.

He frowned. "Maybe, he's in the shower."

"Or he's a heavy sleeper," said Jo. "Let's try calling him."

McKinley did the honors. It was a still morning, with barely enough of a breeze to shift Jo's hair around. They could clearly hear the distant cars on the highway. They also should have been able to hear Swann's phone ringing in the room.

They heard nothing.

"Maybe it's on silent," McKinley suggested.

"Maybe this has gone on long enough," Jo added. "There's no way I'm getting stranded in this town. I'm supposed to be on a pleasant road trip."

"It's kind of nice here," McKinley said. He didn't sound confident.

Jo tried the door. She didn't expect it to open. It was just something she had to check off the list. But it *did* open. The room was dark and cool.

If Swann's still sleeping, she thought, *I'm about to grab a pillow and beat him with it.*

She went inside.

EIGHTEEN

There was no sound at all in the room. That was enough for Jo to know Swann was not in the shower. The bathroom door was also wide open; the lights were off inside.

She hit the switch for the overhead light. It revealed an abandoned room. The bed was unmade, and Swann was not in it.

Jo went into the bathroom and turned that light on as well. Swann's toothbrush was there on the counter. It was resting inside its plastic travel case. There was a tube of toothpaste as well. A large tube, half-empty. From the Seattle apartment he had so unceremoniously departed.

Beside the toothbrush was a small black bag with a drawstring. Jo didn't have to look inside to know it was an electric razor.

She glanced around at the rest of the bathroom and said to herself, "Well, at least now I know you're in the habit of putting the seat down. Way to be a gentleman, Swann."

"What was that?" McKinley called out.

"Nothing. Just trying to make myself laugh in the face of devastation."

"Did it work?" McKinley asked.

"Not at all." Jo pulled the shower curtain back. Of course, Swann was not inside.

She went back into the main room. McKinley was sitting on the bed, scratching his chin in thought.

"I checked out the end table," he said. "Every FBI agent I know keeps their important things close at hand. Sidearm. Phone. Wallet and ID. They weren't on the table. The drawer is empty, too. Other than the Bible, obviously."

"Obviously." Jo nodded. "So. No Swann, and none of Swann's things. Mostly. He left his toothbrush and razor in the bathroom."

"But he left nothing else," said McKinley. "He even took his duffel bag with all his clothes."

"But not the bathroom stuff. *And* he left the door unlocked. I know Swann has this idea that we all think he's an amateur. But he's not. What could make a guy like that be so...?"

"Careless?" McKinley finished for her.

"Or maybe *hurried* is the right word. I guess the better question is, where did he go?"

They both looked at the door.

"Maybe Miriam knows," Jo said.

"Couldn't hurt to ask," McKinley replied.

"All right. Let's go see if she's in a talking mood yet."

They left Swann's room. As the door swung shut, Jo had an unpleasant feeling. Like they were sealing Swann's tomb, and burying him forever.

But that was foolish. Wherever he went, she was sure everything was just fine. Swann was a trained federal agent. He could take care of himself.

If his phone wasn't in the room, she thought, *then he must have it with him.*

She tried calling him again on their way to the office. He didn't answer. She got his voicemail message. A stilted recording where he announced himself as Agent Edward Swann and entreated the caller to leave their name and number. She hung up and shook her head at McKinley.

The OPEN sign in the hotel office was on. They went inside and were hit by the scent of cinnamon. Miriam was standing behind the counter. She was wearing a bright smile.

"Good morning, agents," she said. "Where's that tall, younger fellow?"

Jo and McKinley shared a look.

"We were hoping you could help us with that," said Jo. "Agent Swann is not in his room, and he isn't answering our calls. Did you happen to see him leave the hotel at some point?"

Miriam thought about it, then shook her head. "No. I was asleep all night. Well, *almost* all night. Anyway, I never saw Agent Swann leave his room. But I know someone who might have."

NINETEEN

"Who do you know?" McKinley asked. "Someone else who works here at the hotel?"

Miriam beckoned to them. They followed her behind the counter. Miriam had a tiny apartment in the back of the office. She opened the door to what should have been a coat closet. Instead, there was an ancient computer inside. The old tower almost generated enough heat to turn the small room into a sauna.

McKinley pointed to the dust-clogged intake fans. "This might be a fire hazard, ma'am."

"Oh, I wouldn't worry," said Miriam. "This old gal's been running non-stop for twelve years. Ever since my nephew installed it for me, this has been my command center. That's what I call it."

Miriam jiggled the mouse. The screen came on and showed a grid of four panels. They were camera feeds. Extremely low-resolution. It seemed the cameras were just as old and outdated as the PC.

"As far as security systems go, it's not the worst I've ever seen," McKinley said nicely. "Are these the only four feeds?"

"It's wonderful, isn't it?" Miriam beamed. "The problem is, I have no idea how to use it. My nephew showed me when he put it in, but

I only understood about two words of it. If either of you thinks you can work it, have at it. Tea? I was just about to brew a mug for myself."

"No, but thank you," Jo said.

"Suit yourselves. Just let me know when you're finished."

She left, moving into her kitchenette.

"All right, this system is almost half as old as the man we're trying to find," McKinley said, "but I'll try and work my magic."

It didn't take him long to get the hang of it. Soon, he was scrubbing back through old footage.

"Pretty nifty thing her nephew set up here," he said. "He did almost everything right. There's supposedly enough hard drive space to save a whole week's worth of footage at a time."

"Supposedly?" Jo asked.

"Well, he didn't do *every*thing right. He set up four hard drives in a RAID configuration. That's Redundant Array of Independent Disks. It's a way to spread data across multiple hard drives. The problem is, he set it up for RAID 0."

"Just go ahead and tell me, McKinley. You know you want to."

"RAID 0 is one of four ways to use RAID. Unlike the others, it doesn't include redundancy. At other levels of RAID, data is stored in copies across all the drives. If one dies, you still have all your data. But 0 is just about speed. The same data gets chopped up into pieces. Each hard drive handles a section of that data. Well, after twelve years of constant use, hard drives inevitably start to die."

"So we lost some data."

"Right. Or I guess it's more accurate to say that the data never existed. The computer is still trying to use RAID 0, but only two of the four drives are still functioning. So half of the footage is just... gone.

It's not huge blocks at a time, at least. It's just bits here and there. But it wouldn't take a huge block of footage for Swann to sneak out of the hotel room. If we were unlucky, we wouldn't see him leaving at all."

"I'm already feeling very unlucky," said Jo, "but something tells me you have good news for me."

McKinley nodded. "Look at this."

He let the footage play. It skipped and lagged a lot. Jumping ahead as it tried to play the missing blocks and failed. Along with the terrible image quality, it was hard to tell what was happening. All they saw was a dark blob emerging from a room. The dark blob shut the door, then rushed across the parking lot. It quickly vanished from sight.

"Even Swann's own mother wouldn't be able to tell this was him," said McKinley, "but we have our excellent deduction skills. We're the only three guests at the hotel. Both of us are still here at the hotel. The only person this could be is our fellow agent Swann."

"Sherlock Holmes would be proud," said Jo. "Any other angles?"

"None that are useful."

"So, the only thing we can tell from this footage is that Swann left the hotel. I would say this has been an incredibly fruitful venture."

"Wait a second." McKinley pointed at the screen.

In the dark, blurry image of the hotel, a pair of headlights played across the room doors as a car swung out of the parking lot.

"Someone picked him up," said McKinley.

"Or he drove himself... but not in our car. It's still parked outside."

They left the sweaty closet behind. They thanked Miriam, turned down another offer for tea, and went outside. The cold air felt refreshing.

"She's acting like everything's fine," McKinley remarked. "Maybe last night she was having some kind of... episode? Like sundowning syndrome?"

Jo sighed. "I have no idea. Let's just focus on finding Swann."

They gave the Boise office a call, theorizing that Swann might have found a car and driven himself the rest of the way. But no one in Boise knew anything.

"I was annoyed before," Jo said after hanging up, "but now I'm getting freaked out."

McKinley's eyes suddenly went wide. "The waitress! Carmen was her name. Remember how she was looking at him last night?"

Jo smiled. "Swann might have spent the night at her place. You're a genius, McKinley."

"So, now all we have to do is wait for him to come back," he said with a grin.

Jo looked at the sky again. The gray cloud ceiling seemed to have dropped. It hovered over Lapse at an ominously low altitude. Any second now, it would begin to snow.

TWENTY

"Got her right here," said McKinley, staring at his laptop. "Carmen Powell. There's an address listed here on her driver's license. The same one is on her most recent tax return."

They were back in McKinley's room. They were only just getting warm again. But Jo was antsy to head back out into the elements.

She shrugged her coat back on. "Let's go."

McKinley nodded. He moved very slowly, obviously trying to spend as much time in the warmth as possible. They finally went outside and got in the car. Jo fiddled with the heat controls as she waited for it to warm up. They got blasted with cold air from the vents at first.

"We could just wait for him to show up," McKinley said, blowing into his hands. "I know I already suggested it, but..."

In response, Jo put the car into drive and eased it out of the parking lot. The snowplows had been through, tossing snow into the driveway and clogging it up. Scraping the main road down to a glassy smooth sheen of ice. It wasn't very good driving. But they didn't have far to go.

With McKinley's directions, Jo found the place easily enough. Carmen Powell lived in a cute little house at the end of a long driveway.

They couldn't actually drive up it, though. There was a car parked in the way.

"Looks like a 2007 Ford Five Hundred," McKinley said. "Burgundy color. Checks out. That's Carmen's ride."

Jo squinted toward the house. There was no movement. She couldn't figure out what it was, but just looking at the place gave her a sense of desolation.

The agents got out of their car and approached the house. Jo noticed two things at once.

The first thing was the reason why the house gave her the creeps. It was the lack of footprints outside. The wind had been blowing late last night. Whipping powder around. It would have covered up a lot. But this stuff was perfectly smooth. No one had been in or out of this house in the past twelve hours, maybe longer.

The second thing she noticed was the area immediately around Carmen's car. She pointed, and McKinley nodded.

"It's churned up," he said.

"Like a dozen people had a dance party here," Jo added. She scanned the ground a bit further away, up the street. There were some divots in the snow. Maybe footprints. But the wind had smoothed them out. They were too faint to be of any use.

Jo pulled her sleeve up over her hand and tried the door of the car. The handle moved freely, but the door wouldn't budge. She cupped her hands over her eyes and peeked through the window.

"It looks unlocked," she said.

"The door's probably just frozen shut," said McKinley.

Jo nodded and gave the handle a meatier tug. It popped out with the sound of crackling ice. A normal thing in these conditions. Snow falls on a car. The heat of the car melts it. The water flows into the nooks and crannies around the door. Refreezes.

It meant the car had been sitting here still warm at some point. But it wasn't warm now. Somehow, the air in the car felt even colder than the outside. It smelled faintly of perfume and cooking grease.

"Definitely her car," Jo said. "I had a friend in college who worked at a diner. Every time she gave me a ride, her car smelled just like this."

"Is Swann in there?" McKinley asked.

"No, smartass," Jo scoffed. "If he was, he'd be a popsicle by now."

She looked the car over, then stood up and shut the door. "Nothing of Swann's inside. Nothing at all, really. Looking at the snow, it doesn't seem like they made it inside the house."

"But they left the car at some point," McKinley said. "To go where?"

A cold feeling settled over Jo. It had nothing to do with the weather.

"I think we're going to be in Lapse a bit longer," she muttered. "I guess I'll have to learn to like it here."

TWENTY-ONE

Jo was pretty sure her judgment of the situation was correct. Neither Swann nor Carmen had gone into the house. But she and McKinley still walked up the long driveway. Snow fell into their shoes, making their feet wet and cold.

"This sucks," McKinley said with a grunt.

"Now we're on the same page." Jo patted him on the shoulder. "But this isn't that bad. At least we're not getting shot at."

"That's because Ford isn't here," McKinley replied. "Whenever that guy shows up, you know things are about to go crazy."

He was talking about Bryan Ford. He was a former police detective, now a private investigator with his own agency. Ever since Jo moved to her current field office, she and Ford couldn't help but run into each other. He had even worked with her as a consultant on the Graff case.

But Ford was in Seattle. Chasing unfaithful spouses and runaway teens by day and eating spaghetti dinners with his wife and daughter by night.

Good for him, Jo thought. *He gets all the rain. I get all the snow and a missing agent.*

"I really hope this isn't what I think it is," Jo moaned. "I hope he and Carmen are inside, asleep in each other's arms."

"I bet that's the case," McKinley said brightly. "But just for the record, what do you think it is?"

"Remember the six missing people?" said Jo. "Maybe this is something like that. If so, we're up to eight now."

"Who would be bold enough to kidnap an FBI agent?" McKinley asked.

"No idea. Unless they didn't know, but in towns this small, people know everything about everyone. And word travels fast."

The closer they got to the front porch, the more certain Jo became. The wind had deposited snow all the way under the overhang. It went up to the door. And it was completely undisturbed.

Jo pulled the storm door open. She knocked her fist against the main door. It was the kind of knock you use when you want to make sure everyone in the house knows you're there. And maybe even the whole neighborhood.

"Please answer," she said.

No one came to the door.

Jo knocked again. "Carmen Powell. Agent Swann. Open up."

She waited thirty seconds, then let out a sigh.

"They aren't here," McKinley said.

"But I have to be sure. You can wait here in case someone comes to the door. I'll just do a quick circuit."

She left McKinley behind, stepping off the porch and sinking shin-deep in snow. She no longer felt the cold as she lumbered around the corner of the house. All she felt was the buzz of panicked thoughts in her head.

All ordinary procedures were temporarily out the window. It was different when it was one of your own. Despite your training, panic fought hard to take over. You forgot to do the ordinary things. You forgot to take stock of what was important.

She could afford no mistakes.

Jo took a deep breath. She got her thoughts in order.

Carmen's house was small. It was one bedroom, maybe two. Her land backed up onto a swampy-looking forest. But her backyard was surrounded by a wooden fence. It was low enough to climb over, which Jo did.

She dropped down on the other side and looked around. There was a grill and not much else. A very sparse place. But there was a back door to the house. Jo hurried over to it and peered through the glass.

The house was dark. No sign of anyone. She could see all the way to the front from where she stood. She could even see McKinley's shadow shifting around beyond the frosted glass of the front door.

She stepped back and turned in a circle. She couldn't see any neighbors from here. But they had passed other houses on the way in. Maybe someone had seen something.

But there were other things to worry about.

Jo returned to the front of the house.

"I tried opening the door," McKinley told her. "Unlike the car, we didn't get lucky here."

"We didn't get lucky there either," Jo said with a grunt. "But I suppose we should take a closer look. Not close enough to destroy any evidence, though. I guess we should have traveled with a mobile CSI unit."

McKinley sighed. "No kidding. Should we talk to some neighbors?"

"That's just what I was thinking. We can look up if Carmen has family in the area. They might know something, too. But first, we need to start running a trace on Swann's phone."

McKinley smiled. "Already put in the call. Agent Larkin is taking care of it. I assume Grantham will be giving us a call any time now."

"Larkin. Is that the new guy?" Jo asked.

"Larkin's been there longer than you have, Jo. And she's not a guy. Come on, you know Agent Larkin. Kind of tiny, but muscular. Redhead."

"Oh. Well, I've seen her around, but..."

"I get it. You sit next to me, and I'm all the company you need. But you should probably socialize a bit more. You know?"

Jo shrugged. "Yeah. Well... anyway. That was some nice lighthearted banter. But I guess it's time to start knocking on doors."

McKinley gestured down the driveway. "Lead on."

TWENTY-TWO

One of the neighbors was a woman in her eighties who was nearly deaf and wore glasses as thick as milk bottles. Her name was Margaret, and she claimed to always go to bed around nine. In short, she could tell them nothing useful.

Another neighboring house belonged to a couple in their fifties whose youngest child had only recently moved away to college. They were Stan and Thora Brown. Thora was happy enough to show pictures of her three kids to the agents.

While Jo was nodding politely along to Thora's stories, a kitten ran across her feet. A new addition to the family. It seemed the Browns were already in full-blown empty-nesting mode. With no one left to take care of, they had begun acquiring pets.

"There goes the little stinker," Stan chuckled. "Probably gonna climb the curtains in our bedroom again. Crazy cat."

"Do either of you know Carmen very well?" Jo asked, trying for the fifth or sixth time to get things back on track.

"Can't say we do," said Stan. "Very friendly young lady, though."

"Sweet girl," Thora confirmed. "She hasn't been living in that house very long. We see her at the diner sometimes. Don't we, Stan?"

He nodded. "Yep. Sure, do. Thora loves their country-fried steak. I think it's too greasy. I'm a meatloaf man, myself."

McKinley stifled a yawn.

"Well," Jo went on, "did either of you see Carmen coming home from work last night?"

"She's not in... some kind of *trouble*, is she?" Thora whispered.

"She's not in trouble with the law," Jo said. "But we think she has some information that would be valuable to us."

"Well, we didn't see anything," Stan replied. "We both passed out in front of the TV around eleven-thirty. As we usually do. Then the little stinker ran across my face and woke me up around, oh, two or so. I got Thora up, and we went to bed."

Thora nodded. "We didn't see anything."

"I see," said Jo. She was almost pleased. If they *had* seen anything, it meant she would have to stay and listen to them for longer. "You've been very helpful. If you hear anything, we're staying at the Lapse Lodge."

As Jo and McKinley turned to leave, something interesting happened. Thora leaned close to her husband and spoke to him in a low voice. "Is it another one of those disappearances, do you think?"

Jo looked back at the couple. For the first time since stepping foot in their house, she felt intrigued.

"Are you talking about the six people who've gone missing from your town in the past year?" Jo asked.

Thora nodded. "You're here in town about them, aren't you?"

"Actually, we were just passing through," said Jo. "But things have gotten interesting here. Do you know any of the people who went missing?"

Stan looked glassy-eyed. "One of them was best friends with our Susie. A girl named Candy Lawson. She's been gone for a few months now. Susie's been taking it hard."

Jo knew from one of Thora's stories that Susie was their middle daughter. She thought back to the photo she had taken on her cell phone last night. The one of McKinley's laptop screen. She fixed the names in her mind.

"Candy was the only female on the list," Jo said. "If she was best friends with your daughter, you must have known a lot about her."

Stan blew air out of his lips. It made his mustache flutter. "Candy was a nice kid. Had a good head on her shoulders. Real smart. Always reading these philosophy books."

"Oh, yeah." Thora nodded. "Always reading. Asking questions about anything and everything. Always looking for answers. I guess... maybe she just looked in the wrong place."

Thora's nose wrinkled. Her eyes squeezed shut. She began to cry.

Stan hugged his wife and gave the agents an apologetic smile.

"Sorry to take up so much of your time," Jo told them. "You know where to find us if anything comes to mind. Thanks again."

They took their leave, pausing on the front stoop of the Brown house.

"So, two neighbors and not much to go on," McKinley said.

"I think it's time to narrow our search," Jo agreed. "We'll take a two-pronged approach. I'll find local law enforcement and have a chat with them."

"Good idea. What will I be doing?"

"You'll be talking to Miriam at the hotel. She knows a lot more than the tiny bit she told me last night. She's just afraid to say it. You think you can get her to relax enough to spill a few beans?"

McKinley grunted uncertainly. "I'll have a cup of tea with her. Just let her talk at first. Maybe something will come out."

"Good idea." She pulled out the car keys and gave them a jingle. "I'll drop you off at the lodge."

TWENTY-THREE

Grantham called as they were driving away from Carmen's neighborhood. The first thing they heard when answering was a heavy sigh.

"So, Swann got into trouble again," Grantham said.

"It seems that way, sir," McKinley answered. "We think whatever happened to him is tied up in the strange disappearances that have been happening in town."

"Yes, I've pulled up the file on Lapse. Six missing people, all young. Candy Lawson. Samuel Whitaker. Yadda, yadda. I want you two to make sure the name Edward Swann doesn't end up on that list."

"Loud and clear," Jo said. "Sir, we know Swann went out with a waitress from the local diner."

"Carmen Powell," Grantham replied. "Twenty-four years old. Five foot four. Brown hair, brown eyes."

"That's her. There's still a chance they went off somewhere in town together. Swann might turn up."

"Does that sound like the kind of luck we're likely to receive, Agent Pullinger?" Grantham asked.

Jo thought about it. "Probably not."

"Right. We're still working on locating Swann's phone. It may take some time, and it may be unsuccessful. You've got a big storm headed your way, I hear."

Jo reached for the windshield wiper controls. "The snow's just starting to fall now. It's supposed to be a big one."

"You're in unfamiliar territory out there," Grantham warned. "You're possibly working against an unknown assailant. Someone with the grit to overpower and abduct a trained FBI agent. An agent who's in very good physical shape. Be careful, you two. Keep your wits about you. And keep me updated."

He hung up with the usual Grantham abruptness. Neither Jo nor McKinley spoke for the rest of the short drive.

***

After dropping McKinley off at the hotel, Jo headed further into town along the main road. She had an instinct about where the police station might be, and she was right. It was in the very center of the minuscule downtown area, right across the street from the one-garage fire station.

She pulled into the police station parking lot. The building pretty much looked like someone's house. It had vinyl siding and nice shutters on all the windows. It even had an ordinary wooden door.

Jo went inside, ignoring the urge to knock first. Or to find a doorbell to ring.

She didn't need to. The door struck a brass bell overhead, letting out a happy ringing. From across the carpeted lobby, an old woman at a desk swiveled her head around to look.

"Neil, we got company!" she squawked. "I think it's one of them FBI people."

The old woman stood up and crossed the room. With a warm smile, she stuck out her hand.

"The name's Sheri Phelps," she said. "I work here, along with the sheriff."

"Very nice to meet you." Jo shook her hand. "What's your title?"

"Spouse," Sheri said simply. She looked over her shoulder. "Neil! Didn't you hear me?"

Neil arrived through an open door, carrying a cup of coffee. "Keep your shirt on, woman. I might be old and slow, but I'm not deaf."

Jo could hardly believe her eyes. Neil looked exactly like her image of the stereotypical small-town sheriff. He had a handlebar mustache, a pot belly, and a general world-weary look to him. He was also wearing a cowboy hat.

"Keep my shirt on, he says." Sheri rolled her eyes. "Never thought I'd marry a man who told me to do *that*. Should be the opposite."

"Please ignore my wife," said Neil. "She's always fishing for the next humdinger of a line to make herself laugh. I'm Neil Phelps, the sheriff of these here parts."

Jo had to wonder whether he was delivering that line sincerely or sarcastically. She hoped it was the former, to further suit the stereotype.

Neil transferred his coffee to his left hand and stuck out his right. Jo shook it.

"Agent Pullinger, FBI," she said.

Neil's eyes widened. "Well, I'll be tied up and flash-fried. A real-life FBI person, here in my humble workplace. Rumor in town is you're just passing through. Am I to believe that? Because I figured, with the disappearances and all, you'd be keeping tabs on us."

Jo nodded. "I'll be honest with you, Sheriff. We were on our way to Boise. But we seem to have misplaced one of our agents."

The mood in the station immediately changed. Sheri displayed impressive speed and agility as she sprinted across the room, grabbing her keys off her desk.

"Describe the missing agent to me, please," Neil said. He pulled out a pad and pen.

Jo gave him the basic description, including Swann's name. Neil wrote it all down, then tore off the page, and handed it to his wife.

"Where did he go missing from?" Neil asked.

Jo gave him the address of the house.

"That's Carmen Powell's place, isn't it?" he asked. Sheri nodded at him. "That's what I thought. Is she missing as well, Agent Pullinger?"

"She very well could be. They made it to the driveway in Carmen's car. There's some evidence of a struggle there. They never reached the house."

Neil turned to his wife. "Be a doll and go keep an eye on Carmen's car, would you?"

Sheri headed for the door.

"Before you go," said Jo. "You can call my field office in Seattle. Ask for Robert Grantham, and tell them who referred you. Grantham will send you all the help you need."

TWENTY-FOUR

Sheri hurried out the door. A moment later, an engine coughed to life, and she backed out of the lot in a station wagon.

Neil smiled, taking a sip of coffee. "I married a good one. If Sheri's on the case, your missing man is as good as found. Can I get you a cup of coffee?"

"No, thanks," said Jo.

"In that case, why don't we head back into my office? There are some things you might want to take a look at."

He led her through the open door he had stepped through earlier. His office turned out to be a laptop on a card table that also had a coffee pot on it. There were several filing cabinets along the wall.

Neil grabbed a landline handset and put it to his ear. He dialed a number and started speaking a moment later.

"Yeah, hi. Yeah, this is the Sheriff speaking. No, I don't want to make a reservation. Like you ever get enough customers at one time to warrant that, Jerry." He chuckled. "Yes, I am calling for a reason. It's about Carmen Powell. Did she come to work today? I see. Well, thanks. I'd be grateful. Bye, now."

He hung up and raised an eyebrow at Jo.

"That was Jerry. He's the manager over at the diner. Carmen's on the schedule today, but not until dinner time. He says he'll call me when she shows up. Or I guess, *if* is the right word."

He opened the top drawer of a filing cabinet and pulled out a folder. He dropped it in front of Jo.

"There you are," he said. "All the information I have on our strange disappearances. Go ahead and take a peek."

Jo sat down and opened the file. It consisted of six lonely sheets of paper, each with a different person's information on it. The top sheet was for Candy Lawson. There was also one for Samuel Whitaker, Joseph Malone, Theodore Hummel, Connor Foster, and Desmond Brooke.

"They all disappeared within two months," Jo observed.

Neil nodded. "That was a tough time for all of us here. The prevailing theory among the townspeople is that these six are alive and well. They fled town to escape stagnation. To find good jobs somewhere. To have adventures. Can't say I'd blame them. When I was young, Lapse felt like the most boring place in the world."

"What do you think happened to them?" asked Jo.

He shrugged. "Whatever it was, they all fell victim to the same thing. Far too coincidental. Wherever they are, I think they're together. Beyond that... who knows? The real trouble now is, another one of our young people might be missing too. Along with one of your agents. And I'd bet my favorite Stetson that it's all linked up."

He interlaced his fingers, giving Jo a tired smile.

"Then I guess it's safe to say it now," Jo replied. "The FBI is here in Lapse, and we're going to figure out where these people have gone. I'm going to need your cooperation on this, Sheriff."

"Count on it. As long as you call me Neil from now on. And what should I call you?"

"Jo works all right for me," she said.

"Jo, it is. Sure I can't get you a cup of coffee, Jo? No? Then I guess we'd better move right along. I think I know where we should go next, and I think you'll agree with me."

"Hit me," Jo said.

"Well, maybe you know by now..." Neil paused to swallow half his cup of coffee in one go. "...but we already have an FBI agent in town. Retired, of course. A man by the name of Kurt Black. Correct me if I'm wrong, but the way I see it, you can take a fellow's badge away—maybe he'll even give it over willingly—but you can't take away his training. And you can't take the bloodhound out of him, either."

"Agent McKinley and I agree. We assumed Mr. Black would be a good source of information."

Neil nodded along, but there was a strange twinkle in his eye. Jo could normally read people like a book, but everything going on in Lapse had her thrown off balance. She hadn't even told the sheriff about what Miriam had said to her the night before.

Then again, maybe she shouldn't. Lapse was a small town, cut off from everything. Just the kind of place that criminal organizations liked to make their home. And most of the time, the success of those organizations relied on the protection of local law enforcement.

She hated to think that this nice, humorous character could be involved in the disappearances. But appearances were deceptive. And even the smallest misjudgment could bring disaster.

TWENTY-FIVE

Neil Phelps whistled as he poured the rest of his coffee into a travel mug. He topped it off from the carafe, slapped the lid on, and turned to Jo.

"I'll lead the way out to Kurt Black's place," he said. "He's some kind of recluse, that guy. Looked for the most remote property he could find, and it so happened to be in the backwoods of my fair town. *Deep* in the backwoods. Hate to see you get lost trying to get there on your own. Would you like to ride with me or take your own car?"

She showed him her keys.

"Suit yourself," he said. "I like to sing while I drive, anyway. And my singing voice is downright awful. I think maybe you're making the right choice."

They bundled up, and headed outside.

"Now, Kurt's a bit of an odd duck," he said. "We rarely see him in town, and we've never had trouble with him, but... like I said, he's a recluse. Maybe I'll just let you see for yourself once we get there. Just follow me."

He hopped behind the wheel of a huge pickup truck. Jo got inside her Grantham-issued sedan, feeling tiny. She tailed the sheriff out of the lot and down the road. She could already see him tapping and bobbing his head along to his music.

He led her south out of town, off the main road and onto a narrower one. This road was also paved, at least for now, and it didn't seem to be snowing much harder than before.

Everything changed once they hit the dirt roads. The route out to Kurt's house was uncomplicated but long. The sheriff took them through untamed country. Through places that Jo was surprised even had a road, to begin with. Indeed, in some spots, there barely was a road. The limbs of pine trees scraped her car on either side.

Neil's wider vehicle was faring much worse. By two miles into their drive, he had a fresh load of loose needles and sticky pine cones in the bed of his truck.

And then it began to snow harder. Jo dialed up her windshield wipers. Then she dialed them up again. Eventually, she had to turn them onto max speed. The already faint road was swiftly disappearing from sight. All she could do was stick close to Neil, but not *too* close, and drive along in the ruts left by his wheels.

She knew the town wasn't very far behind her. Even so, she felt a million miles removed from anything warm or hospitable. Her sense of disquiet grew with every quarter mile. She found herself wishing she was riding with Neil.

How bad could his singing be?

She turned her headlights on to try and see through the falling snow.

TWENTY-SIX

"There's nothing better than a cup of tea on a cold day. Here you go, dear."

Miriam set a steaming mug down in front of McKinley. They were sitting in her kitchenette behind the hotel office. Already, he had turned down her offers of a turkey sandwich and a bowl of split pea soup. He had accepted the gingersnap cookies, which he was nibbling on now.

"Thank you so much," he said, sniffing the steam rising from his cup. "What is that aroma? Darjeeling, maybe?"

"It's some sort of black tea that comes in a bag," Miriam said. "Can't I get you anything else to eat? You're too thin."

"You're not the first person to tell me that." He chomped down on another cookie. "I eat plenty. I think I just have a fast metabolism."

He sipped his tea, eager for his next caffeine dose.

"So, you're having a bit of downtime, you said?" Miriam stirred sugar into her cup. "Waiting for your agent friend to come back from somewhere?"

"A training excursion," McKinley lied. "He should be back soon, and then we'll be on our way."

"Oh." Miriam pursed her lips. "I hate to be the bearer of bad news, but we're supposed to get a nasty blizzard. Actually, I think it should be starting any second now. It might be wise to spend an extra night."

McKinley smiled. "Of course, you stand to benefit monetarily from such a decision."

"Oh, you know better." She waved a hand, blushing. "I just worry about people, is all. I hate to imagine you three sliding off the road somewhere. Getting stuck out there in a drift, freezing all night. But you're FBI agents. You can take care of yourselves."

She laughed to herself, taking a drink of her tea. Her eyes were glazed over. She was thinking about something. Worrying.

"Well, the tea is great, Mrs...." McKinley paused. "I guess I'll just call you Miriam."

"Oh, I never told you my last name." She smacked herself lightly on the forehead. "It's Whitaker. Miriam Whitaker."

McKinley's mind had already moved on. He was back to stressing over Swann. When she said the name *Whitaker,* his train of thought came crashing backward.

"Whitaker," he said. "Like Samuel Whitaker? He's one of the missing people."

Miriam set her tea down clumsily. It tipped, half of it spilling across the table before she could right it. She grabbed a dish towel from the counter and threw it over the mess.

"Oh, silly me. Always making a mess. I hope I didn't get any on you, agent. If so, I have more of these towels. You can get yourself dried off."

"Miriam," McKinley said.

She kept on swabbing at the spilled tea, cackling to herself.

"Miriam!" he said louder. "Please sit back down. We can deal with the mess in a moment."

All the energy seemed to leave her body. She fell into her chair, sagging like a sack of potatoes.

"Samuel Whitaker," McKinley said again. He grabbed the dish towel and wiped up what remained of the tea.

"My grandson," Miriam said. "His parents are gone now. I was all he had left. And he was all I had. Agent, I just can't let you try and drive to Boise in this weather. You have to stay another night. Please, promise me."

"All right, we will," McKinley replied. "Like you said, we can take care of ourselves. And we can help find your grandson, too. But I need more information. Tell me everything you know. Tell me what you were afraid to tell Agent Pullinger last night."

Maybe she still wasn't ready. Maybe whatever dreadful weight she had hanging over her was still too heavy. Or maybe McKinley's timing was just poor. She started rambling about her clumsiness again and went to find more towels.

McKinley stayed just long enough to satisfy the rules of politeness. Feeling bad, he even let her give him a turkey sandwich. He left, vowing to get the information out of her one way or another.

For now, he had other avenues to follow.

TWENTY-SEVEN

McKinley knew there was food where he was going, but he already had his turkey sandwich. He peeled the plastic wrap off and ate it on his walk. Not only did chewing it help keep him warm, the sandwich actually tasted good. The bread was slathered with butter, but Miriam had gone the extra mile and cracked some fresh black pepper on each slice as well.

I'm sure her grandson has eaten this exact sandwich before, he thought.

The thought depressed him. He almost lost his appetite, but not quite. He scarfed the sandwich down in less than two minutes. Another eight minutes of brisk walking brought him to the diner.

He stood outside the door for a moment, watching the weather. The ground was blanketed in fresh snow, and it was falling faster than ever. But it was all happening in total silence. Any sounds there might have been were muffled, absorbed, smothered out of existence.

The door of the diner swung open and struck McKinley on the shoulder. He stumbled out of the way and looked back, expecting an apology. Instead, he was looking straight into the angry eyes of a bearded man.

"Watch where you're standing," the man snapped. He stomped past McKinley, got in his car, and drove away.

"What was that about?" McKinley wondered aloud.

He turned back toward the restaurant. The door was still open. A friendly-looking, heavyset man was holding it for him.

"Sorry about that, Agent," he said.

"Not your fault," McKinley replied. "Was that guy angry about something?"

"He seemed to get a little mad when he saw you walking up. That was Bill Lawson. Candy Lawson's father. He's peeved that you're all in town, but you aren't here to find his daughter."

McKinley nodded. "Well, that all might have changed. Can I come inside?"

"It's a diner, and we're open. Of course, you can come in. The name's Jerry, by the way. I'm the manager."

Jerry, the manager, sat McKinley down at a booth. McKinley ordered a cup of coffee. As soon as Jerry hurried away, he surveyed the scene.

There were only a few people at the diner. Most of the town was either at work or at home getting ready for the storm, he figured.

For the first time, he considered the possibility that they might be stuck in Lapse for quite a while, even if Swann magically popped up. There could be power outages. Down trees. Utility trucks and snow plows would be diverted to more populated areas first. Places of higher priority. The town of Lapse might be about to get snowed in completely.

"Heck of a time and place for a missing person investigation," McKinley said to himself.

Suddenly, an arm swung into view and set a coffee cup in front of him.

"So, you *are* here because of the missing persons," said Jerry. "I guess I already knew that."

The manager sat down across from McKinley and spoke quietly.

"Tell me. Is Carmen involved in this? She's my best waitress, you know. I'd hate to hear that something happened to her."

"We have no evidence that anything has happened to Carmen," McKinley said. It wasn't a lie.

Jerry bought it. He sighed and wiped his forehead. "Great. I told the sheriff I'd call him when she shows up for work. She might not, you know, because of the storm. But I know she'll call me if she can't make it in."

I sincerely hope that she does, thought McKinley. *And that she and Swann are shacked up at a motel the next town over. Never mind that her car is still here in Lapse. And Swann doesn't have one.*

He watched the approach of the storm through the window, wondering where Jo was now.

TWENTY-EIGHT

Jo was following Phelps up a small hill. Just before she reached the crest, her car suddenly hung up. The wheels spun, but she wasn't moving.

A moment later, she finally began to move, but in the wrong direction. The car slid backward down the hill. Jo turned her head, using the wheel to try and guide her descent. She barely managed to keep herself on the road. She came to a stop at the lowest point in the road, caught between two slopes.

Sheriff Phelps caught on that she was in trouble. He stopped his truck and got out. The old man appeared at the top of the hill, staring down at Jo with a concerned grimace.

She rolled her window down to call out. "I think I'm trapped here."

"Nonsense!" he shouted back. However, his wincing expression told a different story. "Just do what I say, and you'll get out just fine. First, throw the car into reverse. Climb down the slope behind you as far as you can. Then quickly put it in drive and gun it! I've got my park trucked far enough away, so no worries about hitting me."

He disappeared then, leaving her alone. Though Jo knew he was less than fifty yards away, she suddenly felt like the last woman on Earth.

Just her and the forest. And the snow that seemed like it would never stop falling.

Jo followed the direction Phelps gave her. The car Grantham provided wasn't geared for snow, but it had a strong engine. She rocked it backward. As soon as it stopped moving, she put it into drive and rocketed forward.

This time she made the top of the hill by the skin of her teeth. Phelps was already back in his truck. He drove forward, and they were back on their way.

Jo managed to avoid any further pitfalls. The road opened up ahead of them. The forest thinned out, giving way to a cultivated field. In the middle of that field was Kurt Black's property.

She wasn't prepared for what she saw. The former FBI agent lived on a veritable compound. There were dozens of buildings that she could see, and she assumed there were even more that she couldn't. There were huge barns and tiny sheds. Some were brand new; some were crumbling down. There were RV trailers and mobile homes. There was even a yellow school bus.

This is about to get interesting.

Phelps stopped his truck an eighth of a mile shy of the main house. Jo wondered why he was stopping there. Then her car hit the same patch of treacherous ground. She fishtailed, coming to a stop with her rear wheels buried in a snow drift.

Jo sighed, pulling on her gloves and getting out of the car. Phelps joined her, giving her a wry smile.

"No hills around here," he remarked.

"Yeah, I don't think the Phelps maneuver is going to work this time." Jo nodded at the truck. "I figured you would have four-wheel drive. How often do you get stuck in that thing?"

"Never," Phelps said. "I reckon we'll need to call for a tow truck. Just so long as that tow truck doesn't get stuck, and we need to call a *second* tow truck. You probably think I'm telling a joke, but I've seen it happen where three, sometimes *four* tow trucks all show up in the same place."

Jo shrugged. "I would still consider it a joke. Sometimes you just have to laugh, right?"

Phelps chuckled, taking a sip from his travel mug. "There was some smart fella once who said, 'life is a tragedy for those who feel, and a comedy for those who think.' I take it you're the thinking sort, Agent Pullinger?"

"Sometimes," she replied. "But sometimes it's hard not to feel."

"Yup, I hear ya on that." Phelps shook his head, kicking at one of the truck's tires. "Let's go see Kurt Black. We can figure our way out of this mess when we're done."

TWENTY-NINE

"I wonder what he needs all these buildings for?" Jo asked.

They were halfway between their stuck cars and the house. The smell of woodsmoke was faint but growing stronger. They could see no sign of Kurt or anyone else.

"Beats me," said Phelps. "All I know is, he has permits for most of it. Some of it, like that school bus... sheesh, no idea where that came from. Maybe it was carrying a whole load of politicians."

The sheriff began giggling uncontrollably.

"Am I missing something?" Jo asked.

"Oh, just one heck of a good joke," he said. "A busload of politicians drives off the road and crashes into a farmer's barn. The farmer goes to check the scene and ends up burying the unfortunate politicians.

"Later on, the sheriff pays a visit to investigate. He asks the farmer what happened to all the people on the bus. 'Buried 'em,' says the farmer. The sheriff goes, 'They were all dead?' and the farmer says back, 'Some of them said they weren't, but those politicians are always lying.'"

Phelps busted up laughing again. He slapped his knee and wiped a tear from his eye.

Jo cracked a smile. "I hope this one really is just a joke. Not like the tow trucks."

Phelps didn't get a chance to answer. A terrible screaming sound rang out from somewhere ahead of them. It echoed through the cold air, making Jo's skin bristle. Reflexively, she drew her gun and rested her thumb on the safety catch.

"What in God almighty?" Phelps asked sharply. He saw Jo's sidearm. This apparently made him realize he ought to be concerned. He pulled out his own handgun, a revolver.

They both set off toward the house at a jog. Phelps moved well for a man of his age, kicking his way through the deepening snow.

"Sounded like it was coming from behind the house," he observed.

"I agree," said Jo. "Stick together."

The screaming came again. It sounded like a woman or a child being tortured. But there was something weird about it. It sounded almost alien. Like something from a horror movie.

Jo's human instincts told her to run away. But her training drove her forward.

"I thought the banshee was just a legend," Phelps huffed. "Might be we're about to catch a glimpse of one. Wait a second... I think I know what that sound is."

He slowed down. He didn't share his knowledge with Jo, but his sudden calm had an effect on her anyway. She dropped her speed to match his. Together, they walked around the corner of the house.

Behind the huge, two-story farmhouse was a fenced-in chicken coop. The feathery creatures inside were sauntering carelessly about. All but the rooster; he was in a huff about something. Strutting and darting back and forth.

A man was standing outside the coop. He was wearing a dark blue jacket that looked familiar to Jo. It was FBI issue. She had a couple of them in her closet back home. But she couldn't see the big, yellow letters on the back. He had sewn a patch over them. It depicted a cross.

The man wore long, gray hair in a ponytail. A bushy beard sprouted from his cheeks.

At his feet was a snare trap. A fox was caught in it, thrashing about. It opened its mouth and let out another of those horrible screams.

Kurt Black was holding a rifle. He aimed, sighting on the trapped animal.

"This is the last time you try and eat *my* chickens," he said.

THIRTY

Kurt hesitated. He kept the rifle trained on the fox but didn't shoot. He remained perfectly still for a moment.

He turned around. In a flash, he had the gun aimed straight at Phelps.

"Easy!" Phelps called.

Kurt dropped the barrel, taking his finger off the trigger. "Sheriff. What are you doing sneaking up on me on my own property?"

There was an edge of anger in his voice. Jo had the sense he was barely holding it in. She holstered her sidearm. Phelps did the same.

"We heard screams," Phelps explained, raising his hands. "Turns out it was just the fox. But we figured someone might be in trouble."

"We?" Kurt asked. His eyes flicked to Jo. He sized her up quickly. "Oh. I see. I understand the agency is bleeding staff right now, but I'm not going back. I prefer my new life. Sorry, you wasted your time coming all the way out to my corner of nowhere." His tone was thick with bitter sarcasm.

"I'm not trying to bring you out of retirement," Jo said. "This is a different matter entirely. A serious one."

Kurt seemed to ignore her. He leaned his rifle against the chicken wire and knelt down. With a flick of his hand, he disengaged the snare trap. The frightened but uninjured fox went sprinting off into the trees.

"Why'd you go and do that?" Phelps asked. "That rascal's just gonna come right back later on and try to get your chicken all over again."

Still kneeling, Kurt scooped up a handful of snow. He used it to scrub his hands, then performed the sign of the cross.

"Sometimes we have the luxury of being stirred from our passions," he said. "You distracted me. My anger cooled. I realized the fox was simply acting according to its nature. I am the real foreigner here. And if he eats one of my chickens, oh well. Someone's being fed by it either way."

The snow trickled into his sleeves. He rolled them up. His forearms were covered in tattoos. They seemed to be mostly religious iconography. A Christian cross. A Star of David. The star and crescent of Islam. The Yin Yang. There were other symbols Jo didn't know the names of. It was a tapestry of faiths from around the world.

"What's your name, anyway?" Kurt asked with a grunt.

He said it without looking at Jo. But it was obvious who he was talking to.

"I'm Special Agent Jo Pullinger. From the Seattle office."

Kurt let out another grunt. No words. Just a sound of vague disgust.

"Go ahead and tell me what you're after," he added.

"Information," Jo said.

"And you think because I used to work for the Bureau, I know everything that goes on?" Kurt gestured at the forest. "I mostly keep to myself. Stay hidden out here. I don't know what happens outside this property. And I don't care. I've seen enough of the world."

Jo shook her head. She was getting annoyed preemptively. She knew this guy was going to be difficult. "We have two missing people. One of them is a fellow agent. Edward Swann."

"I hope you find him," Kurt replied. He actually sounded sincere. "But if you don't, try not to beat yourself up. Who else is missing?"

"A waitress from the diner," Jo said.

"Carmen Powell," Phelps added.

Kurt whipped around to face them. He looked the way Jo imagined she and Phelps had looked when they heard the screaming fox.

Apparently, Carmen's name struck a nerve.

THIRTY-ONE

"Did something happen to that girl?" Kurt demanded.

"We don't know that yet," Phelps answered. "We just know she's missing. Agent Pullinger, would you mind filling him in?"

Jo gave Kurt the details. Swann leaving the hotel last night, presumably to meet up with Carmen. Her car in the driveway. The sign of a possible struggle in the snow. Their inability to contact Swann.

During this, Kurt moved through several emotional states. Confusion, fear, and sadness. When Jo stopped, he let out a sigh.

"I've been trying to help that girl," he said. "She and I had many talks."

"I wasn't aware you even knew Carmen. I rarely see you interacting with folks in town, Mr. Black."

Kurt shrugged. "I always eat at the diner when I go into town. Saves me from having to cook for myself. It's not like I can get food delivered out here, either."

Phelps nodded slowly, looking around. "Do you get many visitors, Kurt?"

"You're asking if Carmen ever comes out here."

Phelps grinned. "Yeah, I am. I guess with all that special training you can see right through me."

"Almost literally." Kurt indicated the rifle. "It's not smart to creep up on a guy holding a high-powered weapon."

"Yep." Phelps rocked back on his heels. "It's also not smart to try and change the subject when your sheriff is asking a particular question. Might look suspicious, you know."

Jo thought about jumping in. But she was having a great time just watching Phelps at work.

"Touché," said Kurt. "Yes, Carmen has come out here a couple of times. The first time, she arrived under the wrong assumption. I invited her to a study and prayer session, and she assumed this was a romantic come-on. She showed up with a six-pack of beer, wearing skimpy clothing. It's a credit to her that she stuck around to hear me out. The girl is a hedonist, and she needs to be saved."

"I guess she's into older men," said Phelps. "Not that Swann's much older. Isn't that right, Jo?"

"He's in his late twenties," Jo confirmed. "Tall and dark-haired. Athletic."

"Doesn't ring a bell." Kurt grabbed his rifle and started toward the house. "If I see or hear anything, I'll let you know."

"One more question," Jo said. "How exactly would you go about saving a hedonist, Mr. Black?"

"By showing them the light," was his simple response. "I don't preach any religion in particular here. Each of them is an attempt by humans to find salvation. Each has its truths and its shortcomings. I offered Carmen the chance to join me on the path toward that salvation. And that is all. If you'll excuse me, I have work to do."

He stepped into the back door of the house. It slammed shut behind him.

"Well, then," said Phelps. "Guess we got as much as we're gettin'. Time to head back to the cars."

They started trudging through the snow. Phelps managed to get reception long enough to send his wife a text and receive a response.

"She'll get a tow truck headed out our way," he said. "Might be a while. I won't twist your arm, but if you'd like some company, you're free to wait it out in my truck."

She accepted his offer, climbing into the passenger seat beside him. He turned his country music down and got the heat going.

"So, he was trying to save Carmen from herself," he said.

"That rubs me the wrong way," Jo replied. "In fact, everything we just experienced rubs me the wrong way. Maybe I'm just jaded."

"No, I don't think you are." Phelps drummed on his steering wheel. He stared into the distance. "I reckon my gut's making all the same noises that yours is."

His phone rang.

"It's Sheri," he said. He answered it and put it on speaker mode. "Yes, dear?"

"I'm awfully cold right now, sheriff," Sheri purred. "Wish you were with me."

"Yeah, I'll bet," Phelps said. "You should think about turning your heat up. Just like I did. Me and Agent Pullinger are staying nice and toasty in my truck right now."

"Oh." Sheri cleared her throat. "I called the tow in for you. Should be there within forty minutes. You shouldn't have to resort to cannibalism or anything."

"Now, that is a relief. Much obliged. Let me know if anything changes, Sheri."

Phelps hung up. He and Jo went on waiting through a slightly awkward silence.

THIRTY-TWO

When Swann woke up, he was only aware of the pain. His head was throbbing. He was someplace dark. When he tried to look around, everything smeared. He couldn't focus his eyes.

I'm hungover, he thought. *Carmen and I must have had one crazy party last night. Except I'm not in her bed, and I don't think she's anywhere near me.*

He felt to either side of him to be sure. His fingers found nothing but a cold cement floor and the gritty surface of a stone foundation. His rear end was numb, so he must have been sitting here for some time.

The cold had seeped into his bones. He shivered and tried to hug himself for warmth. His arms came up short with the sound of clanging metal. There were manacles around his wrists. He was anchored to the wall.

"Carmen?" he said. His voice was raspy. His throat was dry. He worked his tongue around to generate some saliva. A coppery taste entered his mouth. All too familiar, from all his brushes with perps in Los Angeles.

It was blood.

The flavor of it brought back his memory of the night before. In an instant, he had gone from kissing Carmen to being dragged into the snow and kicked unconscious. Never before in his life had he gone from bliss to agony in such a short time.

He had no idea where he was. But he knew where he *wasn't*. This was not Carmen's house. Whoever knocked him out had dragged him here.

Swann's heart hammered in his chest. Adrenaline caused the pain to fade away. His mental fog cleared, and his vision focused. He was in a basement. There were rafters running across the low ceiling. Everything smelled old and damp.

He twisted around as far as he could, checking out the anchors that were holding his arms. They were thick steel plates, one for each hand. Each plate was held in the wall by four thick bolts.

There was no way he could break free. But he tried anyway, grunting and straining. Trying to bring his hands together in front of him. Like doing a chest fly at the gym. The chains went taut but didn't budge. The only thing Swann managed was to make his head start hurting again.

He relaxed, cursing to himself.

Suddenly, something moved in the shadows nearby. Fear prickled through Swann until he heard the pitiful moan from the shape, along with the clanking of chains.

"Carmen?" he said. "Is that you?"

She shifted and moaned again.

"Carmen!" he shouted. "Talk to me."

"Agent Swann?" she said weakly.

"Yes! Yes, it's me. I'm right here with you."

"Where are we?" she squeaked.

"In a basement somewhere," Swann replied. "It's not *your* basement, is it?"

"My house doesn't have a basement."

"Oh. Then they must have taken us somewhere else. Are you hurt?"

Carmen moved around. She stretched her legs and fingers. She bent her head from side to side. Checking for injuries.

"I don't think so," she said. "I... I think they injected me with something. I just remember..." She let out a frustrated groan.

"You probably don't remember much," said Swann. "If they injected you, it was probably like falling asleep. You just drifted off. Don't worry, though. Everything's going to be all right."

"How can you say that?" she wailed. "I was with you last night. An FBI agent. I thought that was the safest place I could possibly be. Then *this* happens?"

"I'm not talking about me," Swann replied. "I'm talking about Jo Pullinger. She'll be looking for us right now. As we speak. Along with McKinley. They really are the best at what they do. As for me..."

He almost went down a path of self-pity. But he decided to be strong, if only for Carmen's sake.

"Even if they fail somehow," he added, "we'll still be all right. *I'll* get us out."

THIRTY-THREE

A pale source of light flooded into the basement. A cone of illumination flowed down a set of rickety wooden steps. There was a thud as someone stepped down from the upper level. A squeal of rusty hinges as the door clamored shut.

The light was gone. Swann only got a vague impression of motion as the newcomer descended the stairs. He clenched up. Not knowing what to expect but certain it would be painful.

The silhouette came to a stop a few feet away. It reached up, grabbing a pull chain. With a *click,* a weak, yellow bulb came to life.

It was difficult to ascertain much about the figure. From the height and frame, Swann pegged them as being male. Most of their body was hidden by a flowing white robe. The face was covered with a black ski mask.

Hazel eyes stared intensely at Swann. A single lock of hair was visible through one of the eyeholes. A dirty blond color.

The gaze made Swann uncomfortable. He let his eyes wander away. They landed on the hand that was holding the pull chain. It was missing the tip of its right pinky finger.

Swann locked all these details into his mind. It was something to do. A distraction. Maybe it would be useful if he managed to get out of here.

It all depended on what this hazel-eyed menace was about to say. And what he wanted.

The figure returned to the steps. He had set a platter down there. There were two plates and two glasses on it. Each plate held a slice of brown bread. The glasses were full of water.

The masked man first knelt beside Swann. He ripped off a piece of bread and pressed it to Swann's lips.

Swann refused to open his mouth. The masked person got angry and let out a grunt. It was certainly the voice of a man.

Maybe this is the guy who kicked me in the head, Swann thought. *He's lucky my hands are chained down, or I'd knock a few of his teeth out.*

The man tried the water next. He held the cup to Swann's lips. Tipped it up. None of the water got in Swann's mouth. It poured down his chest, making him even colder.

The man pulled the glass away. "No food," he whispered. "No water. That's your choice. I will respect it."

He moved on to Carmen. She resisted at first as he ground a hunk of bread against her sealed lips. But she finally relented, opening her mouth. Letting him feed her. She ate both slices of bread and swallowed down half a glass of water.

She would have drunk more, but the man pulled the water away.

"Not too much," he said.

"Thank you," Carmen said as tears ran down her face. "Thank you very much for the food."

The man stared over at Swann.

Pinky, Swann thought. *That's what I'll call you. Because something tells me you wouldn't be willing to give me your real name.*

"Next time I come down here," Pinky said, "you should think about accepting my gifts."

Swann was determined to remain silent. He clenched his jaw to avoid shouting any of the angry words that kept coming to his mind.

Pinky carried the platter away. He briefly balanced it on his knee so he could pull the chain again. The light went out. In darkness, the two chained people listened to their captor climb the steps.

The door opened. The hinges screamed as it was shut. Swann listened for a minute. He was trying to make sure Pinky was actually gone.

"You have to stay strong," he said to Carmen.

She was still crying. "I was *hungry*."

"For stale bread?" Swann demanded. "Next time, bite his fingers off instead."

THIRTY-FOUR

Every day, at least once, McKinley gave thanks to whoever came up with the idea of free coffee refills.

The waitress just kept coming back, filling his mug up. Even when it was only half empty, she'd "freshen it up" with a fresh pour. It was pretty good coffee, too. A little weak. But when you drank about six or seven cups, the strength was less of a factor.

McKinley was wired, watching the progress of the storm with a mixture of adrenaline and fear. He kept checking his phone. Hoping Jo would get back to him. Hoping she would have good news. Or at least hoping she wouldn't have *bad* news.

He was really starting to worry about Swann. With every hour that passed, the likelihood that he would randomly show up dwindled further. It was a chance about as small as McKinley turning down the next refill. Or of the snow suddenly stopping.

In other words, it was not going to happen.

Worse than Swann not showing up was what his continued absence implied. He was somewhere against his will. Trapped. Held captive. Maybe even dead. Or at least injured.

McKinley had always been highly empathetic. He couldn't even stand watching other people get blood drawn. Thinking about what Swann might be going through right now...

It made him shiver. It made him want to run out there and find the guy. But he had no idea where to look. And he'd probably just get lost in the blizzard. Never to return to the warm world of weak coffee and overcooked eggs.

Finally, his phone rang. He answered it.

"Jo, please tell me something good," he begged.

"Something good," she replied. In the background, the sheriff cracked up. "Sorry, McKinley, I think Phelps is rubbing off on me. We got stuck in the snow in Kurt Black's driveway, and we're waiting on a tow truck. We're going stir crazy out here."

"No cannibalism!" Phelps said.

"Well, at least that's good," said McKinley. "Did you get anything out of Black?"

Jo sighed. "Just a great deal of suspicion. He had a prior relationship with Carmen. He claims to have been a sort of spiritual mentor to her."

"Sounds weird," McKinley admitted.

"I can almost buy it, though," said Jo. "The guy's very much into religion. He has every single religion tattooed on his arms, it looks like. But certain things he said struck me as odd."

McKinley got his wallet out, setting a neat stack of bills on the table. "I'll head back to the hotel now and start digging up more info on him. He was FBI, so there should be a good file on him somewhere."

"Sounds good. I'll be there as soon as I can. You can update me then."

They hung up. McKinley ran some calculations in his head. Pricing out the coffee and his food. He took some of his cash back, leaving enough for a good tip. Then he pulled his coat on and headed out.

The wind nearly knocked him over. He stumbled, catching himself on a handrail outside the diner. Leaning forward, he started in the general direction of the lodge. All hints of his earlier footprints were long gone. Through the swirling snow, he could barely make out the VACANCY sign in the distance.

He had never felt such cold in his life. The wind seemed to push it through him like icy knives. His thick coat might as well have been a screen door. He used both hands to hold his hood in place.

The inevitable happened when McKinley was halfway to the hotel. The vacancy sign disappeared.

He looked over his shoulder. The lights of the diner were also gone. He could still see the building, but it was now dark.

The power had gone out in Lapse.

No heat. No lights. No way of charging his phone or laptop. McKinley's overthinking mind spun through all the nightmare possibilities.

Heat was the first and most important thing. Before doing any research on Kurt Black, he wanted to go and check on Miriam. If she had a generator, she might need help to get it going. Especially if it was as old and outdated as her security system.

THIRTY-FIVE

The tow truck driver was a hulking man named Bobby, and he was Jo's hero. Phelps said he would show up within forty minutes. Bobby cut that time in half, arriving about twenty minutes after the uncomfortable phone call from Sheri.

"Most people don't go driving at times like these," Bobby said sarcastically. He fell to his knees with a grunt. Reaching under the truck, he hooked a metal claw to some piece of structure. "Mostly folks stay at home."

"Do you see this?" Phelps fired back, tapping his badge. "This means I'm out here on official business. The weather doesn't stop criminals from doing criminal things."

Bobby grinned, showing gaps between his teeth. He nodded toward the distant farmhouse. "Is that hermit fellow a criminal now?"

"That's some more of that official business, there. But between you and me, he isn't. Not at the moment."

Bobby nodded. He heaved himself to his feet and went back to his truck to play with the winch controls. There was a humming, whining noise. The truck slowly inched back out of the snow bank.

Bobby reappeared. "Should be good now, Sheriff. Let's get the lady's car out now. Ma'am."

He offered Jo a charming smile. It would have been more charming if he had brushed his teeth at all in the past few years. Either way, Jo could have kissed him. On the cheek, at least.

Her car was out even faster than the truck. Bobby dusted his hands and tipped his hat.

"Now, we best all be getting out of here fast," he said. "Case you didn't notice, the snow's still falling. Just follow me. If you get stuck again on the way out..."

"You'll just rescue us all over again?" Jo asked.

Bobby winked at her as he climbed back into his truck.

Phelps and Jo returned to their respective driver's seats. Phelps waved Jo in, letting her go first behind the tow truck. The convoy made its way out of the forest, bumping along the dirt road. It might have been hidden by snow, but it was still full of ruts and potholes.

Things went better than expected. Bobby's truck had already cleaved a decent set of tracks through the powder. The weight of the machine had packed the snow into a hard, unyielding surface. Jo's comparatively light sedan glided over it easily.

Her mind was free to wander slightly. All she could think about was Kurt Black, though. She imagined what the inside of his house would look like. A shrine in every room? One for every religion? A crucifix in the living room. A Muslim prayer rug in the kitchen.

He probably has one heck of an eclectic library, too.

It all sounded very interesting. But Kurt's relationship with Carmen was her real concern. Sometimes, the most dangerous person is one who thinks they're doing the right thing. The wise man trying to save the sinful young woman.

Her phone rang. She hoped it was McKinley with some fresh nugget of information. The man always came through.

Instead, a female voice greeted her. "Hello, Jo. This is Agent Larkin. Grantham asked me to run a trace on Agent Swann's cell phone."

"Yes!" said Jo eagerly. "Do you have something?"

"We got a hit," Larkin said. "I have a feeling it's not going to be very fruitful, though. I'm seeing it there in town. Right across the street from the diner. I can't be sure of the exact location, but that's what our triangulation indicates. We were able to get a brief GPS connection, but the storm is acting as a smokescreen."

Larkin's voice then fell under a blanket of static.

"Okay," Jo said. "I'll head over there. Thanks, Larkin. I think I'm about to lose you."

Larkin said something else, but it was too distorted to make out. The connection was lost. The phone beeped a few times to let Jo know the call was over.

She had another reason to be glad Bobby was in front of her. If he wasn't, she would be tempted to speed back into town. Under these conditions, it would have been very dangerous.

***

Jo reached the diner and pulled to a stop in what she could only assume was a parking space. It was a relatively flat area between two mounds of snow that might have been buried cars. She got out. The diner was mostly dark. She could see flashlight beams shining around.

Power's out. Not a good sign.

It only seemed to be getting colder. The wind even more ferocious. She crossed the road in a staggering fashion. It was difficult to tell where the edge of it was. At least with the eyes. She figured it out when she suddenly sank in up to her knees.

Jo pulled herself out of the drift and stood up. She scanned left and right, considering the hopelessness of the task. A needle in a haystack.

Then she spotted something. A smooth furrow through the snow. The fine details had been covered up, but the furrow formed a distinctive arc. It was a tire. Someone had driven almost off the road, stopped, then continued. And it hadn't been that long ago.

Jo approached the spot. She dropped to her knees, then pulled out her phone. She gave Swann's number a call and strained her ears to listen. There was nothing at first. Jo turned her head from side to side, trying to detect any slight change in the soundscape around her.

At last, she thought she heard a faint buzz.

Gritting her teeth, she plunged her bare hands into the icy depths. She felt around quickly, to try and find the phone before her fingers went numb. Suddenly she had it. The familiar feeling of a flat rectangle. Swan's phone.

She yanked it out of the snow. The screen lit up for a fraction of a second, during which she saw the battery level. Critically low. Sapped by the cold.

The phone died.

Jo stuck it in her pocket and hurried back to her car. She didn't want to succumb to the temperature now. She would end up as one of those buried humps under the snow, forgotten until spring.

THIRTY-SIX

At that same moment, McKinley finally reached the hotel's parking lot. The wind gusted stronger, trying to pull him down. He bent almost ninety degrees at the waist to keep upright.

The office might have been dark, but it still shone as bright as a Christmas tree in his mind. Warmth and sanctuary. If he was quick, he might even be able to get a hot shower before the lack of power ruined everything.

McKinley shoved the office door open and rushed through, letting out a groan of relief as he stomped the snow off his shoes. The smell of cinnamon was as strong as ever. There was something else, a slightly burnt aroma undercutting the spiced fragrance.

The door behind the counter was open by a few inches. He could only see darkness beyond.

"Miriam?" he called. "Are you all right?"

There was no response. Maybe she was confused. Or hurt.

"Miriam?" he tried again. "I'm coming to the back."

He moved around the counter and pushed the door open. The burnt smell became stronger. It was too dark to see much, so McKinley flicked his phone flashlight on. He followed the cone of light into the kitchen.

Miriam had been making toast. The two slices of bread stood in their toaster slots. Black as charcoal. She must have toasted them once. Saw they weren't ready yet. Stuck them back in. Then she was distracted, letting the toast go too long.

Distracted by what? The power going out?

McKinley moved past the table. Just a little while ago, he had been sitting there with Miriam. If she was in any kind of trouble...

"Miriam?"

He saw her feet sticking into view from behind the sofa. She seemed to be lying face down on the floor.

McKinley rushed over, peering over the back of the couch. The back of Miriam's head was a mess of blood and hair. More blood stained the carpet around her.

A quiet, stoic voice echoed in McKinley's mind. Listing things off. *Blunt force trauma. No sign of a struggle from her. The killer swung more than once, causing the castoff blood spatter...*

He vaulted over the couch and almost fell on his face. Putting his fingers to Miriam's neck, he felt for a pulse. There was nothing, but the body was still warm.

Paranoid, McKinley raised his head and glanced around. The tiny apartment was full of shadows and blind corners. Narrow hallways and doors. Plenty of hiding places.

Or maybe the killer was long gone. It all depended on motive.

McKinley returned to the front office. He popped open the cash register. There was no way of knowing how much money Miriam usually kept, but the till was still healthily stocked. A few fifties and a bunch of twenties. If someone had come here to rob the place, they wouldn't have missed any of this.

He considered other possibilities. Or rather, he tried to. His mind couldn't quite focus. His stomach roiled, threatening to dispel his diner food. Along with the sandwich Miriam had given him.

She was such a nice old lady. Trusting and warm. What kind of monster could do this?

He had left the door to Miriam's apartment open behind him. Through it, he heard a subtle noise. Maybe it was just a vibration through the floor. Either way, he suddenly knew there was someone there.

McKinley turned fast, drawing his sidearm.

A man charged out of the closet that held Miriam's security system. He wore a ski mask over his face. In his right hand was a claw hammer, stained with blood.

Before McKinley could form a single thought, the man raised the hammer above his head.

"We'll make half the sacrifice right here!" he screamed.

THIRTY-SEVEN

Jo heard a *bang* as she was getting back in her car. She paused, trying to figure out the source of the sound. It might have been a gunshot, but she couldn't be sure. Everything sounded stranger in weather like this.

Then it came again. *Bang.*

She slammed the door shut and backed out of her parking spot. She drove as fast as she could, back out onto the main road. North, toward the hotel. Twice her car lost traction and began to fishtail. Jo was on autopilot, fueled by adrenaline. And it turned out this version of her was a better driver. She navigated the deepening snow like a professional.

She lost control again in the parking lot. The front end of the car hit a patch of compressed snow. A ball of ice as hard as a brick wall. The bumper crumpled with a snapping sound.

Jo ditched the car, drawing her weapon as she sprinted toward the office.

The door was halfway open. It was held that way by a man lying across the threshold. All Jo saw at first was the blood, spreading across the white ground. For a moment, she was terrified that something had happened to McKinley.

Then she saw the ski mask and the huge, beefy arms. No way this was McKinley.

She stepped over the man, charging into the office.

"FBI!" she shouted.

"Jo," McKinley said. "It's just me."

He was sitting behind the counter in Miriam's usual spot. The cash drawer was open for some reason.

"McKinley!" Jo holstered her weapon. "What just happened? Are you hurt?"

"Just emotionally and psychologically," he replied. "Miriam's dead."

She stared at him. He said nothing more. Jo went into the back, scouring the place until she found the old woman's body.

The sight made her blood run cold. It wasn't just the horrible nature of the crime, though that was bad enough.

There are no such things as coincidences, she thought.

Whoever it was who killed Miriam, and whatever reason they had for doing it, they were probably somehow tied up in what had happened to Swann and Carmen. These were clearly some evil, nasty people.

People. Plural. Jo was certain of that part. It would have taken more than one crazy person to overpower Swann. The guy was in excellent shape. He was young. His reflexes were sharp.

This was getting worse and worse. It was a strange, dark tunnel with no end in sight. No side paths to take, no escape routes.

She went back to McKinley.

"Tell me what happened," she said.

"I missed." McKinley let out a dry laugh. "Well, not really. The first shot hit him, but it wasn't fatal. It barely grazed his arm."

"You shot him again?" Jo asked.

McKinley nodded. "He kept coming at me. With the hammer he used on Miriam. My second shot hit him in the chest. He almost made it out of the door before he fell over."

"Good work." Jo patted him on the back. "Very good work. Do you need anything? A cup of coffee?"

"No power. No coffee," McKinley said. "There's something else the guy said, though. Something about a sacrifice. I've been trying to figure out what he was talking about."

"Whatever it was," Jo added, "it can't be anything good. Because I'm pretty sure this guy has friends. And they have Swann and Carmen somewhere. Let's just hope they're still alive."

THIRTY-EIGHT

McKinley was still in a state of shock. His face was waxy and pale. He kept hyperventilating, complaining of nausea. Jo dragged a trash can over in case he lost his lunch. Then she gave him some space.

She went back outside, squatting down next to the fallen man.

He was still wearing his ski mask. But it was bunched up around his forehead, leaving his facial features exposed. In his final moment, as he struggled to breathe, he must have pulled the stifling garment up.

Jo tried to summon a shred of human empathy but failed. This guy had murdered a defenseless elderly woman. Then he tried to kill McKinley, one of her favorite people on the planet.

He was a young guy with no distinctive features. He looked like anyone you might see walking the streets. She snapped a photo of his face. She then searched his pockets.

She came up with nothing. The guy was wearing a pair of coveralls with plenty of pockets, but they were all empty. Nothing but lint. No ID. No keys.

"We have a ghost here," she mumbled to herself. "But you couldn't have just appeared out of nowhere."

She got back in the car, rocking it a bit to try and free it from the glacier. She ignored the pieces of fiberglass that dropped off the front end. When it was clear, she pulled the car up close to the body. Blocking sight of it from anyone passing by.

She doubted very much that anyone was out cruising the highways today, looking for a place to rent a room. So this should be enough to keep the public at bay.

With her car positioned, she set off on foot. She slowly made her way around the perimeter of the parking lot. There were only two vehicles that had any business being there. Miriam's, and the car they had arrived in.

There were no other cars. Not in the hotel lot and not parked out on the road.

The killer must have come on foot. There was no telling how far he had walked to get here. When you planned on committing cold-blooded murder, no weather was going to slow you down. He might have been walking all day just to get here.

Jo reached the back of the building. There was a back door to Miriam's apartment, and there were fairly fresh footprints there. Far too large to have belonged to Miriam.

Jo followed them out as far as she could. Across the empty field behind the hotel. They vanished long before she could reach the other side. The field ended at the edge of a forest, usually a great place to find tracks even when it was snowing.

But with no foliage on the trees and all of this sideswiping wind, even the deepest sections of the forest would be covered in a fresh layer of snow.

Maybe the killer had counted on this. Or maybe it was just a happy accident.

Jo finished her circuit of the hotel. It would have been quicker to go through Miriam's apartment. But she was in no hurry to see the body again. She had seen much worse scenes during training. Photos and videos of horrible crimes.

But in person, it was a different story. Those were people she didn't know. People she had never spoken with.

McKinley was exactly where he had left her. He leaned over his trash can, a string of saliva dangling from his lower lip.

"Are you going to make it?" Jo asked.

He gave her the thumbs up. At the same time, he made a horrible retching sound. Jo turned away before she could see the eruption. The noises were bad enough.

"I'm just going to call Phelps," she said. "Take your time."

She went back out into the cold and dialed the sheriff's number.

"Miss me already?" he asked. "Or did you get that little car of yours stuck again?"

"Almost," she admitted. "I'm at the lodge, Phelps. We've got a situation down here. Someone has murdered Miriam Whitaker."

There was a pause. When Phelps spoke, his voice was much thinner than usual. "Oh, lord. Did the killer get away?"

"No. He's dead."

"At least that's something. I'll be right there. Dang, if this isn't turning out to be the most *rotten* day of my career... Just hang tight."

THIRTY-NINE

They hung tight.

Jo cursed the dead man for falling right in the middle of the door-way. They couldn't close the door. The cold swept through the lobby. It instantly swept away every last shred of warmth. With the furnace no longer running, the chill was here to stay.

At least it's good for preserving the bodies, Jo thought. *Who knows how long it'll take for a coroner to get here?*

Five minutes after the phone call, they heard a diesel engine rumbling toward them. Phelps's truck screamed into the parking lot. It skidded to a dramatic stop. The aging sheriff stepped out and hobbled through the snow toward the lobby.

"Pullinger!" he said. "You show up in town, and less than twen-ty-four hours later, I hardly recognize the place! You must have some awful curse on you."

"That is how it feels sometimes," Jo said, sighing. "We have two corpses here, Phelps."

"Yep." He wrinkled his whole face up like a hero in an old Western movie. "I was mostly talking about the weather, but... let's see them."

The first body was obvious. Phelps took one look at the young dead guy in the entryway. He sniffed once, hard, then stepped over him.

"Miriam?" he asked gravely.

Jo led him into the back. Phelps stared at the body of the old woman for a lot longer.

He took off his hat and held it to his chest. "That's just too bad. Miriam was a great woman."

"Were you close with her?" Jo asked.

Phelps turned away, putting his hat back on. "Close enough. She was good friends with Sheri. She'll be devastated by this."

He let out a growl of anger, grinding one heel into the rug. It seemed as close to an angry outburst as he was capable of.

"This is one big, ugly mess," he added.

"McKinley and I are here," Jo reminded him. "We can help out."

"With this?" Phelps poked a thumb over his shoulder. "I hate to be insensitive. Even callous, my wife would call it. But Miriam's already dead. So is the son of a gun who killed her. Far as I'm concerned, and I am a taxpayer by the way, you two agents have more important business to deal with. Find your missing agent."

Jo nodded. "So, what's the plan, then?"

He gave her a sardonic smile. "You're asking me?"

"I am. Like you told me before, you're the sheriff of these parts. McKinley and I are just passing through."

"Huh." He scratched his mustache. "Well, okay then. If you insist. Here's the deal, Jo. I'm going to put in a call to the state police. They're going to send some nice folks to help me process this scene. I'll keep you updated on our progress."

"And McKinley and I?"

"You're going to head over to Carmen's place," Phelps said. "You can keep warm in that car of yours. Keep an eye on the scene where your agent and the waitress went missing. I think that McKinley needs a break, anyway. And you can relieve my wife of her duties. Send her this way."

"The police will need McKinley's story," Jo said.

Phelps shook his head. "He can give it to me. I'll give it to them. If they need it straight from the source, I'll tell 'em where you are."

Jo smiled. "Okay."

Phelps nodded. "Okay. Let's get to it."

They returned to the lobby. McKinley repeated the details of his encounter. Then he and Jo went out to the car.

They promptly received a call from Grantham. Jo was glad to see it. She'd gotten so caught up in everything, the thought of updating her boss hadn't yet crossed her mind.

"Pullinger here," she said.

"And McKinley," McKinley added.

"Glad to hear both your voices," said Grantham. "I've got some bad news for you."

"That's funny, sir," said Jo. "We've got some bad news for you, too."

Grantham sighed. "You go first. Is it something to do with Swann?"

"Maybe. No news on that yet. But the woman who runs the hotel we're staying at was just murdered. We have the perp dead at the scene as well."

"That is... unexpected," Grantham replied. "You think there's a link?"

"No evidence of one right now, but this is a small town, sir."

"Yeah. I see what you mean. Well, my bad news seems a little less bad in comparison. This storm that's hitting you is some freak thing. They're talking about it on the news all the way up in Seattle, even though it's forty-five and rainy here. It means the backup I was sending your way has been held up."

"Not surprising," Jo said. "Any word on when they'll get here?"

"Sometime tomorrow. They'll be in contact with you. Just don't freeze to death, all right?"

Jo turned the windshield wipers on. The high setting. It made no real difference in her visibility.

"We'll try, sir," she said.

FORTY

Jo hung up and reached for the wheel. She glanced at the instrument panel and groaned.

"Of course, we're on empty," she said.

"There's a gas station right up the road," said McKinley. "We'll pass it on our way to Carmen's. I'm sure they've got their backup power running by now."

McKinley was right. As soon as they turned onto the road, they saw the gas station lights ahead of them. Just a few dim ones glowing inside; the floodlights over the pumps were still out. But the sign showing the gas prices was working.

To Jo, it looked like heaven.

She assumed there would be a run on gas at some point tomorrow, once the snow slowed down and the plows were able to get a real foothold. For now, the station was deserted. She pulled up to a pump.

McKinley disengaged his seatbelt. "I'll pump. Do you mind getting me a coffee from inside?"

"Not at all." Jo gave him the keys and headed in.

The inside of the shop was dark and quiet. But it was warm. She tried not to bask in it too long, knowing she had places to be. She filled two of the biggest cups they had, grabbed a few snacks, and headed for the counter. The clerk had already taped up a sign: CARD READER DOWN. Good thing Jo had cash.

She took the supplies back out to the car. McKinley was already finished pumping. He sat in the driver's seat, his head back, with the heat pumping out of the registers. He opened the door when he saw Jo.

"You want to drive?" she asked.

"Absolutely not!" McKinley was out in a microsecond, rushing around to the passenger side. He started sipping his coffee immediately, unbothered by the boiling temperature. "This stuff is *terrible*."

"It's gas station coffee." Jo tried a sip of hers. "Yup. Tastes like wood chips and rat pee."

"What?" McKinley laughed, then took another drink. He raised an eyebrow. "Yeah. I guess it does taste like that. But it has caffeine, presumably. So bottoms up."

They finished the drive to Carmen's house. Sheri was happy to see them, waving and smiling. Until they told her what had happened. Her face fell. She excused herself and sped away to find her husband.

"This sucks," McKinley said. "For them, I mean."

Jo shrugged. "It sucks for you, too. You had to shoot a guy."

"I'm an FBI agent. It's part of the job."

"You usually work at a desk, though. The idea that every FBI agent runs around in the field, getting in gunfights with bad guys... that's just Hollywood. It never feels right to shoot someone. Even if you do it for all the right reasons."

McKinley made a face and looked away. He wasn't ready to talk about it. Jo changed the subject.

"I wonder how long it'll be before the power's back on?" she asked.

"Days, maybe," said McKinley. "Any plumbers that work in Lapse are about to be busy. Plenty of burst pipes, I'm sure. The power company will worry about high-population areas first."

"I just hope nobody freezes to death." Jo popped the lid off her coffee, hoping it would cool down faster. She looked out at the abandoned car parked in the driveway. "I hope wherever Swann and Carmen are, they at least have a blanket."

"Just one?" McKinley asked.

"Well, yeah. They can huddle up under it and share body heat."

"Fair enough. What did you get for snacks?"

Jo was divvying out bags of junk food when her phone rang again. She was surprised when she saw the name on the caller ID.

"Ford!" she answered with a smile.

"Don't wear it out," the private investigator said. "Bryan Ford, at your service. No need to get so excited. Didn't we just see each other, like, a week ago?"

"The Graff thing? That's old news now. It's great to hear from you. You wouldn't believe the time McKinley and I are having right now."

"I might believe it, actually. Early this afternoon, I was visited by the one and only Robert Grantham."

"Wait a second," Jo said suspiciously. "Grantham came to your office?"

"He did. I think the guy either has a soft spot for you two, or else he missed my incredible charm. Either way, he hired me as a consultant again. I guess all the other agents in Seattle are busy with some huge thing. He couldn't tell me much about that, but..."

Jo grinned. "So, you're the backup Grantham is sending."

"Not just me," Ford corrected her. "I've got three guys from the crime lab with me. They party pretty hard, even in a hotel room. Right now, they're sipping screwdrivers and sharing their most gruesome stories."

"I don't hear anyone in the background," said Jo.

"That's because I'm hiding in the bathroom. I can only hear so much about mangled corpses and barrels of acid before I need a break. Good news is, they made my drink extra strong. So I might not remember any of it."

"Well, don't drink too much," Jo laughed. "You're supposed to come help us out sometime tomorrow."

"We'll be in Lapse as soon as we can," Ford promised.

"Good. We're counting on it. How's the family?"

"We're doing well," Ford replied. "Seems like a boring answer, but I've got nothing against that. There have been no calamities. No problems. Just life as normal."

Jo nodded along. She was happy for her friend but slightly jealous. Right about now, she could use a bit more "boring" in her life.

FORTY-ONE

It had been a busy day. Jo had spent it looking for Swann, searching for clues, and trying not to die on the snowy roads. She had completely lost track of time. Suddenly it was getting dark. Night was here, and it wasn't quite six o'clock.

"This is going to be a long one," McKinley said. He sounded excited.

"You like stakeouts?" Jo asked.

"As long as I'm not alone." McKinley popped a BBQ pork rind into his mouth. Jo had thought they were chips when she bought them. She hated pork rinds, but McKinley liked them. "It's kind of cozy, isn't it? Like a road trip, but you don't have to worry about directions."

Jo looked at the clock again. "A very long road trip."

***

It wasn't so bad. They spent their time chatting or listening to the radio. The local country station gave them occasional weather alerts. Sometimes they even played a decent song. She learned that McKinley was a fan of Brooks & Dunn.

As the snow continued to fall, they took measures to mitigate it. Once an hour, one of them grabbed the snow brush and went out. In this fashion, they kept too much from accumulating on the car.

They had no snow shovel, but they found one leaning against a neighbor's mailbox. They figured it would be OK to borrow, and it came in handy. Without it, the stuff they brushed off the car would just gather in huge mounds and prevent them from ever getting out.

These short bursts of physical labor made the long periods of sitting more pleasant. The time passed faster than Jo would have expected. Eventually, they reached a new stage in their struggle: the effort to stay awake.

Together, they came up with a system. It involved stripping off their coats and doing jumping jacks outside in the cold. It worked a treat and kept them from nodding off.

At midnight, a set of headlights stung their eyes. A truck pulled to a stop nearby, and Phelps got out, carrying a bundle of something toward them. McKinley rolled his window down.

"Howdy, Sheriff," he called.

"Howdy back at ya," Phelps replied "Got some coffee here. Some donuts. And a couple of blankets."

McKinley stopped listening at the word "coffee." He grabbed his cup and started drinking it down.

Jo took the blankets and coffee. "Thanks, Phelps. How are things going at the hotel?"

"Not too bad. Should have more to tell you in a couple of hours. The power's still off around town, but most folks who live in Lapse are smart enough to have generators. Those who don't are shacking up with their neighbors. Fingers crossed, we won't lose anyone to the cold."

FORTY-TWO

Hours went by. The masked man did not return. The cold, hard ground continued sapping Swann's strength. At least there was a furnace somewhere. He could hear the ductwork rattling. Warm, dry air stirred around him.

For a while, Swann assumed things wouldn't get much worse. At least not until his captor returned. Until that dreadful moment, he could just sit here and think. He could try and come up with a way out.

Then the power went out.

He didn't realize it at first. He could hear some kind of storm raging outside. Howling winds. Icy snow hitting the outside walls.

The furnace would kick on at regular intervals. The passage of time was hard to grasp, but he never went too long without feeling that stirring of air. It would always come just as he was starting to shiver.

The shivering came. But the warm air did not. Swann assumed that he was just losing strength, getting cold faster. Minutes passed, and he expected to hear the rattling vents at any second. It never came.

Swann got to his feet.

"What are you doing?" Carmen asked. Her voice was weak. She sniffled with cold.

"I think we lost power," he said, grunting. "If I can reach the pull chain, I can test the light. Then we'll know for sure."

But he was too tall. Just by standing, he pulled his chains taut. He couldn't move forward at all.

He crouched down, giving himself some slack, and crab-walked closer to the pull chain. He still came up short. No matter how he stretched his arms, he couldn't reach it.

Balancing on one foot, he lifted the other off the floor. He extended his leg upward, trying to reach the chain with his toes.

"You almost got it," said Carmen.

Swann sighed and lowered his leg. "I'm not *that* flexible. Let me try this..."

He turned so that he was facing Carmen. The pull chain was to his left now. He balanced on one foot again. This time, he was able to extend his free leg fully. And get it just high enough. The cold chain settled between his toes. He yanked down on it.

There was a click. But no light.

"No power," Swann groaned. "At least I got to practice my side kick. Haven't done that since I was about eleven years old, doing karate."

Carmen was quiet. Swann desperately wanted to say something that would make her feel better. He couldn't come up with anything. He wondered if it was just because he was tired. Or maybe their situation really was hopeless.

He settled back into his spot. The floor felt even colder than before. He wanted to sleep but was afraid he might never wake up. Swann forced himself to stay awake, shifting around as much as he could. Keeping his blood flowing. He advised Carmen to do the same.

At one point, he heard a generator kicking on somewhere nearby. He thought about screaming for help. But the person who turned the generator on was probably working with Pinky. Swann had a feeling he was being held somewhere remote. There was probably no shortage of such places around Lapse.

Either way, the generator was a good sound. It meant they would probably have heat soon. He kept telling himself that as he watched the dim sunlight fade, replaced by complete darkness.

Swann had grown up in southern California. When he moved to Seattle, he thought he got his first glimpse of what cold felt like. But it wasn't even close. *This* was cold. It wasn't just an unpleasant feeling. It was a physical force, slowly asserting itself on your mind, body, and soul.

There was no ignoring it.

The only thing he could do was keep trying to escape.

FORTY-THREE

Jo was listening to country music at a low volume. She couldn't even tell which singer it was.

Probably some guy named Travis, Jason, or Luke, she thought with a chuckle.

The passenger door opened. Fingers of icy cold wiggled their way into the car. Jo felt a snowflake hit her right cheek and melt away.

McKinley quickly ducked inside. He knocked his shoes together to get the snow off. Then he pulled his feet into the car and slammed the door shut.

"Cold out there!" he exclaimed. He used his teeth to remove his gloves, rubbing his bare hands together. "Oh, this song's funny. It's about a guy deciding whether he should have another beer or not."

"Does he have a pickup truck, too?" Jo asked.

McKinley shrugged and pointed at the clock. "Quarter to two. I burned off a whole five minutes brushing the snow off our car. Next time I might try and go a little slower. There must be some happy medium between killing as much time as possible and..."

"...and not freezing to death?" Jo asked.

"Yeah. Something like that. I wish Phelps would bring us more coffee now. And donuts."

He got his wish fifteen minutes later. Phelps made his second appearance of the night. The sheriff looked like he had aged ten years since the last time they saw him. Even his mustache looked sad, drooping down past his chin.

Instead of handing their goodies through the window, he opened the backseat and climbed inside.

"Got some hot cocoa for you," he said. "No more donuts. No place in Lapse is open at this hour, even on a good night. And this ain't a good night by any stretch."

"Thanks all the same," Jo replied. She took a sip of cocoa. It was room temp and a little watery. She figured he probably made it for them in one of the hotel rooms. "Any updates from the crime scene?"

"Yep," Phelps groaned. "I thought I recognized the guy you shot, Agent McKinley. But I didn't say anything because I wasn't sure. He looked... *feral.* That's the best way I can say it, I think. Like he went wild since the last time I saw him. But, we got a positive ID back."

"Who was it?" McKinley asked.

"A young man named Joseph Malone. He always went by Joey."

Jo almost choked on her next swallow of cocoa. She set her cup down and looked back at Phelps. "That's one of the missing people."

He nodded. "Guess he's not missing anymore. He showed up here in town to murder the grandmother of one of the other missing kids. It's a whole weird mess, is what it is. Too many questions."

"Like why did he kill Miriam," said Jo.

"And where has he been hiding out all this time?" McKinley added.

Jo was perplexed by it. Her heart rate increased, and her imagination burned with ideas. It was a puzzle to solve. She was totally in her element.

Meanwhile, Sheriff Phelps looked completely depressed.

"I thought I'd never see that boy alive again," he whispered. "Turns out I was right. I guess I should have seen this coming, though..."

FORTY-FOUR

"It's been a rumor for a few months," Phelps went on. "More like an urban legend, I guess. It all started this past autumn. A guy in town—I'll leave out his name—was out in the woods. Looking for mushrooms. We have a festival here, you know. We call it Fungus Funtime. Yeah, I know it's silly, but I won't waste my time trying to explain it to you city-slickers.

"Anyway, this mushroom hunter got kind of lost. The fool thought, since he grew up in these parts, he could go wandering around anywhere. No problem. And certainly no compass or GPS. He wandered and wandered, trying to find his way back home. It got dark. He finally saw a light up ahead. A campfire. He headed over to try and find some help.

"When he got close enough, he saw the people standing around that fire and thought better about joining them. There were a handful of folks, all dressed in strange robes, all standing in a circle around the fire. They were just staring into the flames. Not talking. Not moving. The hero of our story hightailed his butt out of there and finally managed to get home. Came into the station the next morning to tell me about his sighting."

The brief silence was punctuated by the sound of McKinley slurping his hot chocolate.

"Did you believe him?" Jo asked.

"No reason not to," said Phelps. "I tend to believe folks. And this man always had a solid reputation. He's no drunken reprobate. We got a few of those around town, as you can probably imagine. A small place like this. But even if those folks told me about some weirdos in the woods, I'd probably still believe them. But what was I supposed to do about it?"

"It's not illegal to wear robes and stare at a fire," McKinley said.

Phelps pointed at him. "Exactly. Is it peculiar? Sure. But the mushroom huntin' fellow admitted he had no idea where he was. He said he probably wouldn't be able to bring me to wherever it was he saw those odd characters around the fire. He didn't even know if it was private property or state land."

"You said it was an urban legend," said Jo. "Have you heard anything else?"

"Stories." Phelps used the index finger on either hand to smooth out his mustache. "Mostly kids making things up, I reckon. Stuff about a creepy cult in the woods. Stuff like that. Like all myths, it's taken on some spicy flavor over the weeks. Supposedly they're a bunch of cannibals. They lure people into the woods and eat them."

Phelps scoffed and laughed to show what he thought of that idea.

"I like you, Phelps," Jo told him. "I'm even starting to like this town. Just a little bit. I'd like everything to be fine. For everyone to be safe. And I'd like to let you hold onto that dismissive attitude. But I can't. I think these stories might have some truth behind them."

McKinley nodded. "Right. This Joey Malone guy was yelling something about a sacrifice when he charged at me."

Phelps pinched the ends of his mustache and did a twirling motion. Suddenly it was good as new. But he still looked haggard. "If you're asking me to consider the possibility that I'm dealing with a cannibal cult..."

"Probably not," Jo admitted. "If they were luring people out and killing them for food, why would Joey show up in town and murder Miriam in her own business?"

Phelps smirked. "You got a point there. Now I feel so much better. They might be killing the nice folks of Lapse, but at least they aren't eatin' em. Which means... maybe none of the people who went missing recently are victims. Maybe they're willing participants."

"Joey was," McKinley replied. "Maybe it's a whole group. All the missing people are involved."

Jo nodded. "They've been recruiting. Gaining new followers. And maybe they've decided to step up their game."

FORTY-FIVE

"Think about it," Jo went on. "We saw it right here, earlier today."

McKinley pointed at the clock. "Yesterday. It's past two AM."

"We haven't gone to sleep yet, McKinley. And the sunrise hasn't happened, so it's still the same day."

"Hmm." He drank the rest of his cocoa. "Doesn't quite add up, but I'll go with it."

Phelps leaned into the front seat. "If you two are done arguing semantics, I'd sure like to hear whatever theory you're working on."

Jo turned the headlights on. Carmen's car, still in the driveway, was illuminated. "It's too obvious to be a theory. When McKinley and I arrived at her car earlier, we saw markings in the snow. Some kind of struggle. It seemed like multiple people were involved. It would have taken more than one to take Swann down."

"A group of attackers," said Phelps.

"Right. And now we're talking about a group of robe-wearing strangers in the forest. One of them is pretty much confirmed to be Joey Malone. So, we can guess that the other missing people are in the same group."

"And they attacked your friend?" asked Phelps. "Why on Earth would they do a thing like that? Nothing gets fringe groups shut down faster than when they mess with the FBI."

"Then their goal must be to draw attention to themselves," Jo said.

"Mission accomplished," McKinley added. "Maybe they knew the kind of weather that was coming. A good way of delaying any official blowback from the Bureau."

Flashing lights lit up the inside of the car. A snow plow went past behind them, bulldozing the road clear.

"I think that was Bobby again," said Phelps.

Jo turned her head to follow the flashing lights. "He drives a plow, too?"

"Of course. Good way to make some extra cash."

"Our savior," Jo said with a smile.

"Amen to that. This is kind of nice, ain't it? Just sitting in a toasty car, swapping theories? It would be even nicer if they were theories about a murderous cult in someone *else's* town, but I appreciate the comradery. I haven't had much of a chance to deal with FBI folks in the past. You two have made a pleasant impression on me."

Jo looked at him in the rearview mirror. "Thanks, Phelps. Just so you know, McKinley and I aren't leaving Lapse until we figure out what's going on."

"Well, I'm much obliged for that, Agent Pullinger. But I figured you two would be out of here once you found that missing agent of yours."

"If we find Swann," said Jo, "chances are good we'll solve a few other mysteries at the same time. The thing that bugs me more than anything..."

"Why did Joey Malone kill Miriam Whitaker?" McKinley tried. "It doesn't make much sense. We have the family connection. Miriam was the grandmother of Samuel Whitaker, who's also a missing person. Part of Malone's group, presumably."

"Are they trying to sever their old connections?" Phelps suggested. "Trying to make a clean break from their past lives?"

"That could be," Jo said. "But Miriam talked to us. She tried to share her fears about what was happening in Lapse. She wasn't able to get much of it out, but Malone's group might have caught on. He came into town to silence her."

McKinley unbuckled his seatbelt and sat forward. He was getting excited. "The way Miriam talked, it sounded like maybe she was being threatened. There's only one way for a group like this to go hidden for so long: fear. They must be threatening people all over town."

"They never threatened my wife and me." Phelps frowned. "But the mushroom hunter... the reason I didn't give you his name is because he asked me never to give it out in relation to the story he told me. I figured he was just being private, but..."

"Maybe he found a threatening note in his mailbox," Jo suggested. "Before tonight, Phelps, you had the whole thing chalked up as an urban legend. That's exactly how they've wanted it to look. But now they've changed their MO, and abducted an FBI agent."

"Remember what Malone yelled at me?" asked McKinley.

Jo nodded. "The sacrifice."

FORTY-SIX

Swann lost it for a little while. He flew into a frenzy, yanking at his chains. Jerking as hard as he could, as though he might transform into Hercules and break them clean in half.

When he came back to himself, he realized he was in great pain. The cuffs had bitten into his wrists, drawing blood. His knuckles were scraped raw from hitting the wall. He fell to his knees, huffing and puffing. Exhaustion hit him like a truck.

After he caught his breath, he shuffled to the side a bit. He found a narrow moonbeam shining through a gap in the foundation and aligned his left hand with it. In the pale glow, he checked out his injuries. Nothing too bad. If an infection set in, it would take time. In his mind, he'd be out of here by then. Or dead.

Either way, it didn't matter.

As he was studying his hand, he noticed something new. One of the links in the chain was weak. The weld was broken. There was a quarter-inch gap between the two halves of the link.

Swann's heart fluttered when he saw it. It was an opportunity, however slim.

It sure beats punching the foundation.

"It's all right, Agent Swann," Carmen said softly. "Just relax. Conserve your energy."

She had been quiet all through Swann's outburst. It probably frightened her. Swann felt a wave of shame. It gave him even more motivation to get out of there. He wanted to show her that he was in control.

He shifted around until he could get his right hand into the light as well. Unfortunately, there was no weak link on this side. But it was all one chain. It looped through two separate plates in the wall, one for each of his hands, but it was one length. If he got one side off, he could feed the chain back through those loops. And he'd be free.

Much easier said than done.

He did see something on his hand that might help. The knuckles were scraped up from striking the wall. But there was also a small puncture wound between two of his fingers. It looked vaguely round. Thinking back, he could remember hitting something that jutted out from the wall. Something metal.

He stood up and started feeling around. Running his hands along the foundation. It took him a few minutes to find it. A masonry screw had been sunk into the stone. It wasn't sunk all the way, though. It had probably been used for hanging something.

The head was broken off, leaving a jagged length of the shank behind. That's what had stabbed into his hand. It stuck out only a half inch or so. Hardly anything to work with. But as long as it was rooted deep, he might still get a good purchase.

Swann hooked the broken chain link over the screw. He stepped off to the side as far as he could go. Flattening himself against the wall to decrease the angle. This would help keep the chain from popping off of the screw once he started pulling.

"I'm going to try something else now," Swann called. "I might still sound like a gorilla here, but this time it'll be for a good cause. Here we go."

He pulled slowly at first, gradually increasing the tension. Once his muscles began to shake and his bleeding wrist cried out for mercy, he stopped. Squatting in the moonbeam, he checked his progress.

The gap looked slightly wider. The broken link was bending, coming open. As long as he stayed strong, it was only a matter of time before it gave out. He just had to keep going.

FORTY-SEVEN

"Looks like the snow is slowing down," said Phelps.

It was the first word the sheriff had spoken for several minutes. Jo was just starting to think he might have fallen asleep.

McKinley was nodding off. His head jerked backward at the sheriff's voice. "Huh? Oh, yeah. My weather app said it was supposed to quit sometime in the middle of the night."

"Then our backup should be able to reach us." Jo flicked the headlights on again. Just for a moment. Long enough to see that no one was around. The scene of Swann's disappearance was still undisturbed. "I just wish we could be doing something right now. This is killing me."

"Too dark and too cold out there to go off half-cocked," Phelps grunted. "But we *can* do something, as a matter of fact. We can lay out some kind of plan."

"We need to check out Kurt Black's place again," said Jo. "Just about everything we know so far—"

"Which isn't much," McKinley interjected.

"—points in his general direction," Jo finished. "First off, he knew Carmen. And we have these stories about a cult in the forest. A cult is basically a religion that went a step too far, right? Well, Kurt has plenty of religious iconography tattooed on his body. He lives a long way outside of town."

"A long, *long* way," Phelps agreed. "Only reason he gets to put Lapse on his address is because it's the closest place to him with a zip code."

Jo nodded. "Plus, his land is littered with structures. Plenty of hiding places. Who knows what he has out there?"

"Then we'll head back there as soon as we can," McKinley replied. "Only a few hours left until sunrise."

Phelps yawned. "Jeez, only a few? Guess I'd better get home and check on the wife. You two take care of each other, now."

He slapped both agents on the shoulder, then stepped out of the car. He got back into his truck and used the neighbor's drive to turn around. Then he was gone, leaving a dark and empty spot in their backseat.

"You can get some sleep," Jo said.

"I'm fine," McKinley told her.

"I saw you nodding off a minute ago. Just close your eyes, McKinley. I'll wake you up if something interesting happens. Or if I can't keep my own eyes open."

McKinley shrugged and settled in. He balled up his jacket and wedged it between his head and the wall. With his long, thin limbs, he looked awkward and uncomfortable. But he was asleep less than a minute later. Snoring softly.

Jo shook her head to try and stay awake. She'd been fine until drinking the cocoa. The sugar crash was hitting her now. She thought about going outside to let the cold shock her awake. But she didn't want to disturb McKinley. He looked calm. And he deserved a bit of peace.

She gripped the steering wheel. Staring through the windshield, she tried to imagine the falling snowflakes were stars. She was zooming through space, faster than light. Flying across the galaxy.

With her strength of will, she made it through the night. The first hint of sunrise came, sparkling on the snow-covered ground. The storm hadn't quite passed, but it was thinning out. Maybe it would be gone soon.

And replaced with a storm of a different kind, Jo thought.

She had a feeling it was going to be an eventful day.

FORTY-EIGHT

The sun was coming up. Swann paused for a few minutes to enjoy this phenomenon. It happened every day, and he normally took it for granted. But now, it felt like the most beautiful moment of his life.

"We've almost made it, Carmen," he whispered. He was so tired and so dehydrated that a whisper was all he could manage. It had been a sleepless night spent pulling at a chain.

He was making progress, but his body was giving him diminishing returns. There was hardly any strength left in his muscles. His mind was starting to fail him.

He took longer and longer breaks. Falling into a state of half-sleep. He dreamt, but the dreams weren't deep. They were a mere skin over the surface of reality. He hallucinated that Jo was there, urging him on. He asked her for help, but she suddenly vanished. At one point, he thought he heard her opening the door and coming down the stairs. When he looked, he saw no one.

"Almost there?" Carmen asked. She sounded slightly stronger now. She must have gotten some sleep. "What are you basing that off of?"

"Well," Swann huffed, standing back up to start again. "I'm about to break this chain. Any minute now. Then I'll try and find a good way out of here."

"You're just going to leave me?" she asked.

"Of course not. But I'll need to find a tool of some kind to break you free."

She only sniffed in response.

"I know you have no faith in me," Swann said. "That doesn't matter. Because I have faith in myself now."

She let out a moan. "It's not you, Agent Swann. I know you're trying. But I know what's coming. We can't get away."

He stared at her. Now that the sun was rising, he could make out the shape of her face in the shadows. "What do you mean?" he asked.

She sighed. "Nothing. Sorry, I said anything. I'm just rambling."

"You're getting fatalistic," Swann snapped. "You're giving up. Don't do that."

He was angry. The anger made him stronger. He hooked the weak link of the chain on the broken screw. It was so close now. The gap was over an inch wide. The metal on the other side of the link was showing signs of stress. There were small cracks on the surface.

"It's some kind of crappy pot metal," he growled as he started pulling. "But it's still metal. This is hard."

"Now, who's getting fatalistic?" Carmen shot back.

"Yeah, yeah. Don't worry. It's going to break. Just one or two more tries and—
"

He should have seen it coming. Unless it was superheated, metal tended to be firm. It rarely tore gradually.

The chain popped in half with no warning. Swann fell to the side as his left hand came free. His ankles tangled up, and he collapsed to his knees.

"Just like that," he said casually. "Nothing to it. Just three or four hours of work. Maybe five."

"Who's counting?" Carmen sighed. "Maybe I should have been, actually. Something to do."

"Don't worry about that." Swann stood up and walked backward, away from the wall. The chain slithered out through both brackets and fell to the floor. "I'm free now."

He went directly over to Carmen and knelt beside her. She stared up at him. Her face was pale, and her eyes were very wide and round.

"Doing okay?" Swann asked.

"What do you think?" Carmen replied. "Let's just say I was having a way better time when we were making out in my car."

"Yeah..." Swann looked up at the ceiling. "This isn't much of a second date, is it? But if I move fast enough, maybe you can still have breakfast in bed. First, let me check your chains. Maybe there's a weak link in yours, too."

He looked over every inch of her bonds. The chain was solid.

"Damn." Swann shook his head.

"No biggie," Carmen said cheerfully. "I don't think yanking a chain for another five hours would be a smart way to escape, anyway."

"Right. I'll go look for a tool. Maybe a crowbar or something..."

He stood up and turned around.

That's when he heard the sound of clapping coming from somewhere in the basement.

FORTY-NINE

Swann's eyes darted left and right, trying to find the source of the sound. The basement was full of brick support pillars. They held up the floor of whatever was above. They also provided plenty of hiding spots.

Maybe it's another hallucination.

The thought ran through his head. But he dismissed it right away. The adrenaline that came with his escape from the chain had shocked him into lucidity. His mind was purring along now. He felt strong and fresh. And one sleepless night was not enough to cause any long-lasting symptoms.

No. The clapping was real. A moment later, he got to see who was making it. It was Pinky again, still dressed in his white robe and ski mask. He stepped out from behind a pillar and proceeded to clap a few more times.

"Bravo!" he called out. "I was rooting for you the whole time, Agent. I like to see people do well and achieve great things. It makes me feel happy about the future of my species."

Swann's body hummed with anger. "Your species? We're not part of the same species. I'm a man, and you're a snake. A little rat hiding in the shadows."

Pinky stopped walking. He let his hands hang at his sides. "A cheap insult. Water off a duck's back. I know what I'm doing. I understand my purpose. Nothing you say or do can harm my conviction."

"What if I punched your head off?" Swann asked. "That might harm a few things."

Pinky clicked his tongue. "They really did train you well. Still so strong after that long night you had. No heat. No water. Straining yourself for hours. Impressive."

Swann forced himself to be calm. He paid attention to Pinky's voice. He sounded like quite a young person.

Dirty blond hair. Hazel eyes. Missing pinky finger. Young.

"You know," Pinky went on, "you're only making things harder on yourself."

Swann sized up the distance between him and Pinky. Twenty feet or so. A considerable span to cover for an attack. But the stairs were closer to Swann. He could cut off Pinky's escape. Corner him somewhere.

"How long have you been down here?" Swann asked.

"Two or three hours," Pinky replied. "You were barely conscious when I entered. I guess you never saw me."

I thought I heard the hallucination of Jo on the steps, thought Swann. *But it was no hallucination. It was this weasel creeping downstairs.*

"You stood in the dark for three hours, watching me, without making a sound?" Swann asked. "That takes dedication. And a lot of patience. Admirable qualities. We could always use more people like you in the Bureau."

Pinky scoffed. "What are you doing? Trying to lull me into some kind of trance? Trying to draw me closer so you can strangle me with that chain?"

"Actually..." Swann lifted the chain, feeling its weight. "I was thinking of bashing you over the skull with it."

"Keep dreaming," Pinky laughed. He reached behind him with both hands to the back of his belt. One hand came back, holding a hatchet. The other was holding a pistol. "I am going to step closer to you now. And you won't try anything unless you enjoy the taste of cold lead. Understand?"

"Swann, let the chain drop.

Pinky closed the gap. He stopped six feet away from Carmen. He waved his gun hand, gesturing at Swann to get back. Swann returned to the spot where he had been chained up.

"Now..." Pinky pointed the pistol at Carmen. "I'm going to give you two options, Agent Swann. You're not going to like either of them, but I think you'll make the right choice."

FIFTY

Carmen squeezed her eyes shut. Other than that, she seemed surprisingly calm. She wasn't trembling or crying. Swann had a terrible idea that she really had given up. It wasn't just talk. She had accepted her doom and would do nothing to stop it now.

It was all on him, and he had to think fast.

"Don't hurt her," he said. "I'll do whatever you want."

Pinky narrowed his eyes. "Can you at least let me finish talking before you start blubbering? And what kind of line was that? You think this is some Hollywood action movie? I'm not going to hurt Carmen at all. Unless you want me to."

"Why would I want that?" Swann shouted.

Pinky grinned. "Because you're not a man. *I* am. It's you who's the rat, Agent Swann. You're my little rat, stuck in a maze. Caught in my trap. And maybe you'll do anything to get out. Now, here's the deal."

He took another step toward Carmen, cocking the hammer of his pistol.

"If you decide to go along, everything will be fine," he said. "Or you can choose not to go along. In that case, I'll leave you alone completely. But I'll kill Carmen."

Swann put his back to the wall. He slid down it, falling into a seated position. "So, what's the deal? I let you shoot me, or I let you shoot her? Either way, one of us dies. Is that how it goes?"

Pinky chuckled. "Not at all. You don't get the bullet, Swann. Only Carmen can have the privilege of a swift exit. Not you. You made me angry."

"Was it those comments about beating you to death with a chain?" Swann asked.

"No. Those were just entertaining because of how stupid they were. You thought you could escape, Agent. Not only that, you made a real, solid attempt at it. This needs to be punished."

He brandished the hatchet, twirling it in his right hand.

"A finger," he added. "I'll take one of your fingers as punishment."

Swann's heart fluttered. A cold, sick feeling washed over him. He looked at Carmen. She still had her eyes closed. She almost looked like she was asleep. Except now he could see her lips moving slightly. She was whispering something to herself.

She's losing it, Swann thought. *She's broken. I have to save whatever's left of her.*

"The offer has an expiration date," Pinky said. "It goes away in one minute. If you say nothing at all, I'll still shoot."

"Stupid rules," Swann snapped.

"Stupid or not, I'm the one making them. What's it going to be?"

"Hold on. I'm trying to think of a loophole. Something I can say or do that'll make you just shoot yourself instead."

"You're a funny man, Agent Swann. By the way, I *am* counting. You only have forty seconds left."

Swann let ten more seconds go by. He could hardly keep his thoughts straight.

"Do I at least get to pick?" he asked.

"Of course," said Pinky. "I'm a man, not a monster. But sometimes, a man can be worse. Which finger do you choose?"

It was a simple decision, demanded by logic. It only made sense to choose the least important one. "Pinky finger. Left hand."

"Very well." Pinky changed direction, walking closer to Swann. "Put your hand out on the floor. Palm up. Curl the other fingers in."

Swann followed these directions. The only reason he didn't freeze up was that part of him still thought it was one big joke. There was no way any of this was happening.

Pinky didn't go for an overhead swing. Instead, he gently rested the blade of the hatchet at the base of Swann's little finger.

What's he going for? Swann wondered.

Suddenly, Pinky raised one foot and stomped down on the blunt side of the hatchet. The blade was driven down, hitting the concrete floor with a cracking noise.

Swann rolled away. The pain was sharp and terrible. He immediately pressed his wound against his side, trying to stem the bleeding. He bit his lip to stop himself from screaming.

"And that's it," said Pinky. "I'll discard the finger so you don't have to see it. By the way, we're always watching. Try and get away again, and we'll do much worse to you."

He stepped into Swann's view again, holding up his hand. He showed the missing pinky finger.

"See?" he said. "I know how it feels. Losing this finger hasn't altered my life at all. You just have to get through the pain."

He stuck the hatchet and pistol back under his belt. He climbed the stairs, stepped through the door, and closed it behind him.

"Are you all right?" Carmen asked.

"I will be," Swann gasped. "In a little while. It could have been worse."

"I'm sorry," said Carmen. "Hey! He didn't tie you back up. You're still free."

Swann didn't say anything. He knew why Pinky didn't bother chaining him back up. He knew Swann had no chance of getting out of here either way.

But that didn't mean he was beaten.

FIFTY-ONE

The time was six AM. McKinley was still asleep and showed no signs of waking up anytime soon. Jo eased her way out of the car. She pushed the door shut slowly until she heard it click.

"Good enough."

She turned to face the rising sun. It shone through a blue crack in the otherwise gray sky. With Seattle's winter weather being what it was, it had been a while since she felt this warmth on her skin. Hopefully, wherever Swann was, he could feel it too.

Jo strolled a little way up the road. Her shoes crunched in a thin layer of snow. Bobby's plow had pushed most of it to the side. There was a wall of ice just beyond the edge of the pavement. It was as high as Jo's hip, and she was a tall woman.

The wind had died. The air was still. Jo did a few jumping jacks and managed to work up a sweat. Back home, she had been keeping up with her jogging regimen. She was used to exercising in the mornings and didn't want to miss out.

She went as far as she could go without losing sight of the car. Then she started running. She went past the car, seeking a good turnaround spot. Maybe she could get a mile or so in before McKinley woke up.

There was a curve in the road ahead. She stopped there, looking back to check if the car was still in sight. She paused to catch her breath. The cold, dry air wasn't doing her throat any favors.

Jo heard an engine behind her. The crackle of tires in the snow. She turned to find a tall white van ambling toward her. Even though the windshield was tinted and impossible to see through, she knew right away who it was.

She stepped off to the side to give the van space. It pulled up beside her. The front passenger window rolled down, and Bryan Ford grinned out at her. He was a handsome man in his early forties.

"Morning, Jo," he said. "Did you have your morning Joe?"

"Not yet," she replied with a laugh.

Ford handed her a cup of coffee through the window. "There you are. Just the way you like it. I think. Where's McKinley?"

Jo gestured toward the car. "In dreamland."

Ford nodded. "Got a cup for him, too. Jo, say hi to Rupert."

The driver waved at her. He was a stocky guy with thin blond hair.

"Hello, Rupert," Jo said. "Good to meet you."

"The other boys are in the back," Rupert told her. He had a British accent. "Where would you like us?"

"Just follow me," said Jo.

She jogged back to the car. The van tailed her at five miles an hour. As they were approaching, the door opened, and McKinley stepped out. He blinked groggily, stifling a yawn.

"Jo," he called. "I think someone's following you."

Ford stuck his head out of the window. "It's just me. And I've got your caffeine fix here."

McKinley was suddenly alert. He accepted the cup that was handed to him and popped the lid off. He sipped it and made a face. "Wow. That's hot."

"It's *fresh*," Ford corrected him.

McKinley squatted down. He scooped a bit of snow into his cup and let it melt. Then he tried it again. "There we go. Perfect."

"You know," said Ford, "a dog might have peed in that spot."

Rupert laughed, and the two of them high-fived.

"It wasn't yellow," McKinley said in a worried tone of voice.

"Could have been a well-hydrated dog," Rupert added. "Shall we get out, Bryan?"

"We shall," said Ford.

They got out of the van. As Rupert went to open the back doors, Ford joined Jo and McKinley by their car.

"Get much sleep last night?" he asked.

"None," said Jo. "By the way, how did you get here so early? I figured you'd be a few more hours."

"We didn't get much sleep either," Ford replied. "I got up to use the bathroom around four. When I checked the weather, it said we were all clear. Road conditions looked passable. So I woke up the others, and we decided to head out."

"Well, thanks for making that call," said Jo. "I'm glad you're here. Even if I had been lying in the world's most comfortable bed last night, I don't think I would have slept."

"You're worried about Swann."

Jo nodded. "I saved him once. From Graff. Maybe it's silly, but now it feels like more than just looking out for a fellow agent. You know what I mean?"

Ford nodded. "Don't worry. If he's findable, we'll find him. You and me."

"What about me?" McKinley asked.

Ford smiled. "You have an important job too. You're going to over-see Rupert's team here. I know I'm just a consultant, but Grantham gave me pretty clear instructions."

McKinley sighed. "I get it. This is an important operation. Not a good time to field-test the desk jockey. But I'd feel better if I was out there with you."

Jo knocked him on the shoulder. "You already bagged one bad guy, McKinley. But Ford's right. Your job is just as important as ours. Here..." She pulled Swann's phone out of her pocket and gave it to him. "Hand this off to Rupert. He might be able to get something off of it."

McKinley held the phone like it was a precious historical artifact. He carried it toward the van, moving slowly.

"Time to hit the road?" Ford asked.

Jo nodded. "Of course."

FIFTY-TWO

They got in the car. Ford took McKinley's former seat. They were both around the same height, tall and slender, so he didn't need to adjust anything.

Jo backed out slowly, paranoid of getting stuck again. But Bobby the plowman had done a fantastic job. It wasn't long before she was cruising toward the main road.

"I'm going damn near the speed limit right now," she said. "Incredible."

"Looks like Lapse got hit hard," said Ford. "We saw some downed power lines on our way in. And no sign of anyone working on them. It'll be a while."

"Got any good news?" Jo asked.

"Hazel lost another baby tooth. The tooth fairy ran out of small bills, so she got five bucks this time. She reacted how I would if I won the lottery. Jumping for joy and shouting at the top of her lungs."

"What's she going to blow it on?"

"Oh, it's already gone." Ford whistled. "She got herself a whole box of ice cream sandwiches. With Neapolitan filling."

"Never had those. Sounds fancy. Any other news?"

"Since the last time we saw each other?" Ford shrugged. "Not much to report. But I did hit something of a milestone. This is the furthest I've been from my family since Kelly and I reconciled. It's illogical, but I have to admit it was hard telling her I wouldn't be home for dinner."

"I'm sure she took it just fine," said Jo.

"She did. Especially when I said it was to help you out. If there was a Jo Pullinger fan club—I mean, besides whatever that deal with Graff was—she might be a high-ranking member. But don't let it go to your head. I think the main reason she likes you so much is because she knows you won't let me get into trouble."

"Isn't that a sweet sentiment?" Jo chuckled at first, but a dark thought clouded her mind. "I wasn't able to keep Swann out of trouble, though. Let's hope for your family's sake that I don't mess up again."

Ford leaned his seat back, folding his arms behind his head. "You know that wasn't your fault. If it makes you feel better, I promise not to run off with a young waitress in the middle of the night."

"Good." Jo swallowed her negative feelings back. "Because if you did, I'd have to report it to your wife."

"If you did that, you'd have to start looking for a new partner. And write me a nice, heartfelt eulogy. So, where are we going?"

They were on the main road through town, heading past the diner.

"I'm taking you to meet a new friend of mine," said Jo. "Sheriff Neil Phelps. Let's see if he's dragged himself to work yet."

FIFTY-THREE

Jo recognized Phelps's truck and Sheri's station wagon. They were parked neatly side by side out in front of the police station. Nearby, parked at an extreme angle, was a dark blue SUV.

"Wonder who that could be?" Jo said.

"Who?" Ford asked. "Let me remind you, I've never been to this town before."

"Never mind. Let's go inside."

They entered the station with their coffee cups in hand.

Sheri was standing in the middle of the lobby, her arms wrapped around a woman in her fifties who was sobbing uncontrollably. Sheri herself looked exhausted, but she soldiered on. Rubbing the woman's back. Whispering kind words.

Sheriff Phelps lingered off the side. He stood awkwardly, one foot against the wall behind him. His thumbs hooked through his belt loops. He looked lost. He perked up a bit when he saw Jo come in. His smile turned to a curious squint when he saw the strange man beside her.

"Excuse me for a moment, ladies," he said quietly, tipping his hat. He stepped past the front counter, joining Jo and Ford. "I wish I could say good morning to you two, but my mama taught me never to tell a lie."

"Is that Joey Malone's mother?" asked Jo.

Phelps winked at her. It went strangely with his morose frown. "That's her, all right. Barbara Malone. My sister—God rest her soul—when she was in her teens, she used to babysit Barbara. She's a good, ordinary person. She doesn't deserve this."

Ford was hit especially hard by this sad sight. "No one deserves it, Sheriff Phelps."

"So Jo has already introduced me," Phelps said.

"She has. I'm Bryan Ford."

They shook hands.

"FBI?" asked Phelps.

"Private Investigator. Used to be a detective with the Seattle PD. Jo and I have worked together a few times in the past. Sometimes it seems like we just can't get away from each other."

Jo nudged him. "But we always get the job done."

Phelps let out his usual chuckle. "Let's hope this time is no different. Just gotta get through this tough part, then we can be on our way. You know, the parents of missing kids always just want to know what happened to them, either way. Good or bad. But I think right now, Barbara wishes she had no idea."

It was a somber note to leave on, but time was wasting. Phelps grabbed his keys and shrugged on his fur-lined jacket. "I'll lead the way again. I asked Bobby to drive out that way last night. But depending on when he went, we might still have a few inches of accumulation to contend with."

"You sure Sheri's all right here by herself?" Jo asked.

Phelps smirked. One side of his mustache twitched upward. "You kidding me? I may be the sheriff, but she's the strong one in our relationship. She'll be just fine."

Jo and Ford got in their car and followed the Sheriff's truck. It was a familiar route now, and Bobby's plow had made it almost easy to navigate. Almost. Jo still had to pay attention at a few parts, but she fell into a rhythm.

"Are you going to let me in on where we're going?" Ford asked.

"Sorry," said Jo. "We're going to pay Kurt Black another visit.""Right. I got an update from your field office about that. You've got some reason to suspect this guy's involved? A former FBI agent?"

Jo shrugged. "It's not an easy job. People choose it for a variety of reasons. I think Kurt probably went into the Bureau because he thought he could make the world a better, safer place. Then he learned that's essentially impossible. We all learn that. Some people take the news harder than others."

"You think he snapped?"

"I think he found a new purpose. A *spiritual* purpose. He's the kind of guy who could amass a following without even trying, just by virtue of who he is. That's what we're afraid of. These missing kids may have wandered away from their lives to join Kurt Black in his self-imposed exile. Once you see his place, I think you'll be able to buy it too."

Ford planted both hands on the dashboard. "Then let's go off-roading."

They went over a hidden pothole. The car jumped up and down. The suspension cried uncle.

"There actually *is* a road under there," said Jo. "Believe it or not."

Ford nodded. "And maybe it leads straight to the answers we're looking for."

FIFTY-FOUR

Ford whistled when he saw the sprawling property. "You weren't kidding. This place is a proper compound. He could have a fleet of decommissioned Abrams tanks in there."

"Let's hope not. But when you consider why one man would need so many structures... your mind wanders into some interesting territory."

Ford shrugged. "Maybe he's a hoarder. I watched an episode of one of those shows about hoarding. Some guy had about three dozen huge warehouses on his property, full of worthless junk he'd bought at auctions over the years. And it wasn't even the only property he owned."

"A lot of these buildings are old," said Jo. "And Kurt hasn't lived here that long. Only the newer structures are ones he's built. Still, he went looking for this kind of property. I wonder why?"

Now that the road was plowed and there was no chance of getting stuck, Phelps led them all the way up to the main house. They got out and stretched a bit, shaking off the bumpy ride.

"Smoke," said Phelps, pointing at the chimney. "He's home keeping himself warm. Let's go knock."

But Kurt beat them to the punch. They were climbing the front porch's steps when the door swung open. It banged into the wall, causing a piece of a shingle to snap off.

Kurt stomped out in a pair of slippers and a bathrobe. He was holding a cup of coffee in one hand and a revolver in the other.

"Whoa, there." Phelps put up his hands. "What's the gun for?"

"You had yours drawn when you trespassed on my property yesterday," Kurt said calmly. "I just figured that's the way you liked greeting people. Thought I should show some hospitality." His tone was as dry as sandpaper.

"Well, you can put it away," Phelps urged.

Kurt leaned back into the house, setting the gun on a shelf. He took a drink of coffee, watching them like a hawk over the cup's rim.

He lowered the cup. "I don't know who that guy is."

"Me?" Ford asked. "My name's Bryan Ford."

"You're the backup." Kurt nodded. "I guess I should be thankful that the storm has slowed things down. Otherwise, I'd have a dozen of you rats crawling all over my land right now."

"We'd need a search warrant for that," Jo told him.

"No, you wouldn't. You're the FBI. You can do whatever you want."

"Mr. Black, the only thing we want is to find the two missing people," Jo replied. "Are you worried about the possibility of your property being searched? Are you hiding something?"

He shook his head. "I'm an American taxpayer enjoying the privilege of owning land. I just don't want you stepping on that."

"We won't, I promise you that," said Phelps.

Kurt grunted. He stared at Phelps for a moment and seemed to soften up.

"I heard about Miriam," he said. "Tragic."

"Yup." Phelps nodded. "I've made plenty of promises in my career, Kurt. I promised Barbara Malone that I'd find her son. Well, I did. I found him dead. I also promised Miriam Whitaker that I'd find her grandson. At least I might still be able to make good on that one."

Kurt bowed his head. "Yes. You might. I wish you the best of luck with that."

Phelps let out a long sigh. "Samuel Whitaker. Did you ever get a chance to meet him, Kurt?"

"Not that I know of," Kurt replied. He tapped his foot impatiently.

"Well, you'd know him if you saw him. He's got sort of dirty blond hair. Hazel eyes. And he's missing one of his little fingers. An accident with a table saw, as I recall."

FIFTY-FIVE

Kurt shook his head. "Doesn't sound familiar. You're fishing for information that I don't have."

Jo watched him carefully. As a former agent, he had plenty of training and experience that would make him an almost perfect liar. There were no tells. Maybe he hesitated just a bit, but that could be passed off as a genuine attempt at recollection.

"Come on," Phelps said with a laugh, "just think. You must have run into him at some point. He's a smart kid. Well-spoken. Doesn't that sound like anyone you know?"

"It sounds a bit like me when I was younger." Kurt peered into the distance, a nostalgic smile curling his lips. "I want all of you to know that I wish no harm on any living creature. I appreciate what you did for me yesterday."

Ford leaned close to Jo. "Um... what did you do for him yesterday?"

"He's talking about the fox," Jo said. "He was going to shoot it for trying to attack his chickens."

Kurt put his hands together in a prayer position. "No one's perfect. We're all prone to bursts of brutish anger. I was going to kill that poor animal, but your arrival startled me out of the moment. So far, my peaceful track record since leaving the Bureau is intact. I feel at peace."

"Glad we could help," Phelps quipped. "I'd say your hunger for peace doesn't extend to your fellow man."

"Are you talking about the gun?" Kurt's foot tapping intensified. "I said I *wish* no harm on any living creature. That's not to say I'm incapable of delivering it. I will say one final thing to you, Sheriff. I've done nothing to hurt Samuel Whitaker, Carmen Powell, or whoever that missing agent is."

"Swann," Jo put in.

"Whatever. I really don't care what his name is. But I'll be praying for him either way. Now I would like very much for the three of you to leave. I moved out here for a reason. To hide away from an evil world. I won't allow that evil to ever step foot over this threshold."

He moved back into his house. Holding the door open, he stepped slightly to the side. This afforded them a clear view of a rack on the entryway wall. It was filled with guns. Pistols, rifles, shotguns.

"Do you have licenses for all those?" Phelps asked, pointing.

Kurt grinned. "They're just for show, Sheriff. None of them fire."

"Because they can't, or because you won't?" Phelps asked.

He got no answer. Kurt shut and locked the door. There was a small window on the door as well, but Kurt pulled the curtain shut over it.

"If I can play the part of Captain Obvious for a second," Ford said, "he seems like a very private person."

Phelps growled angrily. "And that's the problem, ain't it? With these privacy freaks, you can never tell if they're hiding something. Now is it just me, or did we once again waste our time by coming out here?"

Jo sighed. "Without even a visit from Bobby to brighten our moods."

"Come on," Ford urged. "Let's lighten up here. I wouldn't say we wasted our time at all. It's always good to have a second opinion on something. And I agree: this guy has to be hiding something."

"He can probably hear us still," Phelps pointed out. "We ought to step off the man's porch. I'm an American taxpayer too, and I respect his right to privacy. Even if it does tick me off just a tad."

FIFTY-SIX

"We're going to come back," Ford said.

They were in the car, following Phelps back to town.

Jo nodded. "Yes. We are. And our third visit isn't going to be a courteous one."

"Any ideas coming to mind?"

"Not quite. But we *need* to check out those outbuildings. That property is so huge we could probably spend a whole day searching through it. And he'd never even know we were there."

"It wouldn't exactly be... legal," Ford added.

"Not exactly. But I don't care about producing admissible evidence here. I just want to know for a fact that Swann and Carmen aren't being held there."

"Then we'll make a plan," Ford agreed. "A very careful plan. You might have the protection of an FBI badge, but I don't. If Kurt catches us on his property, he could make it pretty ugly for me."

"Then maybe it should just be McKinley and me," Jo suggested.

Ford scoffed. "Yeah. Okay. I didn't come all the way down here just to build a snowman. Hey, maybe we should stop and get a carrot on our way. Maybe some chunks of coal, too."

"Or maybe we should call McKinley." Jo picked up her phone and dialed him.

"Agent McKinley speaking," he answered in his clean, professional voice.

"You know it's me," Jo replied with a touch of annoyance. "Did you get a chance to do any more research on Kurt Black?"

"Actually, I was distracted by finding a dead body and then shooting a guy. Luckily, I just sat down and did some research a little while ago. Black's record is exemplary. He's received the Shield of Bravery and the Medal of Valor. He's never been in any kind of trouble. Seems like he really did want to make the world a better place."

"An overachieving, idealistic hermit," Ford said. "Sounds like cult-leader material to me."

"You could probably say that about a lot of retired agents," said McKinley. "Some of them stick around as instructors. Or they work as consultants like you, Ford. Others decide they've had enough of that life, and they retreat somewhere quiet. I'm not sure about Kurt now."

"None of us are," Jo replied. "But he's the only real suspect we have. You know we have to get a closer look, McKinley."

"I know."

"Then you should meet us at the hotel as soon as you finish up there. Ford and I are going to come up with a plan. And one other thing: Phelps can't know about this."

"It's for his own good, right?" McKinley asked.

"Of course. He doesn't need to be involved."

Jo ended the call with McKinley. She looked forward, staring at Phelps through his rear window. Part of an FBI agent's job was to know when to let local law enforcement in, and when to box them out. It wasn't always easy, especially when you ran into a guy as likable as the sheriff of Lapse, Oregon.

FIFTY-SEVEN

"Cats have nine lives," Swann whispered. "Humans have ten fingers."

With his right hand, he took turns pressing his thumb against the tips of his opposing fingers. He counted them all out. He did the same with his left. Or tried to. He had to stop when he reached his middle finger. It hurt too bad.

"Are you okay?" Carmen asked. "You sound…"

"Hmm?" He sat up, his back scraping the wall. He blinked a few times, bringing her into focus.

"Unhinged," she finished. "That's the word."

At some point, she had tied her dark hair into a ponytail. At first glance, she looked well put together. Sitting there cross-legged on the floor. Other than the shivering, she might have been relaxing at home.

"No, I was just thinking," Swann told her. "But I was doing it out loud. Most thoughts probably sound really weird if you vocalize them. When people say cats have nine lives, it sounds like a lot. Maybe nine fingers is still a lot, too."

"I think it's enough," Carmen sniffed. "Swann… I know you're in rough shape. And I hate to ask, but do you think you could look around? You know, for something more to cover up with. I'm really cold."

"Oh, sure." Swann smiled and nodded. But he was a bit worried. The last time he tried to stand up, ten minutes ago, he got lightheaded and collapsed. He took a deep breath and pushed off the wall.

This time, he managed to stay on his feet. He took a test step and still felt all right. The wound no longer bled as long as he kept his hand elevated. He walked across the basement with his left hand up by his face.

"Dark down here..." he said as he squinted around. There was a tiny old wood stove. Cast iron. The door was open, and there was nothing but ash inside. Besides, the chimney was no longer connected. Even if they got a fire going, they'd just choke to death on the smoke.

Might not be the worst way to go, Swann thought.

He kept looking. In a corner, he discovered a stack of old crates. There was nothing inside but a few mouse nests. But the pile was half-covered with a tarp. He dragged it over to Carmen with a smile on his face.

"Here you go," he said. "It stinks pretty bad. And there are some holes in it."

"I won't complain." She took it from him, quickly wrapping it around her shoulders. She folded some of it under her backside. An extra layer between her and the frigid floor. "What about you?"

"I'll look around a bit more," he replied.

"Do you think you can try freeing me again?" she asked, biting her lip. She gave him puppy-dog eyes.

"Not yet, Carmen. Not until I know there's a way out. If I get caught wandering around, I'll be the only one who gets punished. It's better that way."

"It's not fair," she pointed out.

Swann shook his head. "Listen, kid..."

"Watch who you call a kid. You were kissing me last night, remember? I'm like two years younger than you, if that."

"Fine. But I'm also an FBI agent, which makes me the authority here."

"Do you feel like an authority?" she asked.

"I did right up until I got my finger chopped off. Anyway, if I still had my FBI shield, this is where I'd show it to you. You don't need to worry about me. And I'm still going to get us out. I made a promise."

He went to the nearest window. There were bars on it. He grabbed hold of the bars and pulled himself up. The window was boarded on the outside. He couldn't reach any of the nails, and the wood was solid.

"No luck there," he mumbled.

There were three other windows in the basement. He checked them all. They were the same as the first. No way out. If he had a tool, a hatchet, or something...

But I don't, he thought. *Which leaves only one option. Two, technically, but there's no way I'm going to keep sitting around.*

He headed toward the stairs. Carmen didn't realize what he was doing until he took a step up.

"*No!*" she hissed. "Remember what he said? He'll kill you!"

"Or I'll kill him," Swann said.

"With no weapons? The guy has a gun!"

Swann held up a hand. "Be quiet. If he's close by, I don't want him to get tipped off."

He continued climbing slowly, trying to be silent. His heart was beating so hard he was sure Pinky would hear it. When he was halfway up, a wave of fear almost pushed him right back down. But he thought about Carmen. He thought about what it would feel like to be a hero.

He kept going.

FIFTY-EIGHT

The staircase was dark. Swann didn't realize he was at the top until he bumped his head into something. He cursed, rubbing his sore scalp.

Very good start to this supposedly stealthy mission, he thought.

He felt around. And soon discovered what had hit his head. It was no ordinary door at the top. It was a trapdoor directly above him. He touched the cold hinges, then slid his hand across to the other side. There was no latch on this side.

There must be one on the other side, though. A way for Pinky to lock them in. If the latch was engaged, the game was over. Swann felt confident he could smash his way through the trapdoor with enough effort. But it would create way too much noise. And take too much time.

He put his left hand against the latch side of the door. He balled his right hand into a fist in case he had to defend himself. Then he stepped up, using the strength of his legs to push on the door.

There was a grinding sound as the rusty door scraped against its frame. It swung open by a couple of inches. Swann stopped, his heart pounding. He stepped up a bit further, pushing the top of his head into the door.

His eyes were now level with the floor above. He turned to either side, scanning everything. The room above was shadowy but lit well enough by bleeding sunlight. He could tell there was no one there. At least, not in his sight.

Swann took a deep breath and stepped up once more. He opened the door wide enough to climb through, then quickly made his way up. He took another look around to make sure he was still alone. Once that was accomplished, he swung the door fully open and slowly rested it on the floor.

Now his escape route was fully open. If he heard someone coming, he could dart back downstairs and pull the trapdoor shut over him. If he was careful, they'd never know he left the basement.

Unless they have cameras, he thought. *But I doubt it. This place looks dilapidated.*

He was in a barn. Most of the sunlight was coming through holes in the ceiling. The rafters were thirty feet over his head, and he could see old bird nests dotted around. A single electrical conduit came through from outside, ran down the wall, and went into the basement. That was what fed the furnace and the overhead light.

It looked like recent work. Pinky had made preparations, getting the basement ready for guests. Apparently, he hadn't anticipated that they would lose power.

Swann took in all of this in the space of a few seconds. Then his eyes landed on the door. He headed straight for it. More sunlight bled through here, making his eyes hurt. He almost laughed with relief.

Something else caught his eye.

He didn't know how he hadn't seen them before. Maybe he just thought they were ordinary barn implements. On second glance, it was clear they were also new. He could still see sap oozing out of the cuts.

Two wooden constructions had been erected in the middle of the barn. Side by side. They looked like crucifixes, with extra planks near the bottom for your feet to rest on. Holes had been drilled through the sidebars. Chains had been fed through these holes. To hold a person in an upright position.

If that wasn't bad enough, there were also huge piles of sawdust under each crucifix. Swann spotted a pile of firewood stacked against the wall.

They're pyres, he thought, stopping in his tracks. *They're going to burn us. They're going to let this whole barn catch on fire and fall down on our heads. Why?*

He no longer felt the cold or the throbbing pain in his left hand. He felt only panic. He ran for the door, his feet pounding loudly on the floor. At that moment, he didn't even care if he got shot from behind. Anything beat what waited for him on the crucifix.

FIFTY-NINE

Swann changed his mind when he heard the click of the hammer. He was nearly at the door. He could have reached out and touched it. But he could almost feel the cold steel of the gun barrel on his back.

He turned around.

Pinky stepped out of the shadows behind the two pyres. He was dressed more warmly now, a scarf wrapped around his neck and a pair of wool gloves on his hands. He was still holding the same handgun as before.

He stopped ten feet away from Swann. His hazel eyes stared at the agent for a moment. Then he blinked and looked away, letting out a sigh.

"I was actually starting to nod off," he said. "I didn't even hear you come up. If you hadn't started running like that, you probably would have gotten away."

Swann looked at the door again. It no longer seemed like a beacon of hope, leading him to safety. It looked more like a trap to drag him into ruination.

"I doubt it," he said.

"Why's that?" asked Pinky.

"Because you're not alone. Am I right?"

Pinky scoffed. "I cut my own finger off with a table saw. You think I'm handy enough to build those two crosses on my own? Of course, I have friends. They're nearby. They probably would have seen you trying to escape, but there's no guarantee. But I don't think you would have gotten far either way."

Pinky walked over to the trap door and peered down it. "You wouldn't have left Carmen. You would have come to your senses and come back for her. Right?"

"Probably," said Swann. "But I would have found a weapon first. So you're lucky you woke up when you did."

"And you're *unlucky*," Pinky said with a chuckle. "This has been very boring for me. I drew a short straw with this job, watching over you two. But I have been enjoying our talks."

He gestured toward the crosses. "Sorry, you had to see those, Agent Swann. But part of me is glad you did. Father believes it's always best to know your fate, however dark it may be. Sometimes that's the only thing a person has left."

"Who's your Father?" Swann asked.

"You expect me to tell you?" Pinky asked with a snort. "Nope. But you'll meet him soon enough. Don't worry. Things may look bad, Agent Swann, but you still have a choice."

"Let me guess," said Swann. "I can run and let you shoot me. Or I can go back downstairs like a good little slave and wait to die painfully."

Pinky shook his head. "Actually, I was going to say you can join us. We can teach you everything we've learned over the past few months. Maybe you'll start to see things our way. And we can find someone else to take your place. Maybe one of those other agents."

"They'll find me," Swann growled. "And they'll shatter any illusion this little power trip has given you. You're a worm. If you're *lucky*, you'll get to spend the rest of your life in prison."Pinky laughed. "Doesn't sound that lucky. The other agents do pose a threat, which is why we're in kind of a hurry here. Tying up some loose ends before the big show tonight. You have until then to make up your mind."

"So I have options," Swann said with a relieved smile. "That's good. I feel a bit better now."

Pinky smiled back. "Good. We're not exactly trying to make you suffer here. We're just after the symbolism. You'll understand."

"The symbolism of burning us at the stake?" Swann pointed at the stack of firewood. "Are you sure that's enough? Any idea how much heat it takes to immolate a human body?"

A shadow of doubt crossed Pinky's face. He turned away from Swann to inspect the wood pile.

And that was just what Swann wanted him to do.

SIXTY

Swann rushed toward Pinky. The rotting floorboards splintered under his feet.

Pinky turned back and raised the gun. Too slow. Swann caught his wrist, shoving his hand away. The first shot went off. The bullet flew through the wall, letting in another thin shaft of sunlight.

The sound made Swann's ears ring. He saw that his finger wound was bleeding again, but he felt no pain. Still holding Pinky's wrist, he shoved his other forearm under Pinky's jaw. He shoved the man backward, toward the other wall.

Pinky was smaller than Swann. He was skinny, maybe even frail. His wrist felt thin and bony, like Swann could snap the bones just by squeezing.

But he had some fight in him. As he was being driven backward, Pinky launched a knee into Swann's crotch. Swann grunted in pain. His eyes watered. But he refused to flinch.

Pinky tried again. This time, he aimed a kick at Swann's right shin. This blow was not as painful as the first, but it was more debilitating. Swann stumbled. He limped, favoring his left leg for a moment.

His charge was ruined. He still managed to throw Pinky against the wall, bringing a shower of dust. But Pinky was able to slip away easily, dancing to the side.

However, Swann's hand was still on his wrist. Pinky tried to wrench away. This caused the second shot to go off. The bullet just barely grazed Swann's shoulder, digging a shallow trench out of his flesh. It burned with pain and oozed blood onto his shirt.

"Give it up!" Pinky screamed, pulling again. "Maybe I'll let you live if you stop now."

They were in a tug-of-war match. Swann stood tall, using one hand. Pinky was leaning all the way back, with both hands on the gun. With his lower body weight, he was at a disadvantage. But now both men were fighting for their lives.

"You'll let me live so you can burn me alive later?" Swann growled. "I don't think so. Come here."

He stepped forward, grabbing at Pinky with his free hand. He got a handful of Pinky's white robe. Swann pulled his assailant toward him. He twisted to his right, trying to throw Pinky to the floor.

Pinky kept his grip on the gun. He swung low to the floor, then sprang back onto his feet. Through a twisting motion, he managed to pry the gun out of Swann's hand.

But he was still halfway through the motion. Facing away. Swann followed him, staying at Pinky's back. He wrapped his arms around the other man, squeezing him.

Pinky groaned in pain as his rib cage was compressed. He lurched forward, trying to free himself. Strange beast-like noises issued from his mouth. He was terrified. He was panicking now.

That was both a good and a bad thing. Good because it meant Swann had a chance, and both of them knew it. Bad because a panicked person was at their most dangerous.

Pinky made his first gambit. He aimed his pistol downward and fired, obviously going for Swann's foot. And he came very close. The bullet carved out another furrow, this time in the rubber midsole of Swann's shoe.

The bullet punched down into the basement. Through the new hole, they heard Carmen scream.

Swann looked at the trapdoor. He tried to judge the distance. Tried to get his bearings. Were they directly over Carmen? Could she have been hit? He didn't think so.

Pinky tried his next tactic. His arms were pinned to his sides, so he couldn't do much with them. But he still had his mouth. Bending his neck as far as it could go, he sank his teeth into the bloody stump of Swann's missing finger.

The pain was incredible. Swann let go involuntarily, jumping backward.

Pinky turned on his heel. His teeth bared in a snarl. He lifted the gun and aimed it dead in the center of Swann's chest.

"That's enough!" Pinky shouted. "Just settle down!"

His face was red with anger. His chest rose and fell rapidly.

Swann felt just as angry. "You bit me," he said in disbelief.

"You gave me no choice," Pinky replied. He took a deep breath. "That was a nice try. You're just as strong as you look, Agent Swann. Even after a sleepless night on a cold floor. Even after I took one of your fingers."

Swann hung his head in shame. "I could have crushed you. I could have squeezed you so hard your sternum caved in."

Pinky smiled. "But you had to let go. You didn't get a choice. Reflexes are almost impossible to control, aren't they?"

Swann looked at his hand. It was bleeding heavily. Blood trickled onto the floor.

Pinky made a disgusted noise. "Sorry about that. I'm not very proud of what I did. But we're both still alive. It could have been worse. Now *move.*"

He herded Swann back to the trapdoor.

"Down," Pinky ordered.

Swann climbed down the steps.

Pinky lifted the door and prepared to lower it. "Watch your head. Good. I won't forget the latch this time. Have a good day, Agent Swann."

He let the door fall shut. A moment later, Swann heard the click of the latch.

That was his last hope of getting out of here, and he had blown it.

He made his way down the stairs slowly, feeling depressed. Suddenly, he remembered something.

It was *not* his last chance. Jo was still out there. And he knew she was looking for him.

SIXTY-ONE

Jo pulled into the parking lot of the Lapse Lodge. She parked in the same spot as before, as evidenced by the tire ruts in the snow and the shattered fiberglass dotting the snow-covered area.

Ford was typing out a text. It gave Jo a moment to reflect. She watched the door of the lobby. The crime scene guys had shut it when they left. The body of Joey Malone was long gone, though his blood still stained the snow.

"All right, good to go." Ford put his phone away. "Just updating Kelly."

"What did you tell her?" Jo asked.

"That I have no idea when I'll be back."

"I'm sure she'll understand," Jo said.

"Oh, she will. And I know someone else who's going to be *very* happy about it. My assistant, Dessie. She's watching the office while I'm gone, but I've told her not to accept any new cases until I get back. So she's probably got her feet up right now, watching a movie."

"Easy street," Jo said with a laugh. "Wouldn't that be nice? Instead, we find ourselves in a completely foreign situation. Staying at a hotel whose owner just died. Is it okay to keep sleeping here? We can't exactly pay for additional nights."

"I think it's fine." Ford shrugged. "Think about it from Miriam's point of view. Money doesn't matter to her now. Maybe nothing matters. We already bagged the guy who did her in."

Jo sighed. "Listen to us. Talking about a tragedy like it's something we saw in a TV show."

"You think that reflects poorly on us?" Ford asked. "I don't. I think it's the opposite. We've got a lot of responsibility, but we're still just normal people. We witness terrible things, and we compartmentalize them. We won't do any good by losing our minds, right?"

"Right." Jo nodded.

"Are you good now?" Ford asked.

"I think so."

"Are you sure? Because I can always give you a slap. Or find a bucket of cold water to dump on your head. Anything to help a friend."

"I feel so loved. Come on, let's go inside and wait for McKinley." Jo sighed and got out of the car. Her breath formed a plume of frosty mist in front of her face. For all the sunlight that was now beaming down on Lapse, the temperature was hovering barely above zero.

Ford shivered and rubbed his hands together as they crossed the parking lot. "Jeez, do people really live here? Pretty weird that you can drive hundreds of miles south of Seattle and somehow find yourself in the arctic circle."

Jo didn't even crack a smile. She was feeling as low as she ever had before. Helpless and lost. And the fact that she felt this way made her feel even worse. Like she was some kind of rookie on her first case.

Her spirits were lifted as soon as she opened the door of her room. Warm air rushed out to greet her. She could hear the furnace humming behind the walls.

"Power's back on," she said brightly.

"Thank God for small blessings," Ford groaned. He kicked his shoes off, jogged across the room, and tossed himself onto Jo's bed. "I'm calling this one."

"There's only one bed in the room, Ford," Jo pointed out.

"Oh. Well, I'll take the floor." He slithered off the side of the bed and flopped onto the floor. "Ah. That's not so bad."

Jo shut the door and hung her coat up. She took off her shoes and hopped forward to avoid the growing puddle of melted snow in the entryway. Wet socks were one of the worst things in life.

She lay across the bed, draping an arm over her eyes. "Ah... I don't think a hotel bed has ever felt this good. Especially since it's not a frozen slab. I wonder how they got the power back already?"

"Maybe they heard Jo Pullinger was in town," Ford said. "And they decided to expedite it. To hell with Pendleton or whatever the next town is called. Is it just me, or is it feeling a lot like nap time?"

"My body says, yes," said Jo, "but my mind says no. I just know as soon as I'm about to drift off, I'll start thinking about Swann."

"I know what you mean. Let's find a distraction." Ford reached up, hooking the TV remote off the nightstand. He hit the power button and went through the channels. "Here we go. Some old black-and-white movie. Looks about as boring as watching paint dry. It's perfect."

Jo barely paid the movie any attention. She was lost in her own thoughts.

It was clear that Kurt Black's property was the best lead they had. The *only* lead they had. They had to wait for nightfall to check the place out, or else Kurt would see them and come out with one of his big guns. Until then, she could either rest up so she could be on her A-game, or she could go wandering through the arctic temperatures. Hoping some random clue would land in her lap.

As soon as she established this logic in her mind, she was able to drift off to sleep.

SIXTY-TWO

There was a knock on the door.

Jo sat up, her heart thumping in her ears. It was dark in the room. The TV was still on, showing an entirely different movie. It looked like something from the 70s.

Through the window blinds, she could tell that night was almost upon them. The sunlight had dwindled to a soft reddish glow.

Another knock. Ford sat up on the floor, snorting and wiping drool from his mouth. "Kelly, Hazel's sleepwalking again."

"Ford," Jo said quietly.

He looked at her. "Oh. I'm here in Lapse. Crap."

A third knock came, and this time it was accompanied by a voice. "Uh, guys? Can you let me in? If you're in there. I checked the other two rooms already."

Jo didn't remember locking the door, but she knew she must have. Muscle memory. She got out of bed and hurried to the door, pulling it open. A wave of cold hit her. McKinley stepped inside, pushing the door shut behind him.

"Whew!" he gasped. "It got even colder out there. I would have been here a bit sooner, but I thought we could all use a bite."

He handed Jo a paper sack that smelled like greasy meat. She dug two burgers out, handing one to Ford. They all sat on the edge of the bed together. They unwrapped their dinner and wolfed it down.

"What took so long at Carmen's house?" Jo asked.

McKinley blew out his lips. "Man. Those guys are really thorough. I had a great time watching them work. And I got back before dark. I assumed that's when you planned on making your move."

Jo balled up her burger wrapper and tossed it into the garbage can. "That's exactly right. I'm a bit worried about the cold, but we can't waste any more time. Ford and I will head out to Kurt's property. We're going to search as much of it as we can. We'll go all night if we have to."

McKinley nodded. "Another reason I was late... I made a stop at the local hardware store. You'll want these."

He pulled two extra pairs of gloves out of his coat pocket, along with two black ski masks. As Jo and Ford were trying theirs on, he pulled a third mask out.

"You think I'm just going to sit around here and wait for you guys to come back?" McKinley asked.

"Actually," said Jo, "I was thinking you might stay in the car and keep the heat running. We'll have to park a ways out from Kurt's place, but maybe Ford and I can jog back whenever we need to warm up.""That's also not happening," McKinley replied. "We have a lot of stuff to search out there. An extra set of eyes is going to come in handy."

Jo nodded. "So, it's settled. We're all going."

"Correct," McKinley agreed. "One thing that isn't settled... are we really not letting the sheriff know? A fourth set of eyes would come in handy, too."

"And that's exactly what I'm worried about," said Jo. "Best case scenario, if we tell Phelps, he'll want to come with us."

"Would that be such a bad thing?" Ford asked.

Jo frowned and licked a bit of ketchup off her finger. "It could be. Phelps is a good man. I trust his character. But he's a small-town cop. Not exactly the caliber of person we need on this particular assignment."

"All right, fine," said Ford. "But what's the worst-case scenario if we tell him?"

"He tries to shut us down," Jo replied. "Then we'll be in the unfortunate position of having to tell him to get stuffed. I don't want to do that. I like the guy. Not telling him is the easiest way. If we find Swann and Carmen, we can let him know we were there."

"If we don't?" asked McKinley.

"Then there's no reason for anyone to know about it. Are we ready?"

"One more bite." Ford unhinged his jaw, shoving the last quarter of his huge burger into his mouth. He said something else then, but it was too muffled to make out.

SIXTY-THREE

They didn't speak much during the first couple of miles of the drive. Jo took the wheel. She felt that was only right. It was her operation, her plan. And she'd been doing all right driving in the snow so far.

The stars were twinkling in a clear sky. McKinley had already checked the forecast before they left the hotel. But Jo asked him to check again.

"No chance of snow for the next three days," he reiterated. "We'll be good. We won't get stuck."

"Good," she said with a sigh. "Because getting stuck would be a huge problem. Especially, if it's when we're trying to make a quick getaway. But I guess I don't need to tell you guys that."

"Nope," said Ford, from the backseat. "I've seen lots of action movies. Horror, too. The car always stalls out or gets stuck in the mud when someone's trying to get away. But that won't happen here. I have faith."

"So do I," Jo agreed. She smiled and nodded. "I think we're going to find them."

"What if we don't?" McKinley asked.

Ford reached forward, rubbing McKinley's shoulders. "No need to overthink, my friend. If Jo says we're going to find them, we're going to find them."

"I didn't say we were going to find them," Jo replied. "I said I *think* we're going to find them. Somebody call Grantham now. Let him know what we're doing. If he tries to pull the plug, we can just pretend like we're losing signal. I joke because I know what he's going to say."

McKinley got their boss on the phone.

"Agent McKinley," Grantham boomed, his voice undiminished despite the distance between them. "I hope you have some kind of positive update for me."

"No, sir," McKinley answered. "But it's not negative either. It's just an update."

"Quit being cute and just tell me," Grantham said.

"We're going to be conducting a stealth search of Kurt Black's property," said McKinley.

"Kurt Black," Grantham said slowly. "As in, the ex-FBI agent who's just minding his own business?"

Jo jumped in. "Sir, we have reason to believe Kurt could be running a cult. Joey Malone might have been a member of that cult. And there are surely others. They're most likely holding Swann and Carmen for some kind of ritual sacrifice."

"Yes, I have the file here in front of me," Grantham said. "I'd stake a good amount of money that Kurt Black is innocent. But I will give your mission my stamp of approval. I want to be updated as soon as humanly possible, Agent Pullinger. Understand?"

"Absolutely, sir," said Jo. "But before I go... how much money would you stake, exactly?"

Grantham sighed. "Now you're being cute as well. It's a good thing I like you two. If this mission of yours goes sideways, I'll even take the blame for it. And here's my final word. If I'm right, you buy me dinner. And vice versa."

"I don't know, sir," McKinley added. "'Dinner' is kind of a broad term. Some places are pretty expensive."

"What's that?" said Grantham. "You're breaking up. Can't hear you."

The call ended abruptly.

"Son of a..." McKinley stared at his phone, shaking his head. "He used the trick you were going to use, Jo."

Ford laughed. "Hard to pull one over on Robert Grantham. But keep trying."

"That's all right." Jo drove onward into the dark. "We're about to enter the boondocks here. We would have lost signal soon either way. McKinley, did Rupert and his team find anything useful at Carmen's house?"

"Fingerprints inside the car," McKinley said. "Some of them match Swann. The others are still unidentified, but they were all over the steering wheel and gearshift. So they're most likely Carmen's. Other than that, not much. A few fibers that might be useful once we have something to compare them to."

"In other words," said Jo, "everything's pretty much riding on what we do or don't find tonight. That makes me feel a lot better."

They were soon driving down narrow dirt roads. The forest crowded around them. Choking out every bit of moonlight that tried to reach them. Even the car's headlights seemed weak. But Jo knew the way.

When they were still about a half mile out from Kurt's property, she found a decent spot to pull off the road. She inched the car forward, slotting it between two low evergreen trees. The curtain of needles served as a decent hiding place.

The three of them bundled up in their gloves and ski masks. They zipped their jackets up tight and kept their sidearms in hand as they jogged down the road.

SIXTY-FOUR

Checking on Carmen was the first thing Swann did when he returned to the basement. She was fine. The bullet had come through a few feet away. Close enough to scare her, but that was all.

"You're bleeding again," she said.

"I know. He bit me."

Carmen made a face. "That's so nasty. Don't worry. I'll take it up with him next time he comes down here."

Swann smiled and nodded, going along with the joke. He didn't know how to tell her that the next time Pinky came, it would be to lead them to their deaths. He didn't know if he *should* tell her.

***

Over the next several hours, Swann wrestled with that question.

The power came back at one point. That was a good thing, at least. The furnace started blowing again. It was a weak appliance, and the basement was a huge space. It was enough that they didn't freeze to death. But they certainly weren't comfortable.

Swann spent most of that time on his feet. He paced back and forth. He wandered around the basement. Checking every nook and cranny for the tenth time. Unfortunately, no incredible secrets were revealed. No hidden lever to pull that would drop them down into a hot tub and shove a mug of cocoa into their hands.

Mostly he just searched so that he could feel useful. If he went back to sitting around, he might lose his mind. Then he'd really be screwed. They both would.

Of course, he might lose his mind either way. Because he knew what Pinky had in store for them. He had seen the crucifixes and the pyres beneath them.

Carmen had no idea. Not yet. Swann had to make a choice. Should he tell her? Or should he let her find out on her own if all else failed and they were unable to get away?

He weighed the pros and cons. There was a certain dignity in knowing your fate. But other than that, he could think of no good reason to tell her. As for *not* telling her, he could think of many good reasons.

Or maybe you're just passing the buck, Swann thought. *Taking the easy way. Maybe you're abandoning her in some way, trying to make it better for yourself.*

Swann had always struggled with a defeatist attitude. No matter what he did, he could think of reasons why it was wrong, why he was a failure.

This time, he decided to be brave. He decided to change. There was dignity in that too. Even if it was the last thing he did.

He made up his mind. There was no way he would tell Carmen about the pyres. If he did that, it would be the same as admitting they had no chance of survival.

SIXTY-FIVE

The edge of the forest stood ahead of them. Jo dropped to a prone position, crawling forward on her elbows. She reached the edge of the clearing and peered across it. It was a wide-open space, well-lit by the moon. If they went sprinting across at the wrong time, they could easily be seen.

"There it is," she said.

She peered toward the main house. Several of the windows glowed with an inner light. She could make out a few of the outbuildings. The others were lost in the distance, and the shadows of the trees dotting the property.

"Looks unassuming," McKinley said, crawling up beside Jo. "Like any other bumpkin's property."

Ford approached as well, falling to one knee. "Are you guys really going to belly-crawl the whole way?"

"Kurt's a paranoid person," Jo said. "And we've already been sniffing around. I wouldn't be surprised if he's keeping watch."

Ford shrugged, lowering himself onto his stomach. "So, what's the move?"

Jo scanned the edge of the clearing. "We can cut along the edge. Staying just inside the trees. Once we get off to the side of the main house, we can cut in."

"Then let's do it," McKinley said.

They retreated into the cover of the trees. Then they started jogging again, finding their way by moonlight. There was no wind. If there were any forest creatures here, they were dead silent. The only sound Jo heard was their breathing and the crunch of their feet in snow.

She glanced to the side now and then. Gauging her angle. When she could no longer see the lights from the main house, she stepped back out into the open.

"This is good," she said. "But let's make it quick."

"Roger, Roger," Ford replied.

They sprinted across the open field. Jo relaxed a bit as soon as they reached trees again. She approached the side of a barn and scraped along it. Ford and McKinley followed close behind.

Jo stopped at the corner of the barn and peeked around it. The main house was directly ahead of her, though hidden by snowy bushes. To her left, a lane of cleared ground stretched into the distance. Kurt had come by with a plow of his own, granting himself access to a few outbuildings.

"Are we checking this one out?" Ford asked, touching the side of the barn.

"Not yet," Jo whispered. "Before we go digging, let's make sure we know where Kurt is. Follow me."

She moved slowly now. Past the bushes, toward the foundation of the house. One of the glowing windows was a few feet to her left. She sidled over. McKinley and Ford were both tall enough to see through the window, but Jo had to stand on her toes.

The window was situated in a hallway. Looking straight through, Jo could only see a wall. But if she craned her head to the side at just the right angle...

"There he is," she muttered.

McKinley and Ford grunted to show they could see him too.

The door at the end of the hall was open. They could see only a very narrow angle of the room beyond. Kurt happened to be standing in just the right spot to be seen.

He was situated in front of a lectern. The kind of thing you might see in a church. But instead of a Bible perched on it, there was a spiral notebook full of scribblings and symbols.

Kurt was dressed in a white robe with flowing sleeves. His hands were raised, and his eyes were closed.

"He's praying," McKinley said.

"We already knew he was a religious guy," Ford replied. "Nothing fishy so far."

Kurt opened his eyes and lowered his hands. When he spoke, it was loud enough for the agents outside to hear.

"Thank you all for joining me in that silent prayer," he said. "You've been with me for so long, I fear I've begun to take your presence for granted. Rest assured. I appreciate every moment we have together."

"He's not alone," Jo hissed to the others. "They're in there with him. The missing kids!"

SIXTY-SIX

"Looks like Grantham owes us dinner," Ford growled.

"Quiet," McKinley warned.

Inside, Kurt turned a page in his notebook. It was his very own Bible. The holy tome of whatever strange religion he had created.

"Now," Kurt went on, "I'd like you all to hear some thoughts of mine. These are things I've been thinking about a lot lately, but especially the past day or two..."

Suddenly, the lights went out. Everything was cast into darkness. Jo could no longer see anything inside the house.

"Great," Kurt shouted. "The power's out. Again. No worries. If one of you would kindly fetch the candles..."

A softly orange light sparked to life. Someone handed Kurt a candle. The warm glow created shadows in the hollows of his cheeks.

"Thank you," he said. "We'll get the generator going in a little while. This is an important lesson, I suppose. No matter how rich our spirits grow, no matter how close we come to the divine, we'll never be free of mundane concerns. Such as heat.

"Anyway, as I was saying, I've been thinking a lot about the meaning of everything we do. The world is dominated by distrust, fear, and hatred. It always has been and always will be. We are not allowed to just exist out here, seeking our truths. No. The world will never leave us alone. But we can rise above it.

"There are many ills in this world. Chaos and cruelty are everywhere. But soon, there will be a symbolic killing of those ills. A final departure. A statement that we will make: we are no longer part of that world. We reject it. It might try crashing in on us, but we'll hold fast."

He shut his notebook and took a sip from a mug.

"The air in here is still warm," he said. "It will be for a while. Let's go into the parlor and sit for a few minutes in quiet reflection."

Kurt stepped away from the lectern, disappearing to the left. He was followed by three figures who also appeared to be dressed in white robes. They moved too quickly for Jo to identify them.

"Did either of you get anything?" Ford asked.

"Two men and one woman," said McKinley. "That's what I saw."

Jo nodded. "Two men and one woman. Three men, if you count Kurt. Let's just move away before they come out to turn the generator on."

They headed back in the same direction, past the bushes.

Ford whistled. "Yup. Looks like a cult to me."

"They'll see our footprints," McKinley whispered.

"Nothing we can do about that," Jo said. "Let's just hope they aren't paying too much attention."

Ford gestured at the barn in front of them. "I guess searching these buildings might be a bad idea. Too close to the house."

"That's all right," McKinley said. "If they're keeping Swann and Carmen somewhere, it'll be deeper in."

"It's safe to assume," Jo agreed.

She led the way, taking them along the plowed path. She passed by a handful of buildings. The itch to search them all was there, but she ignored it.

"If I play Captain Obvious yet again," said Ford, "it's cold out here. I think there's an icicle growing in each one of my nostrils right now."

Jo looked over her shoulder. She couldn't see the main house at all. It was at least the length of a football field away now. Maybe that was enough.

"Let's go inside for a minute," she said.

The closest building to them was a huge warehouse with a steel roof. There was a big roll-up door on it. It would have made a racket to try and open. Luckily, there was a small side door around the corner.

"It's probably locked," said Ford.

"Wanna bet?" Jo asked.

"Grantham already owes us dinner. I'll quit while I'm ahead. Just check the door."

Jo tried the door. It opened right up. The air inside was warm and dry; the warehouse was climate controlled, at least when the power was on. That was Jo's first clue that it housed something important.

"Either of you got a flashlight?" she asked.

McKinley did. He clicked it on, shining the cone of light around.

"Holy crap," Jo gasped.

The warehouse housed an arsenal. There were racks everywhere. Each one piled with guns. And that was just the walls. The floor itself was jam-packed with vehicles. There were two APCs, a SWAT van, an armored truck, and a Humvee.

McKinley clicked the light off. He was breathing heavily.

"Kurt pretty much said he was ready to face the world," Jo said. "Now we know why. He's got enough firepower in here to wage one hell of a war."

SIXTY-SEVEN

In the distance, they heard the sound of a door slamming shut.

All at once, they rushed into the warehouse. Ford closed the door.

"They're coming," McKinley moaned.

"It's all right," Jo urged. "That was just them going out to start the generator. They have no idea we're here. Can I have the light?"

McKinley groped around in the dark until he found her, then transferred the flashlight to her hand. She turned the light on, bringing the racks of weaponry back into view.

"Are you sure that's a good idea?" McKinley asked.

Jo nodded, playing the light along the walls. "This building is tight, McKinley. And there are no windows. They won't be able to see anything."

He groaned. "I know I wanted to come out here, but this sucks. I'd rather be making a rubber-band ball right now."

"Hey, you don't go into the field very often," Jo said softly. "You're just rusty. Take a deep breath."

McKinley did as she advised. He pulled air in slowly, filling his lungs. He let it out again.

"Better?" Jo asked.

"A little," he replied. "But I'd feel even better if we grabbed some of these guns."

Ford rushed to the nearest rack. "I'll drink to that, McKinley. Check this one out. AK-47. Never shot one of these before. It's probably as old as I am, but it looks brand new. They don't make 'em like they used to."

"Pretty sad when a gun ages better than you, huh?" Jo said. She joined him at the rack, reaching out to touch the barrel of a shotgun. "Ooh. A SPAS-12. Iconic. At least Kurt has good taste in weaponry."

McKinley approached. "Shotgun's no good. You want to be able to take these freaks down from a distance. I'll take the M4."

The guns were behind glass doors, but they weren't locked up. McKinley pulled down his M4 carbine and popped out the clip.

"No ammo in here," he said.

Ford pointed down. There were lockers under each of the display cases. "Bullets are probably in there."

Jo dropped to her knees. She tried to pull the locker open, but it wouldn't budge. She looked closer.

"There's a keyhole," she said, and then she sighed. "They're locked. We aren't getting any ammo. Put the guns back, boys."

Ford set his AK-47 back carefully. He saw that McKinley was frozen and pulled the M4 away from him.

This motion startled McKinley out of his trance. He backed up, crashing into the side of the Humvee. "This isn't good," he said frantically. "Kurt will have the key. He'll be able to open these lockers. They'll come after us with the big guns. We need to leave. We need to call for backup."

"You already did," Ford replied. "I'm the backup."

"We need *more* backup," said McKinley. "We need the army."

Ford smirked at Jo. She stepped up to McKinley, grabbing him by the front of the jacket.

"Listen," she said. "We can't wait for backup. Swann might be here somewhere. He can't wait, either. We can't abandon him. We just have to be smart. The way we were trained to be. Got it?"

McKinley nodded. He took another deep breath. "Sorry. I'm all right. I won't lose it again."

She clapped him on the shoulder. "Good. Let's be fast here. Find Swann and Carmen. Get out of dodge. Before you know it, you'll be back in Seattle. Sitting at your desk, bored to tears."

Ford had gone to the door. He opened it and stuck his head out to look and listen.

"Anything?" Jo said quietly.

He shook his head. "All clear. Let's move out."

SIXTY-EIGHT

Jo led the way again. The itch she felt now was to get past as many buildings as possible. To put more distance between her and the house. Again, she refused the urge. They looked inside each and every structure. Even the tiny sheds.

She would have expected some of them to be empty. But they all had something in them. From old farming equipment to tool chests and car lifts. There was even a second house in one larger building. It was like a giant studio apartment with a kitchen and everything.

"He's got everything out here," Ford said.

"A whole compound," Jo replied. "Enough room for his little cult to grow into an army. I'm sure that's exactly what he's going for."

"He would need to keep finding new members," McKinley pointed out. "Do you think he's trying to recruit Swann and Carmen? The whole thing about the sacrifice could just be a scare tactic."

Jo closed the door to the studio apartment building. "Who knows? If we can shut his operation down tonight, it won't matter."

***

The property seemed to go on forever. They tried to be systematic and thorough, but the outbuildings seemed randomly arranged. They couldn't be sure they had checked every one of them.

Once every few minutes, they stopped to listen. For any sign of pursuit or cries of help from Swann. They heard nothing other than the increasingly distant hum of a generator.

"How long have we been searching?" Jo asked.

Ford pulled up his sleeve to check his watch. "About forty-five minutes since we set foot on the property."

"I guess we're making good time, then," she said. "But it doesn't feel like it. My toes are numb. How about that one?" She pointed to a dark shape looming in front of them. "Have we checked that place yet?"

"Don't think so," McKinley said, sniffling in the cold. "Maybe it's warm inside."

As they came closer to the building, Jo spotted a series of gaping holes in its roof. "Don't think it's going to be warm in there, McKinley."

It was a rundown old barn. The door was hanging askew; one of its hinges was gone. It let out a tired groan when Ford pulled at it.

"This old thing's going to give us away," Ford said. "Anyone have an emergency can of WD-40?"

Jo brushed past him, stepping into the barn. The rotting planks sagged under her weight. She sniffed at the air, detecting a faint lingering aroma.

"Gunpowder?" she said.

McKinley entered next. "I can't smell anything. My nose is filled with snot."

"Then blow it."

"No way. It'll get all over my ski mask."

Ford stepped inside. He pulled a few tissues out of his pocket and handed them to McKinley. "Here."

"Where'd you get those?" McKinley stammered.

"I'm a dad. We always carry things like this. I'm just mad I didn't bring my WD-40. I usually always have a can handy."

McKinley lifted his mask long enough to blow his nose. "That's a joke, right? About the WD-40?"

"It's whatever you want it to be," Ford said.

Jo shut the door as tightly as she could. Then she flicked the flashlight on, getting a look at the room.

"Trap door," Ford said, pointing. "Jo. Over there. Shine the line so I can see."

But she was locked in on something else. Ford followed her eyes, then let out a series of bad words.

"What are those?" McKinley asked.

"Crosses," Jo said. "Crucifixes."

"With piles of kindling under them," Ford added. "Pyres. It looks like something from the Salem witch trials. I think we found the site of that sacrifice we were talking about."

SIXTY-NINE

Swann didn't realize he was sleeping. He just knew he was somewhere warm and nice. It was a park in Seattle he used to like running in. There was a great one-mile loop that took him past a duck pond.

He was there now. Jogging along in the sun. He didn't feel tired. He wasn't out of breath. He felt like he could run forever. Around the whole world and right back to where he had started.

There was a sound. A rumbling. A vibration overhead. He looked up at the Seattle sky, sunny for a change. There were no clouds in sight.

Then how come I hear thunder?

His eyes snapped open in the dark basement. He was suddenly very tired. And very cold. He remembered now. The power went out again. Winter was seeping back into the basement. His whole body felt frozen. He could barely move.

There was a bit of warmth against him, though. Carmen. He remembered that, too. Sitting down next to her. Wrapping his arms around her for warmth.

There was that sound again. Thunder. He looked up but could only see the ceiling.

Then, with a thud, he heard a sprinkling of dust falling down the steps.

Adrenaline burst into Swann's body. He had fallen asleep against his own will. He had wasted time. Pinky had said the sacrifice would happen tonight. The time had come. They were coming down to haul Swann to the cross to be burned alive. Carmen, too.

There was no more time for thinking or planning. There was nothing left to do but fight. To die trying.

Swann made himself stand. Carmen slumped to the side and didn't make a sound. His legs shook and almost buckled. He needed a weapon, and there was only one thing he could think of. The chain that had held him to the wall.

He found it, curled up on the floor. He wrapped one end around his right fist, holding the rest in his left hand so it wouldn't drag on the floor and give him away.

There were more footsteps. Multiple sets, moving around above him. It wasn't just Pinky, now. He had brought his friends to help him out.

"Swann?" Carmen's feeble voice called.

"*Shh.* Don't make a sound," Swann ordered her. He was happy to hear her voice. He was worried she had succumbed to the cold.

The stairs were open. But there was a low wall running along beneath them, forming a storage nook. Swann crouched by that wall. In this position, someone coming down the steps wouldn't see him. Not until they stepped off two feet away. Well within striking distance.

The chain was heavy. Great as a bludgeoning weapon. But Swann didn't know if he had the strength to use it properly.

He waited, holding his breath.

SEVENTY

"Trap door," Ford said. "Should I say it again?"

"We heard you the first seven times," Jo told him. She pulled the flashlight beam away from the crucifixes. She found the trapdoor. Unlike the rest of the floor, it looked solid. Relatively new. The hardware was heavy metal. There was a latch, and it was held shut with a heavy padlock.

"We're going to have to smash it open," said Jo.

"Or we just rip that door out of the floor," Ford suggested. "The wood around it looks weak."

"Sounds ridiculous. And every bit as noisy." Jo bit her lip. "Swann could be down there."

"It seems like the logical place," Ford said. "If he is, then it'll be worth every bit of noise we make. We can grab him and run."

"What are you guys talking about?" McKinley called.

"Sorry, didn't realize we were whispering," Jo replied. "We're trying to figure out how to get into this trap door. We're probably just going to have to smash it open. Any suggestions?"

McKinley let out a dry laugh. "No amount of coffee and research is going to help us now. Sometimes you just have to break stuff. Before you do anything, let me make sure the coast is clear."

He ducked out through the door. They heard his shoes crunching away in the snow. A moment later, they came crunching back. McKinley came inside and pushed the door shut.

"Don't hear or see anyone," he said.

"That doesn't mean they aren't close by," Ford said in a low voice.

"Are you trying to get me to freak out again?" McKinley asked.

Ford shook his head. "Not at all. I'm just starting to freak out a little myself. I'm thinking about how I have a wife and daughter at home who have no idea I'm in a dangerous situation right now. They're probably safe in bed, all cozy, without a care in the world. All right, just smash the thing."

"Don't you want to do it?" Jo asked.

"Not really," he grumbled.

Jo shrugged. She handed him the flashlight. "Just make sure I can see what I'm doing."

She waited until he had the beam steady. She turned her handgun's safety on, then used the butt like a club, striking the padlock clean in the middle. It broke, popping open. Jo brushed the lock aside, then held up her gun.

"Not even a scratch," she said.

"You're a pro," Ford replied. "Now, let's get that creepy trap door open so we can all go down and get picked off by some subterranean monster."

Jo grabbed the edge of the door. "Where's your sense of adventure?"

"I must have dropped it somewhere while we were running around freezing our cheeks off," Ford told her. "That looks heavy. Let me help you."

McKinley appeared beside them. He waited until they had the door open, then gestured them aside politely.

"I'll go down first," he whispered. "I feel the need to make up for earlier. You know, when I almost lost my head. Let me do this part."

Ford shrugged. "I have no problem with that. We'll back you up."

"I'll call you down once I know it's safe," McKinley said.

He started down the steps. He moved boldly at first, descending at a normal speed. The closer he got to the bottom, the more timid he became. But he kept on going, stepping off at the last step and turning to the left.

"Can't see much," he said. "Want to toss that flashlight down?"

He reached with one hand back up the stairs. Ford took one step down, lining up the toss.

There was a strange sound from the basement. A metallic clanking. McKinley's eyes darted to the side. He let out a curse, ducking to the side just as something huge and heavy came swinging within an inch of his face.

It was a thick metal chain. It somehow found its way around McKinley's neck. He was yanked to the side, out of sight.

All Jo and Ford heard were the sounds of him choking.

SEVENTY-ONE

"They got him," Ford gasped.

"They?" Jo asked, pulling the flashlight away from him.

He looked at her, confused. But she was already running down the steps, pulling her ski mask up, letting it bunch around her forehead. Ford followed a second later. He still had no idea what she was thinking, but he wasn't going to let her go down without backup.

At the bottom of the steps, Jo turned the light on. She shined it around until she found McKinley. His feet were off the ground, kicking around frantically. He had managed to get his fingers under the chain, stopping it from strangling him.

Jo looked past McKinley's panicked eyes. She saw the tall, broad-shouldered man standing behind him. It hadn't even been forty-eight hours since she last saw Swann, but he looked completely different. He looked like a wild animal.

She shined the light upward, onto her face. Letting him see her.

"Swann!" she shouted. "Let him go. It's us. We're here now."

The feral man stared at her for a moment. Abruptly, he released McKinley.

McKinley collapsed forward. Swann shot out a hand, catching his arm and steadying him. He even picked McKinley's dropped sidearm off the floor, handing it over.

"Sorry," Swann said. "I should have recognized your voices. I guess I was in another dimension there. You all right, McKinley?"

"Never better," McKinley rasped, rubbing his throat.

Swann winced. "I'm really sorry. I had no idea it was you. All I could think about was fighting back. I thought we were about to be sacrificed."

"We?" Jo asked hopefully.

Swann pointed. Jo shined the light toward the back wall and saw the ratty old tarp with the scared young woman huddling under it.

"I told you, Carmen," Swann said. "Jo came for us. We're safe now."

"Not safe yet," Jo replied, moving the light away from Carmen's eyes. "We still have to get back to the car. It's pretty far, and the cold is as much an enemy as the cultists."

"Tell me what you know," said Swann.

"We'll talk as we work," Jo told him.

They approached Carmen. She stared up at them with half-closed eyes, dazed. It didn't take long for Jo to see the issue.

"The chains are fed through these steel plates," she said. "That's what's really holding her. The chain will be the weak point, but it'll probably still be easier to pry those plates out of the wall. They'll only be as strong as the masonry they're drilled into."

She looked at Swann.

"How did you get free?" she asked.

"I got lucky. One of the links on my chain was already kind of broken. I found a screw sticking out of the wall and worked at it until it broke. Unfortunately, Carmen's chain is solid."

His words were clear and concise, but it was easy to see he was fading. He was unsteady on his feet. He was keeping his left hand hidden. Jo suspected he was obscuring an injury from them. But it could wait for now.

"Here we go," Ford said, searching through his pockets. "Dads are always carrying things with them. How about one of these?"

He produced a liquor flask, handing it to Swann.

"What is it?" Swann asked.

"Some good old Kentucky bourbon," said Ford. "Just have a couple of sips. Enough to numb you up a bit. Not too much."

Swann unscrewed the top and took a drink. He sighed with satisfaction, then handed the flask back.

"Thanks, Dad," he said.

"Anytime." Ford grinned. "We saved your butt at the Seattle marathon. Now we're saving it again here. But that's just because we're heroes."

"You are," Swann stammered weakly. He let his head drop. "And I'm just not cut out, am I?"

Ford made a face. He handed the flask back to Swann. "Here. You need this more than I do. Not too much, now. Just sit down for a minute, all right?"

Swann took the flask and sank to the floor. He put his back against the wall. But he didn't take another drink. He looked just as dazed as Carmen now, staring around like a lost child.

Jo took McKinley aside, lowering her voice. "We need to find something to get Carmen free. Do you think you can go up and take a look around? Some kind of pry bar. Even something improvised might work."

McKinley nodded and ascended the steps. The basement fell into silence.

SEVENTY-TWO

Swann sat down beside Carmen and fell asleep. He dreamed again. This time, he was in the basement as it had been. Just him and Carmen. Alone and chained up. Without a hope in the world.

His mind immediately accepted this dream. It became his reality. He didn't even feel disappointed that he was still trapped. He was too tired for that.

Someone touched his shoulder. Shook him awake. He opened his eyes and saw Jo Pullinger. She was squatting beside him, her green eyes sparkling with concern.

Not for the first time, he was struck by her looks. She was pretty, but that wasn't it. It was a quality she had, something that radiated from her. She was tough. She was a fighter. She was mighty. She was everything Swann wanted to be.

"Sorry I woke you up," Jo said. "Just making sure you aren't going anywhere."

"Where would I go?" Swann asked with a tired smile. "I'm chained to this wall. I can't move much."

Jo's forehead wrinkled with concern. "Swann, you already freed yourself."

"You came for me," Swann said. "Thanks. But I need to wake up now. Carmen needs me to keep trying."

Somewhere out in the darkness, a door opened. Footsteps thudded on the steps. Swann's body constricted with fear. But it was just McKinley. He gave Swann a nod as he went by. There was a crowbar in his hands.

Swann pointed at McKinley. "I almost killed him."

"Not really," Jo said. "Everything's fine. And we really are here, Swann. You're already awake."

Swann's thoughts crystallized. He began to feel and think. It wasn't very pleasant. It came with a lot of pain and sorrow. But it was necessary.

"Are they working on freeing Carmen?" he asked.

McKinley and Ford were standing over the dazed young woman. Talking amongst themselves. Ford took the crowbar and started prying at the plates holding her chain to the wall.

"Guess that answers my question," Swann added. He looked back at Jo. "How's your heart been?"

"This old thing?" Jo smiled, touching her chest. "It hasn't been bothering me much lately. Probably because I've spent most of my time sitting on my butt. But I've been going for my morning jogs. I think they're helping."

"Nothing too strenuous, I hope," Swann said sympathetically.

Jo laughed. "You sound like my doctor."

With a groan of metal and crumbling brick, one of the plates ripped free. The other one followed suit soon after. Ford handed the crowbar to McKinley and came over toward Jo and Swann.

"Well," he said with a sigh, "we can't get those manacles off their wrists. So they're going to be dragging chains with them unless we find a tool that could cut them off. But that's the best we can do for now."

"It's a start," Jo said. "Next thing we need to think about is—"

Carmen suddenly began to scream at the top of her lungs. It was a startling sound, making everyone jump in fear.

Swann understood straight away what had happened. Carmen woke up from her sleep and saw a strange man with a crowbar standing over her. He would have screamed too.

Despite his weakened state, Swann reacted first. He jumped up and ran to Carmen. Falling to one knee, he pulled her to his chest.

"It's all right!" he shouted. "Carmen, these people are my friends. They're here to help us."

Carmen was staring at the staircase. Maybe expecting someone to come down. Her screams continued for a moment, though her face looked oddly serene.

"She's in shock," Swann said once she quieted down. "She probably has no idea where she even is anymore. Just that she needs to be afraid."

SEVENTY-THREE

Ford was next to reach Carmen. He pulled something else out of his pocket. A fun-size bar of chocolate. He unwrapped it, holding it out. Carmen took it tentatively, giving it a nibble.

"That's better," Ford said. "Come back to us, kid. We're here to get you out. You're free from the wall now, but I'm afraid you'll have to lug that heavy chain with you."

Swann tried to stand up. The blood rushed out of his head. He hit the ground like a sack of dirt. McKinley and Jo rushed to his aid, but Swann sat up under his own power.

"You all right?" McKinley asked. "It would be pretty sad if you died right after we got here."

Swann chuckled. He tried to focus his eyes on the other agent. But his head seemed to be spinning.

"I'm all right," he said. "Just dizzy."

"Probably from the blood loss," Jo said.

"From that gash on his head?" McKinley asked. "It probably did bleed a lot."

"No." Jo grabbed Swann's left hand and held it up. "He's been trying to hide it from us. But then he fell asleep. Look what they did to him."

Ford looked over and frowned. "They cut off his finger? What kind of freaks are we dealing with here?"

"The religious kind," Swann replied. "They're some kind of cult. They wanted to burn us at the stake."

Jo gently released his hand. "We saw the pyres. And we know who's behind all this, too. Kurt Black. He used to be an FBI agent."

Swann let the information sink in. He digested it and tried to figure out what it meant.

"Getting out of here could be very dangerous," Jo went on. "The man has an incredible amount of firepower squirreled away. Our best shot is to get out undetected. And fast."

"Then what are we waiting for?" Ford grumbled. "I've got a life out there. We all do. So let's get moving."

"I'm with Ford," McKinley said.

Jo shook her head. "We can't go yet. If we bring Swann and Carmen out there like this, they'll freeze to death. We at least need to find them *something* to wear."

Ford groaned. He stared at Jo, then at Swann. Then he stood up and pulled off his top layer of clothing.

"Here," he said, handing it to Swann. "You and I are about the same height. This stuff should fit. And I figure you could use a bit of a break from this basement. Just don't fall over again."

Swann started pulling the clothes on. As his head poked through the neck hole of the jacket, he gave Carmen a worried glance.

"Don't worry," Ford added. "I'll stay with her. You three go and bring back something warm."

He patted Swann on the back, sending him away. But then he remembered something.

"Oh! I'll take that flask back, if you're done with it. Hooch might make you feel warm, but it's a false warmth. It won't do you much good topside."

Swann tossed the flask back to its owner. It was a clean throw. He was gaining back some of his dexterity. Life was slowly returning to him.

"Let's go," he said to Jo and McKinley.

SEVENTY-FOUR

"What was that?" McKinley whispered. "Did you hear it?"

Jo paused at the top of the steps. She was standing on the third step down. Her head and shoulders poked up through the trapdoor.

She hadn't heard whatever sound McKinley was talking about. Then it came a second time. A revving, grinding sound echoing through the night.

"Some kind of engine," Jo replied.

"Snowmobile?" Swann asked.

"Could be. Or just the generator."

"It sounded far away, at least," Swann pointed out.

McKinley pulled the ski mask back down over his face. "It did. But we're in the middle of nowhere. Kurt's closest neighbor is further away than our car. Whatever we're hearing, it definitely originated from this property."

Swann wobbled on his feet. He caught himself on the edge of the trap door. "That makes me feel a lot better. Can we hurry up and do this?"

Jo eyed him up. "If you're sure you can make it."

He nodded, clenching his jaw resolutely. "I can make it."

The sound came again. It was hard to tell, but it seemed closer. Or maybe it was just the wind carrying it further.

"On second thought," said McKinley, "I think I'll stay right here. Keep an eye out."

Jo gave the thumbs up. She climbed up into the barn, beckoning to Swann. He stepped up unaided and even led the way toward the door. He was more than ready to leave this place behind. Even if it was only temporary.

***

"I guess McKinley's staying behind," Ford said.

He left the foot of the steps and joined Carmen. With a grunt, he lowered himself to the floor. He wiggled around a bit, trying to find a comfortable position. But there wasn't one to be found.

"I'm too old for this," he said with a sigh. "I know I can't afford to turn into the curmudgeonly old guy just yet. I've got a seven-year-old kid back at home. But damn, it's tempting sometimes."

He twisted the cap off his flask and took a sip. The liquor burned down his throat. It was the only warm thing he had felt for hours.

"How old are you, Carmen?" he asked. He looked at her. She stared back at him with big eyes but didn't speak. "Do you have a mother out there? A father? I know you live alone, but..."

He trailed off, trying to give her a chance to speak. She looked down at the floor and stayed silent.

"Let me guess," Ford went on. "Your parents blew it. Maybe not your mom. Maybe she's still cool in your mind. But I'll bet your dad screwed up somewhere along the line. Alienated you. I almost did that once. A big thing happened that pushed my family apart. It could have stayed that way. Forever, maybe."

He took another drink, letting his thoughts wander.

"What made it change?" Carmen asked.

He smiled at her. "I guess my wife and I just decided to stop being stubborn. It's always a two-way street. She had to decide to take another chance. I had to believe in myself enough to make it happen. And it did."

Carmen scooted closer to him. "Why are you here? You should be with your family."

"We all should," said Ford. "A friend needed my help. I came. That's my job."

Carmen nodded. Her cheek brushed his shoulder. "I don't have parents. I don't remember them much. They died when I was a kid. The same age as your daughter."

That was Ford's cue. He put his arm around her. He figured they could both use a bit of support. Right now, Carmen must be feeling as lost and alone as she ever had. And he was here with her. Somebody's daughter. Somebody's baby girl who never got a chance. Maybe she thought she found a new father figure with Kurt Black. But even that had gone wrong.

"Who took care of you?" he asked.

"Aunts and uncles." She sniffed, rubbing her nose. "But it never lasted long. I was too much for them to handle. So starting at age sixteen, I was on my own. I did a lot of bad things to get by."

"You're still here," Ford said softly. "That's what matters."

Carmen smiled. "I'm here. And so are you. It's a weird world, isn't it?"

SEVENTY-FIVE

Jo and Swann approached the door of the barn.

"Did you search any of the nearby buildings?" Swann asked.

"We did," said Jo. "But we weren't looking for clothes. We were just looking for you."

"How about guns? Did you find any of those? They took mine."

"We did, but they were useless. The ammo was locked down."

Swann cursed. He darted out into the snow, and Jo followed. They headed for the nearest building. A rotting tool shed that leaned at a severe angle. A stiff breeze would have been enough to knock it down. The doorway was out of whack. Swann had to give the door a strong tug to get it open.

"You could have taken Ford's sidearm," said Jo.

"And leave him defenseless?" Swann lifted his arm. He had wrapped his chain around it. "At least I have this. I've been daydreaming about slamming Pinky over the skull with it."

Jo moved into the shed first. She shined the flashlight around. There wasn't much to see. It was a six-by-six room. The only thing inside was a rusty push mower.

"Who's Pinky?" Jo asked.

"The guy who did this." Swann showed his left hand with its stump. "He has a missing finger too."

"Can you tell me anything else about him?" Jo asked as she checked behind the door. There were coat hooks there, but they were empty. "His appearance?"

"He's got hazel eyes and dirty blond hair," Swann replied. "He's kind of small and scrawny, but he's surprisingly strong."

Jo nodded. "All right. So we've now got an ID on another one of these people. The guy you call Pinky is Samuel Whitaker. He's Miriam's missing grandson."

"Miriam? As in, the old lady who runs the hotel?"

"Yup. Except she doesn't run it anymore. She was murdered by Joey Malone, another member of Kurt's cult."

Swann said another bad word. He stepped out of the shed and led them to the next structure in line. It was another shed, directly next to the one they just searched. This one was newer. Obviously, it was meant as a replacement, but someone had been too lazy to haul the old one away.

Their luck turned. The shed was lined with gardening tools. Kurt, or maybe the previous owner, had been clearing away some kind of nasty brush. They had left a couple of flannel jackets behind, along with a pair of work boots. There was also a pair of bolt cutters in a corner.

Swann grabbed the coats. "It's something. Should be enough to get us all back to the car. How far did you say it was?"

"About a mile," Jo replied as she picked up the bolt cutters. "Give or take. It's an estimate."

Swan grinned. "The day before we left Seattle, I did my fastest mile ever. Five minutes flat. I don't think I'll get anywhere close to that tonight, but I'll give it my best shot."

"Just don't leave us all in the dust," Jo said with a laugh. But she didn't feel the humor at all. She only felt a clock ticking over her head. A giant blade getting ready to fall on her. It was time to get out of there before the cult came to perform their sacrifice.

They ran back to the barn, favoring speed rather than stealth. They had heard no more of those distant noises. For now, they seemed to be in the clear.

McKinley was on the stairs, his gun propped on the edge of the trap door. He raised the muzzle toward the ceiling when he saw them come in.

"It's about time," he said.

"We were gone for about two minutes," Jo said. She herded McKinley down the steps.

"Look what we found," Jo said, holding the bolt cutters in the air.

"Lucky find," Ford said with a smile as he took the cutters.

Ford cut Swann's manacles off first and then Carmen's. Swann then gave Ford's clothes back. While Ford helped Carmen into one of the flannels, Swann donned the other. The work boots were too big for Carmen, so he put them on. He left his dress shoes on the floor.

"Now they have a memento to remember me by," he said. "The one that got away. Sayonara, suckers."

He was suddenly in a chipper mood. Grinning from ear to ear. But the smile dropped off his face when a new sound reached them from outside.

Voices. People approaching the barn.

SEVENTY-SIX

"We need to get out," Jo said. She drew her sidearm.

Ford and McKinley did so as well. Swann picked up his chain, holding one end of it. He gave it a practice twirl.

"What about me?" Carmen whispered. "This chain is too heavy. I can't lift and swing it."

"Stay behind me," Swann said.

Jo took point. She set the pace. Fast enough to get out of the basement before they were caught. Slow enough that they made minimal noise. As soon as everyone was up, she quietly shut the trap door. If the cultists came in and saw it closed, they would assume their captives were still downstairs.

The voices were getting closer. But they were still a ways off. Jo listened intently, holding up a finger to keep the others silent.

"I can't make out what they're saying," she finally said. "But they don't sound upset."

"They sound... excited," Ford said, making a disgusted face. "I guess that means they have no clue that we're here."

Jo listened again. Trying to pinpoint the direction the voices were coming from. She pointed. "They're heading for the main door."

"Hopefully, not the only door," McKinley said. "Should we go back down and set an ambush?"

It was a tantalizing thought. If she, McKinley, and Ford all set up in the right spots, they could get one heck of a crossfire going. Put all the cultists down with no injuries to anyone else. But that was in a perfect world. The ideal realm of the imagination.

In most cases, it was better to run than to fight.

She pointed past the pyres. Toward the dark recesses of the barn. "Go check if there's another exit."

McKinley nodded, darting into the shadows.

Jo waved at the others to follow him. They would at least be hidden from sight at the back of the barn, even if they found no way out. As they moved away, Jo tiptoed to the main door.

It was still slightly open. The latch was long gone, and the door hung at an odd angle. It gave her a wide viewing angle. She couldn't see much. Just trees, snow, and darkness.

Then an orange glow appeared in the distance. Others soon joined it. Flickering sources of light. Jo narrowed her eyes and watched for another moment.

Four figures appeared, all dressed in white robes. They were carrying torches that guttered in the cold wind. She couldn't see any of their faces. They were all in ski masks as well. But she recognized the tattooed forearms of Kurt Black.

They were coming fast. Less than fifty feet from the barn now. They were coming to tie their prisoners up. To set the pyres ablaze and make their sacrifice.

Someone touched Jo's arm. She jumped, startled. Turning to the side, she saw Ford. He gestured toward the back of the barn.

Jo nodded and followed him. There was a side door, and Swann was holding it open for them. They hurried out into the frosty air. As a group, they crept away into the night.

But no matter how quietly they moved, Jo was keenly aware of the tracks they left behind.

SEVENTY-SEVEN

Ford pointed at something ahead of them. "Over there. We've gotta get out of the open."

There was a grimy motorhome with four flat tires. They rushed behind it, putting their backs to the wall and catching their breath. It had been a mere fifty-yard dash between here and the barn, but Jo was completely out of breath.

Running for your life took a lot out of you.

Jo didn't want to stop at all. She wanted to keep moving. But Carmen was already having problems. She had fallen twice on the run over. Swann had to pick her up both times. Now she was sobbing, barely keeping it together.

"You have to be quiet," Ford whispered to her. "We can carry you if we have to, so don't worry about that. Right, Swann?"

He looked at the young agent. Swann was still on both feet, but barely. He was under the siege of many symptoms. Lack of sleep. Lack of food and water. Exposure to cold. Blood loss. If not for his training and his will, he would have collapsed before they left the barn.

Jo bit her lip. She was going to get these two out of there. But things could change. She might have to make tough choices. She considered stashing them in a decent hiding place. Picking them up later once she got to the car.

She scraped along to the side, glancing around the corner of the motorhome.

The barn's side door was in the same condition as the main one. It hung open. She could see the glow of torchlight inside, moving about. The voices started again, but this time they were tinged with worry and anger.

They move fast. They already know we're gone.

"Be quiet!" Kurt's authoritative voice suddenly rang out. "We don't need anything out of the basement. What are you three so up in arms for?"

Jo knitted her brow. She stepped out a bit further, trying to make sure she didn't miss a word.

Someone else responded to Kurt. She only caught a snippet. "...FBI agents."

"You know what happened to Joey," Kurt responded. "He was a fool. He lost it, and I couldn't save him. I failed. And now those agents are going to be coming for me. And for all of you. It's time to light the symbolic fire and move on."

Symbolic? Jo wondered.

"Wait!" Kurt shouted. "Where are you going?"

Three figures came bursting through the side door, their torches aglow. Jo ducked back behind the motorhome, readying her pistol. Carmen was still sitting, catching her breath. Swann had to lean against the wall to stay upright. It seemed they would have to fight after all.

A moment passed. She heard no footsteps. She took another look.

"Where'd they go?" Ford asked.

Jo could see the faint light of the torches, moving away. "They're heading back to the main house."

"Why would they do that? They have torches. They must have seen our prints."

"No idea," said Jo.

Kurt appeared at the side door now. He stepped out slowly, shaking his head and muttering.

"Kids... try so hard to teach them... maybe there's a reason none of us fit in. We're all broken. None of it makes sense."

He stuck the end of his torch in the snow, killing the flame. He left the blackened stick there, jutting out of the ground. He turned and hurried after the cultists.

SEVENTY-EIGHT

As soon as Kurt was out of sight, Jo turned to the others.

"Time to go," she said. "Carmen, can you stand?"

"Maybe," the waitress groaned. She held up her hand. Swann grabbed it and pulled her up. "Thanks. I think I can stand on my own. Sorry."

Ford smiled. "Don't be. Do you think you can run?"

She chewed her lip. "I dunno. Maybe a light jog."

"Good enough." Ford beckoned to her. "Let's move."

McKinley checked his phone. He grimaced. "No signal. No GPS. But I think the most direct way off the property is this way." He sliced his hand toward the trees.

Jo needed to hear no more. She headed in that direction, setting the pace at a slow trot. Like soldiers trudging through the third hour of a forced march. Exhausted but driven onward by some tireless beast within them.

At least, that was how she assumed Swann and Carmen were. She still felt fresh and sharp. And she needed to stay that way.

"Kurt's property is surrounded on three sides by clearings," Jo said. "Once we get to a clearing, we'll know we're at the edge. We'll run across to the forest on the other side. And we'll use the trees for shelter as we head for the car in as straight a line as possible. Sound good?"

"Excellent," Ford agreed.

"Yeah, we'll do that," Swann said with a sigh.

"Whatever you say," Carmen added.

"I put a pin on the car before we left it," McKinley said. "But it won't do us any good unless I can get a signal."

"Well, keep checking," Jo said. "But don't let it slow you down."

***

During their search of Kurt's land, they had lost track of exactly where they were. It turned out they had traveled deep onto the property. After trudging forward for what felt like a mile, they were still entrenched in the same maze of trees and scattered structures.

However, this corner of the property had been entirely neglected. The buildings were almost hidden by snow. Their roofs were either collapsed or in the process of collapsing. No trails had been plowed out. No fallen trees, limbs, or brush had been cleared away.

It was a veritable ocean of snowdrifts. They were deep. Sometimes Jo sank all the way up to her knees. Not only that but there were hazards hidden beneath. Logs and boulders. Bits of old machinery and tools. At one point, McKinley nearly impaled himself on a rusty pitchfork.

"This sucks," he said, ripping the abandoned tool out of the snow and tossing it aside.

"You can say that ten more times," Ford agreed. "We should be just about out of here, though."

He looked back. Carmen and Swann were bringing up the rear. Swann stayed behind him, pushing Carmen forward. Helping her over or around obstacles. Jo was tempted to take his place. To give him a break. But she had a strong feeling that Swann wanted it to be him.

"We'll break out of these trees any second now," Jo said.

She kept a positive outward attitude. On the inside, she was getting worried they had made the wrong call. They had decided to head straight off the property. Take the long but theoretically safe path back to the car. Instead, maybe they should have taken the shortest path out.

It would have been much riskier, but they had guns. And they probably would have been in the car already. Instead, they had traveled almost a mile in the wrong direction. And they still had a long way to go.

No choice now but to keep going. The cultists have had too much time to get ready now. Going back would be a death sentence.

In life, most people got second chances. If you were a plumber and you installed a leaky valve, you could shut the water back off and try again. If you were a chef and you messed up an order, you could make a new plate.

Jo didn't have that luxury. Not tonight. Every tiny choice she made, on a second-by-second basis, she had to live with for the rest of her life. However long that life may be. There were no re-dos. It was a tough pill to get down, but she'd already swallowed it years ago.

She was okay with whatever happened to her. She just didn't want any of the others to be subjected to it.

"Any second now," she said again.

SEVENTY-NINE

It was hard to see the end of the trees. But a path of brighter moonlight stood ahead of them. They charged for it with renewed energy. Even Carmen managed to hop over a few logs with no help from Swann.

Jo stopped at the edge of the clearing. She leaned against a tree and took a deep breath. She had expected to feel a surge of relief at the sight. Instead, it looked like no-man's-land. Dangerous and hostile.

"Wow, I'm out of shape," Ford gasped, doubling over. "I haven't run this much since that day at the Seattle Marathon. And I guess I've still got a bit of running ahead of me. This looks hairy."

"We'll be completely exposed," McKinley agreed.

Swann brushed past them all, heading into the open. "Then maybe we should get across fast."

His heroic moment ended abruptly when he saw that Carmen was struggling again. He stopped, watching her. Ford waved him on, then moved over to Carmen. He put an arm around her, holding her up.

"Yeah, I'm wiped out, too," he said. "We'll just get through this part together, okay?"

She pressed herself into him, trembling. "Do you... have any more chocolate?"

He laughed. "I was hoping to ration it out a bit. But here you go, kid. Have at it."

He reached into his pocket and shoved a handful of candy at her. She dug in, unwrapping the small rectangular bars and shoving them into her mouth. The sugar did her a world of good. In a moment, she was keeping up with them on her own. She no longer needed Ford's help.

"How did everything get so messed up?" she wondered aloud. "I had plans for once in my life. Now I'm here. It's all just... wrong."

They let her vent. Not even Ford tried to butt in. Though his fatherly instincts made it hard. His cheeks were just about puffed up from holding in the words of encouragement.

On they went. Jogging at a steady clip with no issues. Jo would have felt hopeful, but the trees on the other side never seemed to get any closer. Finally, she looked back.

Kurt's property looked just as far away now. It was hard to tell their progress by looking forward. It only became clear when looking at how much ground they had covered.

"Almost there," she said with a grunt, picking up the pace. "Can we move a little faster?"

McKinley nodded. Before taking off, he checked his phone again and let out a triumphant laugh. "Got a signal! I can see the car now. As long as I don't lose reception again, I can guide us right back to it."

A distant revving sound caught their attention. A moment later, it was no longer quite so distant. And it wasn't alone. The sharp, whining sound was familiar. And it made Jo's blood run cold.

"Those sound like snowmobiles," she said. "Now I'm no longer asking. I'm ordering you all to run like the wind."

She ran. But not as fast as the others. She moved slower on purpose, to get behind them all. A group was only as fast as its slowest member. A minute ago, that had been Carmen.

Better that the slowest member be someone with a gun.

EIGHTY

Suddenly, they reached the trees. One second, the trees looked just as far away as ever. The next second, they seemed to rush forward to swallow the agents up.

Jo stepped behind a tree and waited. She listened to the cry of the snowmobile engine. Close now. Almost close enough to feel, like an insect buzzing in her ear. It was a terrifying sound. A scream in the night.

She glanced to the side. The others were hidden away as well. Catching their breath after the sprint. Jo decided to give them time until she saw the first hint of a snowmobile headlight. Then it was time to run again.

It had taken them about three minutes to cross the clearing. And that was with taking half the distance at full tilt speed. The snowmobiles could get across it in a third of the time. Maybe faster. It all depended on if the cultists knew where they were going.

Jo leaned out from behind her tree and watched. The engines grew louder and louder. It seemed like they should be popping out any second. She caught a few glimpses of light. Slicing sideways through the trees on the other side of the clearing.

The cultists were searching the edge of Kurt's property. They were moving around the place just as systematically as the intruders had. Only a lot faster.

It didn't take them long to decide their quarry was no longer on their side of the field.

Headlights appeared between the trees. Four snowmobiles erupted into the open, howling across the gap between groups of trees.

"Go!" Jo called.

Everyone ran again. Carmen was suddenly right back to where she had been before. Stumbling along weakly. This time, Ford just picked her up. He slung her over his shoulder and labored onward.

Jo took up the head of the pack. She had a plan. There was no time to tell the others about it. So, she just led them along the path she wanted to take.

It seemed like a terrible route. It carried them over every single obstacle, avoiding none of them. Jo took a spill, bashing her knee on a log. She rolled back onto her feet, limping until the pain disappeared.

"Too slow," Swann huffed beside her. "Need to find another path."

"So will they," Jo told him, stabbing a thumb over her shoulder. "Either that, or they'll crash and die on all these fallen trees."

He had no energy to smile. But he managed a chuckle. "I guess that's smart."

"Nothing about this is smart," Jo said. "Let's just clear up that misconception."

Swann frowned. "Sorry about all this. It's my fault."

"No, it's Kurt Black's fault. Now you should shut up. Save your energy."

They were running up a hill. It was slow going, but they finally reached the top. Just as the snowmobiles entered the forest behind them.

"Here you go," Ford grunted as he lifted Carmen from his shoulder, gently pushing her toward Swann. "Take her. Follow McKinley back toward the car."

"What about you?" Swann asked.

"We'll be right behind you," Ford told him.

He looked at Jo. They nodded at each other as McKinley, Swann, and Carmen continued running.

"About time to set up an ambush," Ford said.

They took up positions behind two trees, right next to one another. Jo put her back against the trunk of her tree and raised her gun to a ready position.

The cultists began to ride up the hill. The engine sounds became more labored as the machines fought against gravity. Jo peeked out, watching as they swerved this way and that. Avoiding the obstacles.

"Now we know why they didn't follow us right off the bat," Jo said. "They were going for vehicles."

"I like it better when the bad guys are stupid," Ford groaned. "How many do you count?"

"Four," said Jo. "None of them look like Kurt. Which means they must have picked up another friend on the way."

"Could be another contingent out there somewhere. Circling around. How long do we wait?"

Jo didn't answer. She was watching the progress of the snowmobiles. Judging the distance. She knew the effective range of her sidearm. She knew her own shooting abilities from countless hours at the range.

She also knew that Ford wasn't quite as good a shot as she was. It was also dark. The glare of the headlights made it difficult to judge distance and depth. So, she waited until they were well within range.

EIGHTY-ONE

"I'll go first," Jo said. "We're too close together. As soon as I come out and start shooting, you dart into cover a bit further away. Once you're there, start taking shots."

Ford nodded. "After you."

Jo took a breath. She dropped down to the side, going to one knee. This brought her low to the ground. It also brought her head and shoulders out from the tree's cover. That was fine for now. They wouldn't know she was there until the shooting started.

She had a moment to line up her first shot. Just a moment. She held her breath, bending her head to the side to line up her eye with the gunsight.

One of the cultists was bolder than the others. He was charging up the hill, performing risky maneuvers that could have easily pitched him off his ride. But he kept going. He was good. And his skill would be his downfall.

Jo took the shot. The gun kicked in her hand, making her bones vibrate. It sounded like an explosion. The sound waves knocked snow out of the branches above her. It rained down the back of her jacket, cold on her neck.

It was a fantastic shot. It hit a moving target two hundred feet away, down a hill, in the dark. The bullet landed in the cultist's chest with enough force to halt the momentum of his body. The machine under him kept going, crashing hard into a tree. The man himself fell straight down. He slid lifelessly down the snowy slope.

Jo glanced to her left. Ford was on the move. He stayed low, scrambling along the crest of the hill. He got himself behind another tree, flattening his body against it.

He nodded at Jo. Then he peeked out, taking aim. He squeezed off two shots. One of them missed completely. The other hit the engine of a snowmobile. It emitted popping, grinding sounds along with a plume of smoke as it slid to a stop.

The person on the dead machine jumped off and hit the deck, crawling into cover.

The whining sound of the two remaining snowmobiles grew deeper as their engines cycled down. The riders were drawing to a stop. They stepped off, unslinging assault rifles from their shoulders.

"Crap," Jo hissed.

She fell back into cover as long bursts of automatic weapons fire ripped through the forest. For a long, tense moment, it seemed to be snowing again, except it was bullets rather than snowflakes.

The two shooters sprayed the top of the hill down. They didn't know exactly where the shooters were hiding. A lucky thing. Jo didn't feel that lucky when several of the bullets hit the tree she was hiding behind. She felt a heavy thud reverberating through the wood.

She caught Ford's eye. He was holding his breath, his cheeks puffing out again. She wondered if he was thinking of his daughter. What would the rest of her life be like if he died right now?

Or maybe he knew Jo wouldn't let that happen.

They were situated at the very top of the hill. The landscape sloped down in either direction. If they moved directly away from the shooters, they could enjoy a moment of safety.

The shooting stopped. Either the cultists were out of ammo in their clips, or they realized they weren't hitting anything. Jo had to hope it was the former. It would give them more time.

She signaled to Ford. With her hand, she indicated the far side of the hill. Then she made a downward sweeping motion.

They dove for it. Going prone, they quickly crawled down the other side of the hill. Once they were far enough along, they tucked to the side and rolled. Letting gravity do the work.

At the bottom, they got to their feet and stumbled forward.

"Dizzy," Jo said.

"But not dead," Ford pointed out. "Unless this is the afterlife. Pretty sucky one, if it is."

EIGHTY-TWO

"Check this out," Jo said. She pointed to a huge cluster of trees ahead of them. The whole thing had fallen over, creating a jungle gym of trunks that stretched fifty feet in either direction. "We can climb up there. Mosey our way along. Hop down somewhere else. It'll throw them off our trail for a little bit."

Ford jumped up onto the lowest log. He offered Jo a hand. She took it, allowing him to pull her up.

"One down, two to go," he said as they shimmied along. "Really nice shooting back there."

"You weren't so bad yourself," Jo replied. "Now they have one less vehicle."

Ford shrugged. "That guy can just hitch a ride with one of the others. But that shot you hit..."

He whistled.

"I killed someone's missing kid," Jo said. "I don't feel that good about it."

"But you don't feel that bad either."

"I guess not. But the fact that I don't feel that bad makes me feel kind of bad. You know?" She shook off her bad thoughts. "I guess everyone is someone's kid, though. And these people think murdering helpless old ladies is a good idea."

"At least Kurt didn't seem too fond of what Joey did," Ford added, climbing between two thick branches. "What was it he said? Something about Joey going off the reservation."

Jo nodded. "This whole thing is weird. I thought we pretty much had it figured out, but I've got a strange feeling now."

They reached the base of the tree. A huge root ball, still covered with soil.

"End of the line." Ford hopped down. Before he had a chance to offer Jo his hand again, she was falling to the ground next to him.

"This way," she said, pointing past the root ball. "Hopefully, we can catch up to McKinley and the others before the cultists do."

The snowmobiles were once again revving up. But they didn't seem to be moving just yet. The enemy was regrouping, getting ready for the next attack.

***

Jo pointed at the ground. "Tracks."

They followed the trail through a narrow valley and up a steep hill. It ended abruptly in a small clearing. The footprints of three separate people went veering off in different directions.

A moment later, Jo heard the clink of Swann's chain.

"You guys can come out," Jo called.

Swann eased out into the open. He was carrying Carmen, holding the chain in his other hand. She looked unconscious.

McKinley appeared next, cursing as he shoved his phone into his pocket. "Are you two all right? We heard a lot of gunfire."

"We made it away unscathed," Jo told him. "But barely."

Ford nodded. "Those guys are packing some mean weaponry. We almost got shredded. Good thing we're so smart and good-looking."

"What does being good-looking have to do with not being shot?" McKinley asked. "The halo effect isn't that powerful. Anyway, I was going to call Sheriff Phelps."

"It's too dangerous out here for him," Jo said.

"This is his job," McKinley argued. "If it's not too dangerous for us, then it isn't for him either. But you can relax. I couldn't get through. I lost the signal."

EIGHTY-THREE

"It disappeared as we were crossing the field," McKinley went on. "But I got one last look at our location. I have a rough idea of where we are."

"How are we going to get back to the car now?" Swann asked, grimacing with the effort of holding Carmen up.

McKinley smiled, gesturing into the forest. "Easy enough. If we go this way, we're bound to find the road. If we see our footprints from earlier, we can follow them to the car. If all we see are tire tracks, we follow them instead."

"I guess that is kind of easy," Swann grumbled. "Minus the guys trying to kill us."

"Jo took one of them out," Ford announced proudly. "And I disabled one of their snowmobiles. So, they have a slight handicap."

Swann shifted Carmen's weight around. "So do we. Maybe we're all even now."

"Are you good with her?" Ford asked. "Want me to take a turn? Believe it or not, I'm used to carrying unconscious women. Have to do it with Kelly all the time. She pretty much never makes it through a movie night. I have to take her upstairs to the bedroom. And she's the world's heaviest sleeper."

"I can do it," Swann rasped. "I'm part of the reason she's in this mess. I'm pretty sure our date is ruined, but I can at least get her home."

***

Adrenaline only lasted so long. It could only get you so far. After that, you were on your own.

The group moved on at a painfully slow speed. Jo could handle it for the time being. She no longer heard the sound of engines. If the cultists were giving chase now, it was on foot. She liked her chances with that a bit better.

But something in the back of her mind told her that was wishful thinking.

"How's everyone doing?" Ford asked.

"Not bad," McKinley said in a chipper tone. "But I could use a cup of coffee."

"So you're the same as you are every other second of your life," Jo replied. "That's encouraging. You're doing well."

"Maybe Grantham will give me a commendation," McKinley mused. "Or at least a gold star sticker I can put on my laptop. What do you think?"

"I think you should tell us how much longer until we get to the road," Swann groaned. His foot sank into a deep patch of snow. He fell forward, barely twisting around in time to avoid crushing Carmen beneath him. He landed on his back, cursing loudly.

"I don't know," McKinley said. "I don't have GPS built into my skull. But I'll be first in line when they come out with that technology."

"Great, I'm happy for you," Swann said, throwing out an exaggerated thumbs-up. "I thought the Seattle marathon would be the hardest physical thing I did for a while. Ford, maybe I'll let you take a turn after all."

Jo helped Swann to his feet while Ford lifted Carmen. The fall had startled her back into a semi-conscious state.

"Are we there yet?" she asked.

"Not yet," Ford told her. "What do you say we do a bridal carry this time? That way, my shoulder isn't stabbing into your gut the whole time."

"That's going to fry your biceps," Swann warned him.

"Good," Ford answered. "Maybe I'll get as buff as you are."

The sound of engines returned. Everyone dropped down reflexively, hiding in the shadows. They listened, expecting the cultists to come barreling toward them.

Instead, the sound faded into the distance. Moving in the direction of the road.

EIGHTY-FOUR

"Signal's back!" McKinley announced.

They had been trekking through the woods for another ten minutes. Jo was starting to feel like they should have found the road by now. She assumed the others felt the same. Ford kept happily saying they'd find it "any day now." Swann kept muttering under his breath.

The cold was their main enemy now. It had been a while since they heard the snowmobiles. Fear was still with them, but the constant stream of adrenaline was gone. They were getting cold. Moving slower. Jo had to keep her arms moving. Pushing blood back into the fingers to keep them dexterous. In case she had to shoot again.

"Check our location first," she said. "Then you can put in a call to Phelps. Let him know our situation."

McKinley was already opening his map. He used his teeth to pull his gloves off and frantically zoomed in, panning around. Looking for the pin he dropped earlier.

He stomped his foot into the snow. "Lost it again! But I managed to see where the car was. The road should be right up ahead."

"Told you," Ford said. "Any day now."

"I'll be able to make a call as we're driving back to town," McKinley added. "The most I've been able to get is one bar out here. Probably not enough to make a reliable call anyway."

The road was even closer than McKinley made it sound. Jo climbed a short hill and took three steps forward. Suddenly she was there, looking across a narrow lane of churned-up snow.

"Are those your tire tracks?" Swann asked.

Jo shook her head. "Those are from snowmobile skids. They headed this way."

"Could be waiting for us at the car," Ford said, grunting with exertion from carrying Carmen. "Swann, take my gun."

He turned his body, showing his hip holster. Swann pulled his sidearm free.

"Feels good to have a real weapon in my hands," he said.

"Don't get used to it. I'll need that back. By the way, you were right. My biceps feel like they're about to rip off the bone."

Jo headed up the road. She kept her gun thrust forward, pointing it downward at a forty-five-degree angle. Ready to be raised and shot at a nanosecond's notice. She was on red alert, her eyes flicking between every tree. Every little shadow that could be hiding a cultist.

Nothing happened. No one jumped out at her. No bullets flew past her head. But that didn't make her feel any better. The confrontation was inevitable, she knew. This moment of peace was only pushing it further into the future.

She would rather have just gotten it over with.

Or maybe it wouldn't happen at all. Back at the barn, Kurt had said something interesting. He had talked about lighting the symbolic fire and "moving on." Moving on where? Perhaps they had a location in mind. A bug-out spot. Maybe they were already long gone, cruising through the night. Escaping the consequences of their actions, along with the fallen comrade Jo had shot.

It was a possibility. But not strong enough for her to alter her tactics.

Her eyes found wider tracks in the snow ahead. They veered off to the left and into the trees. She followed them and discovered the car right where they had left it.

She had been moving ahead of the others. She jogged back to them.

"Found the car," she said. "Undisturbed. The only footprints are the ones we left earlier on our way to Kurt's. The snowmobiles went right past."

"They must have seen the tire tracks," McKinley said.

"Just like they saw our footprints at the barn," Jo agreed. "Once again, they've opted to get ahead of us. They're probably setting up an ambush somewhere. The way we did to them."

Ford helped Carmen to stand up. He grunted, shaking out his arms. "They want us all packed in nice and tight in our vehicle. That way, they can pick us off easier."

Jo had considered that possibility. "Could be. But we'll just have to take the chance. We can't take much more of this cold."

EIGHTY-FIVE

Jo found the car keys in her pocket. She jingled them in her hand. "Everyone pile in. I'll drive."

"Sure you don't want someone else to take a turn?" Ford asked, holding out his hand.

"At this crucial moment? No way. I have the most experience on these roads. Except for her." Jo gestured to Carmen. "And she looks like the living dead."

Jo got in behind the wheel. She turned the engine on and cranked the heat. It felt like a lifetime since she was last in this seat. In reality, it had been a couple of hours. Long enough for the seat to feel like a block of ice. The engine was cold too. The air coming through the vents felt like a blast chiller.

Swann and McKinley helped Carmen into the middle of the backseat. They slid in beside her like bookends. Ford took the passenger seat up front, shivering and fiddling with the vents.

"Colder in here than outside," he said. "At least the wind was calming down."

Jo slapped his hand away from the controls. "Give it a minute. In fact, let's give ourselves a minute too. Is everyone all right?"

"Better than expected," Swann replied. "I feel like death. Ironically, that actually means I'm alive. I should have been charcoal by now, so thanks for coming."

"Hey, don't sweat it." Ford waved a hand. "We'll get you next time, too. Don't worry about that."

Swann groaned. "I know you're just giving me a hard time. But you won't need to save me ever again. I'm done messing up."

The car slowly heated up. As soon as the vent air turned from cold to slightly warm, Jo got back on the road and headed toward town.

The warmth did wonders for Carmen. She woke up and began talking. Asking about everything she had missed.

"Not much," Swann told her. "We just walked right out."

"They just let us get away?" she stammered.

"Not quite," Jo said. "They're somewhere up ahead of us. We don't know where. But we got away from them once. We can do it again. And again. As many times as it takes to get you safe."

Carmen let out a whimper of fear. She said nothing else.

"How much further?" Ford asked.

Jo stared forward, trying to get her bearings. It all looked the same. Then they drove through the ditch she'd nearly gotten stuck in before. When Phelps gave her pointers on how to get free.

"Ten minutes," she said. "McKinley, get a signal yet?"

"Let me check... Yes! Two bars. Let me call Sheriff Phelps." He dialed the number and waited for a concerningly long time. "He didn't answer."

"Do you have Sheri's number?" Jo asked. "Try her."

"Right..." McKinley found her number and called. Another long wait ensued. "Huh. That's odd. Neither of them answered."

"It's late," Ford pointed out.

"It's only eight," Jo shot back.

Ford shrugged. "They're old."

"Not *that* old. McKinley, can you find the number for the station itself? Try that."

"On it." He put it on speakerphone this time, so they could all hear the incessant ringing.

There was a crackling sound, and Phelp's started to talk. "You've reached the Lapse police department. Neither the sheriff nor his favorite deputy are able to make it to the phone. Just leave your name and number, and we'll be with you in two shakes of a lamb's tail."

Jo gestured at McKinley to cut the call. He hung up.

"I'd try Rupert and his team," he said, "but they're probably back in Seattle by now. They won't be able to help us."

If Carmen were still asleep, Jo might have said what was on her mind. But for now, she kept it in.

EIGHTY-SIX

The closer they came to town, the more Jo was able to relax. She considered turning the radio on. It would be a nice way to calm down. But it was still too soon to let her guard down.

They were almost there. She could see dim lights glimmering in the near distance. If they could reach a public space, they would be safe. They could gas the car up and leave this town behind forever.

Unfortunately, that would count as dereliction of duty.

The car went over a few bumps. It thudded down, landing on a smooth path of asphalt. Courtesy of Bobby and his plow. They passed a couple of houses. Someone was out shoveling their driveway. Someone else was sprinkling salt on their front walk. The salt wouldn't do much good. The temperature was still too low.

"We made it," Swann said in disbelief.

Ford hit the radio power button. A quiet, melancholy country song filled the sudden quiet. They were all thinking the same thing. They were technically out of the woods. But they weren't out of trouble.

"What's next?" Ford asked.

"We need to get Carmen somewhere safe," Jo replied. "She lives alone, so her house is no good."

"The diner," Carmen piped up from the backseat. "It'll be full of people right now. Trying to stay warm and charge their phones. It'll be safe there."

"And I can get a coffee to go," McKinley said cheerfully. There was an undercurrent to his voice. A dreamy quality. He knew they didn't have time. But in his own way, he was trying to cheer himself up.

**

As Carmen foretold, the diner was packed. There wasn't a parking space to be had. People were crammed in very close together. It was a wonder any of them had been able to get out of their cars.

Jo pulled up in front of the entrance. "I'll just stop here. I shouldn't be blocking anyone. I doubt anyone's in a hurry to leave."

Swann popped his seatbelt off. He hopped out of the car. Nearly fell over. Then leaned back inside to take Carmen's hand. "Come on. I'll walk you in."

She was strong and stable by now. But she still let Swann pull her free of the car. She leaned on him, putting an arm around her waist. Jo watched them go inside, smiling. In a parallel universe, they would have made a cute couple.

Maybe there was still a chance. Sometimes going through terrible things together could strengthen a bond. Made it as hard as titanium. But Swann and Carmen barely knew each other. And after tonight, Jo doubted they'd ever be in the same state together.

Only time could tell.

***

Swann ignored the strange looks he got as they walked into the diner. His face was still dotted with dried blood from his head wound. Courtesy of a kick to the cranium by some unknown cultist.

Hopefully, it was the guy Jo shot, Swann thought.

"Carmen!" a waitress squealed, running over. "We've been worried about you! Usually, you call in if you're gonna miss a shift. Are you okay?"

"Not really," Carmen answered honestly. "But I will be in a little while. Could you grab a cup of coffee to go, Megan? Make it fast, please."

Megan nodded and hurried away. Carmen led Swann to a booth near the door. They didn't sit down.

"This isn't goodbye, is it?" she asked.

Swann shook his head. "No. We'll be back to check on you. We'll make sure you're taken care of."

She smiled, slugging him playfully on the arm. "Thanks, Agent Swann."

"You can call me Edward," he said.

"All right, Edward. I know our date was really short. But it was still pretty good. I'd like to think it would have been a fun night."

"Instead, it was probably the worst two nights of your life," Swann replied.

She shrugged. "Sometimes it takes a bad night to solidify things. Make everything clear. You know?"

Megan returned with a cup of coffee. Carmen pointed to Swann. Megan handed him the cup. He thanked her, and she left.

"I guess you have no idea what I'm rambling about," Carmen added. "You should go now."

"I'll be back," Swann said.

She nodded. "We'll see each other again soon."

Swann gave her a hug. She returned it fiercely. He hurried out of the diner and got in the car.

EIGHTY-SEVEN

"Coffee!" McKinley exclaimed. He used both hands to carefully grab the cup from Swann. "Thanks. I owe you one."

"You just helped save my life," Swann told him. "I'm pretty sure I still owe you at least five more cups of coffee."

"Is Carmen all right?" Jo asked, looking at Swann in the rearview mirror.

He nodded. "I think so. She's at least safe."

"Good." Jo put the car in drive and circled around the parking lot. "Now we can talk about the reality of the situation. We called Phelps and Sheri on their cells. Then we called the police station. No answer on any account."

"They're in trouble," Ford growled.

"Of the cultist variety?" Swann asked.

"Anything else would be a huge coincidence," Jo replied. "They knew we'd seek the help of local law enforcement. I think they drove those snowmobiles straight to the station. That's where they are now, waiting for us."

"Holding Phelps and Sheri hostage," McKinley added. "We could wait them out. Get some more backup. They're unlikely to harm the sheriff and his wife."

"Swann, can you confirm that?" Jo asked. "What sort of profile would you assign to these people?"

"Purposeful," Swann answered. "They didn't hurt me just to be cruel. There's a reason for all of it. They won't harm anyone unless it suits their reasons. But we don't really know how their minds work, do we?"

"Phelps and Sheri could be in danger," said Jo.

Swann nodded. McKinley cursed and took a drink of coffee.

Ford hit the button again, killing the music. "So we go in. Take them out of this world that they apparently hate so much. Save the Sheriff and his favorite deputy."

"It sounds simple when you put it that way," Jo said. "It almost sounds easy. But they have assault rifles."

"And I don't even have a gun at all," Swann added.

Ford shrugged. "So it'll be an uphill battle. These are kids with a few screws loose. We're trained FBI agents. Well, you three are. But I've got heart. My mom always said so."

Jo smiled. "She was right. You've got heart."

"Yeah. I'm like a bulldog."

"Nah. You're too tall and skinny."

"All right, I'm like a greyhound. Except I'm not fast. But hey, I also don't look like a rat." He pulled the magazine out of his gun and checked it for rounds. "How far to the station?"

Jo pointed ahead. "It's just up the road."

"Then I don't have time to call my wife and kid. Which means you are all just going to have to keep me alive. Got it?"

"Got it," Swann echoed. "But if you go down, I'm taking your gun."

Ford nodded. "That's fine. Just make sure you avenge me."

Jo shook her head at all the drama. She was feeling good. Not excited or positive, but loose. Ready to fight. She felt certain they could win in whatever fight was coming.

Swann's comments had made her feel better. These people were purposeful. They were intelligent. They had some kind of ethical code, however screwy it might be.

There still might be a chance for some kind of peaceful resolution.

EIGHTY-EIGHT

Jo pulled the car to a stop along the side of the road. The police station was directly beside them. None of the streetlamps around town were glowing. But the moon was out in a crisp, clear sky. By the moon's light, they could see everything they needed to see.

"That's the Sheriff's truck," Jo confirmed. It was parked near the front door. "And that's Sheri's station wagon next to it. I don't see any snowmobile tracks…"

"They could have come from the back side," Ford said. "Through the trees. Maybe they stashed the vehicles behind the building."

They watched in silence for a minute. Nothing moved on the outside of the building. There was a dim light glowing inside. Every so often, they saw a hint of movement. A silhouette that seemed to be pacing inside.

"Someone's in there," McKinley whispered.

"Could be Phelps," Swann suggested. "Maybe they didn't come here at all."

He sounded giddy with the possibility. With a missing finger and no gun in hand, the last thing he wanted was to face these people again.

The silhouette stopped moving behind the window blind. A thumb and a finger came between two slats, pushing them aside. Someone was peeking through.

"We've been spotted," Jo said. "I'm sure they're about to send a welcome party."

"Let's hope it's just Sheri with a plate of cookies," Ford said. "I'd even go for oatmeal raisin right now. I know, I know. It's a bold statement. But it's true."

The front door of the station swung open. The person who came out was not Neil or Sheri Phelps. It was a man in a white robe and a ski mask. He was holding an MP5 submachine gun.

"That's Pinky," Swann hissed. "Samuel Whitaker, I mean."

"Is it? I wonder who I shot?" Jo asked.

Whitaker reached out a hand. He made a beckoning motion. Jo did nothing.

McKinley leaned over. "He wants us to come closer."

"I know," Jo replied. "But he hasn't specified whether we should come on foot or bring the car in."

It took Whitaker a moment. But he understood the confusion. He let his MP5 hang briefly by its shoulder strap. With both hands, he pretended to hold a steering wheel.

Jo nodded and pulled the car the rest of the way into the lot. She eased it forward until Whitaker held up a hand. Then she stopped and killed the engine.

"Now what?" Ford asked.

"Now we get out," Jo said. "Put your guns away."

With a series of reluctant sighs, the agents holstered their sidearms. They kicked their doors open and stepped out, letting Whitaker see their hands.

"Took you long enough to get here," he barked.

His gun was firmly back in his hands. Aimed in their direction. With a quick spray, he could easily put a couple of bullets in each of them if he was good enough. Jo didn't know about that, but she didn't feel like finding out.

Just have to play along for now.

She assumed these people were at least smart enough to give Whitaker a backup. She saw it a second later. It was the same person who had been pacing behind the window. They now had the barrel of an AR-15 pressed against the window.

"Lift up your shirts," Whitaker called. "Let me see what you have."

McKinley and Ford looked to Jo.

"Do it," she said.

They pulled their shirts up. Showing their gun holsters.

"What are those, nine millimeters?" Whitaker said. "Cool. Always wondered what guns you pigs carried. Father never told me."

"Didn't you see mine when you took it from me?" Swann asked.

Whitaker snorted. "That was Joey. Dunno where he put your gun. He took that to his grave. Guess you'll have to get a new one once you get back to HQ. Good to see you again, by the way."

"Did Joey take my phone too?" Swann snapped.

Whitaker grinned. "Nope. That was me. I took your cell and dropped it by the diner so nobody could trace it. Smart. Huh?"

Swann grunted, giving Whitaker a hard look.

Jo, Ford, McKinley, and Swann all kept standing there. Showing their hands.

"What are you waiting for?" Whitaker demanded. "Father's willing to make a deal. He calls it an 'amicable conclusion.' He's waiting."

"You're going to let us keep our guns?" Jo asked.

Whitaker shrugged. "Ours are bigger. And they aren't holstered. You think we're scared?"

Jo decided not to answer that. She led the others up the station steps. Whitaker stepped aside, holding the door for them.

EIGHTY-NINE

The dim light they had seen from the outside was a battery-powered lantern. It was sitting on the front desk. By its weak light, the station looked like a huge cavern of darkness.

Jo's eyes took a second to adjust. When they did, she saw Phelps and Sheri. Their mouths were covered with balled-up washcloths. They were sitting in desk chairs. Back to back. They were bound. The cultists had used duct tape. It was wound around their wrists. Their ankles. Longer strands wrapped around their chests, linking them together.

It was pretty weak binding. Even at their age, Jo thought the Sheriff and his wife could break out of it. But it would take time. Too long, considering the heavily armed cultist in the room with them.

The silhouette by the window was standing near the old couple now. A silent warning: *Try anything, and you're dead.*

Sheriff Phelps. Sheri. Samuel Whitaker, and the silhouette.

There was still one more person in the room. Jo hadn't noticed them yet. She was staring at the silhouette. The cultist with the AR-15. It had been impossible to tell through the window, but now it was obvious. This was a woman. The white robe could not hide her curvier figure. Her cold green eyes stared at Jo menacingly.

"Go on," Whitaker said. "Go in. Past the counter. No funny business."

Jo followed his commands. She crossed into the station's inner chamber. Where the sheriff and his favorite deputy plied their trade. Which had, up until recent days, been boring and uneventful.

That was when Jo saw the final person in the room: Kurt Black. However, he was not sitting on a throne stroking a cat like some cliched evil genius. He was tied up as well. Not with duct tape, though. With proper rope.

Kurt watched Jo through one eye. He'd probably be watching her with the other too, except it was black and blue. Swollen shut. His nose was crusted with dried blood. He looked frightened. Angry. Maybe even a bit shameful.

"Kurt?" Jo said in shock.

"Get in there," Whitaker snapped, nudging Swann with the butt of his gun. "You're still my prisoner. For now. You got a nice break, though. How was it, running through the woods dressed in basically nothing?"

"A lot more fun than sniffing your nasty breath," Swann retorted.

Whitaker laughed. "Good. Now everyone's here. No, no, not like that. Get a little further apart."

He gestured with the MP5. Jo, Ford, McKinley, and Swann stepped away from one another. Forming gaps between them.

"Better," Whitaker said with a sigh. "That went all right, didn't it? No one got hurt."

"Except for him." Jo pointed at Kurt. "Did you do that?"

"Yup." Whitaker bared his teeth. "I didn't enjoy it. But it had to be done. Anyway, I don't want to be a rude host. I'm sure the threat is implied, right? We have big guns. Pointed at various people."

"No funny business," Ford echoed.

"Right. I like this guy." Whitaker smiled shakily. "Not sure who he is, but whatever. Listen... we'd already be long gone. And we would have taken Father with us. But things have gotten out of control tonight, and we wanted to try and make a clean break."

Jo sensed the kid was scared. He had no idea what he was doing. However, he was clever enough to know that it was very, very stupid.

"I understand," Jo said softly. "You're messing with the FBI here, Samuel. Our boss knows everything. If anything happens to any of us, he'll send every force at his disposal after you. You might elude them for a while. You might get out of the country and find someplace to hide. But you'll always be looking over your shoulder. Unable to ever relax or enjoy a moment of your freedom. Think about that."

Jo had believed her words would make Whitaker think twice about what he was doing. Instead, he laughed scornfully. "Save the speech, lady! My people have already disowned all that crap. We aren't part of your world anymore. And we aren't afraid of you."

McKinley stepped in. "Then I guess we don't know as much about you as we thought. Why don't you tell us who you are?"

Whitaker nodded. "All right. I was getting to that anyway. But here goes."

NINETY

"Father came up with the name," Whitaker went on. "He had the idea years before he ever moved to Lapse and met all of us. Our group is called Unet. It's short for Unearthers of Truth. We realize that everything people like you stand for—order, consumption, pleasure, and a twisted sense of justice—is all an illusion. It was never real. It'll all die one day. We want to return to the natural order."

"The natural order doesn't have guns," Ford said with a grunt. "Just saying."

"Neither will we," Whitaker said wistfully. "When everything is set straight, we'll no longer need them. Tonight was supposed to be our cord-cutting moment. Our final break from the modern world."

"The sacrifice," said Jo.

"Exactly. It was like killing two birds with one stone. We chose our victims purposefully. Agent Swann represents authority and order. Carmen represents hedonism. It was all thought-out. Believe me, this isn't some hippy crap. We were cerebral with it."

"How was killing them supposed to serve your cause?" Jo asked.

Whitaker shrugged. "It's all symbolism. By sacrificing them, we were taking a final plunge. We'd be kidnappers and murderers. Never able to rejoin society. It was a final, brave step into our future. Our way of committing ourselves to the cause forever."

"I'd say you did that anyway," Swann told him. "You did kidnap us, but now we've gotten away. You tried to kill us, but you failed. You even cut my finger off. Even if you somehow manage to get away, you've got the mark. You'll never be part of society again."

"Then I'd say everything worked out," Whitaker replied. "And it's funny you should talk about us 'managing to get away.' That brings me to why Candy and I are still here."

Candy Lawson. That's who the female cultist is, Jo thought. *That's another one of the missing kids located.*

Whitaker gestured to Candy. She pointed her gun at Jo. Whitaker stepped over to Kurt, setting the barrel of his gun against the man's head.

"Tell them the deal, Father," Whitaker said softly.

Kurt let out a moan. He licked his lips and began talking. "You will all be allowed to live. You three agents, as well as... whoever that guy is."

"I'm Joe," Ford snapped. "Joe Mama. PI extraordinaire. Can I get a little respect around here?"

Candy Lawson giggled to herself.

Kurt went on. "You'll all be allowed to live. But only if one of two conditions is met. The first option is that you join Unet. They're down to only two members now."

"Not counting those who tried to abandon the cause and were dealt with," Whitaker added.

Jo had noticed someone was missing. There were four snowmobilers. She had killed one. That should leave three. She thought Kurt would be one, but now she wasn't sure.

Maybe another cult member was nearby, watching from the wings.

Or maybe they had tried to "abandon the cause," and Whitaker dealt with them.

"The other option is probably more realistic," Kurt continued. "And this is how it goes. You all remain here, along with one of the cultists. This person will keep an eye on you while I, Kurt Black, and the other cultist make our getaway. After enough time passes, the remaining person will simply turn themselves over to you."

"Why would they do that?" McKinley asked. He sounded fascinated, making a deep dive into a very strange way of thinking.

"Because they're completely insane," Kurt replied. "And I do mean *completely*. I would do what they suggest, even if they'll take me with them."

NINETY-ONE

"Let me get this straight," Jo said. "You stayed in Lapse, waiting for us, on the off chance that we'd agree to be in your group?"

Whitaker sneered. "Yeah, it was unlikely. But we had to try. We have our tenets. Our honor. We don't abandon them when things get hard. That's what sets us apart. We could have just shot you as soon as you pulled up outside, but we didn't do that either."

Ford shifted uncomfortably. "We, uh... we appreciate that greatly."

"So you aren't joining," Whitaker said. "Which leaves us with plan B. I think it works out well."

"Not so fast," said Jo. "We can't just let two of you escape."

"You can keep chasing us if you want," Whitaker told her. "Keep us looking over our shoulders, like you said. Anyway, you don't have a choice right now. Big guns, remember?"

Jo nodded begrudgingly. "All right. Which one of you is staying behind?"

Whitaker puffed up proudly. He was fully ready to put himself in that position. Jo felt an odd surging of respect for the young idiot.

But Candy spoke first. "I'll do it. I'll sacrifice myself."

McKinley took a sudden step toward her, raising his hands. "You can't do that!"

Whitaker laughed, shaking his head. "What's this geek doing? He's crazy."

"You can't," McKinley said. "I saw your father at the diner, Candy. You have no idea how much your disappearance has destroyed him."

With a cruel smile, Candy said, "I don't care. He's a dumb pig just like you are."

McKinley's shock kept him quiet for all of three seconds. Then he tried again. "Think about this, Candy. You'll go to prison for the rest of your life. What's in it for you?"

"They are." Candy nodded at Whitaker and Kurt. "I don't care about myself. The only thing I care about is the survival of my cause."

Ford snorted. "Not a very strong group to carry the torch. An obnoxious kid with nine fingers and an old guy who obviously doesn't even want to be here."

"Shut up, Detective Mama," Whitaker said, chuckling. "You don't know anything. Nine fingers is plenty. Right, Agent Swann?"

"For me, it is," Swann growled.

McKinley went back to pleading with Candy. All his words fell on deaf ears. But what he was really doing was stalling for time. And it was working. It gave Jo a chance to look around.

First, she looked at Phelps and Sheri. They were awake, watching the proceedings. Neither of them was making a noise or putting up a fuss. Smart. It meant the cultists weren't watching them at all. If the time came and they saw a way to help, they could make a move. Maybe.

She scanned the rest of the station. There wasn't much to it. A door leading into the Sheriff's office. It was wide open, and she couldn't see anyone inside.

If there was another member of Unet hiding somewhere, where could it be?

She decided to try some delay tactics of her own.

"Theodore Hummel," she said.

McKinley stopped talking and looked at her. So did everyone else.

"Connor Foster," Jo went on. "Desmond Brooke. Those were three other kids who went missing in Lapse. They're still unaccounted for. Where are they?"

"Oh, this is rich." Whitaker snickered. "Theodore Hummel. Ted, we call him. *Called* him, I should say. You killed him earlier tonight when you shot him in the chest. Desmond went for a 'walk in the woods' a couple of weeks ago and never came back. We figure he bailed on us, just like Joey. As for Connor... there was a fight on the way over. He was starting to question things. He went for my gun. Things happened."

They were the words of a psychopath. But Whitaker sounded sad as he said them. There was something human left in him, though it had been twisted way out of proportion.

"So this is really it," Jo muttered. "You and Candy. And your Father."

Kurt grumbled to himself, staring at the floor.

"Maybe," Whitaker said with a devilish smile. His eyes flicked toward the window. He had seen something there. "Or maybe there's someone else. Maybe there's a surprise that's just about to hit you."

The front door opened. Everyone turned to look.

NINETY-TWO

Carmen entered the police station. She was still wearing the oversized flannel jacket Jo and Swann scrounged for her. She had found a pair of gloves somewhere, along with a pair of boots.

"Sorry I'm late," she said. "They dropped me off at the diner. I had to walk all the way here."

Candy beamed. "Welcome back, sister."

Swann's mouth fell open. Jo felt like she was choking. Ford turned away from everyone, shaking his head.

"Feel stupid yet?" Whitaker asked. "You should. Come here, Carmen."

Carmen averted her eyes from the agents. She crossed the room slowly. Whitaker reached under his robe. He pulled a pistol off his belt and handed it over.

"Take it," he said.

Carmen held the gun in both hands. She looked shaky. But there was something in her posture. The way she held the gun. She had practice with it. If the shooting started, she'd probably hit more shots than she missed.

Jo felt her hand itching. She kept reaching toward her gun. She didn't have any intention of drawing it just yet. She just wanted to know it was still there. Things were going from bad to worse in a hurry.

Carmen screamed to get her friends' attention, Jo thought. *And she acted exhausted to try and slow us down so they could catch up...*

Jo couldn't believe it. She had been outsmarted. Outplayed. She had been lured here under a false sense of confidence. Surely a bunch of kids who lived in the woods would be no match for her training. Her intellect and strategic abilities. Her FBI mindset.

Now here she was, facing three bad guys with some very mean weaponry. The 9mm pistol on her belt might as well be a squirt gun.

Firepower wasn't going to get her out of this.

And right now, she didn't see any way of thinking her way out, either.

It seemed the only choice now was to take the deal.

NINETY-THREE

A minute went by before anyone was able to untie their tongues.

"Carmen, why?" Swann demanded. "What's going on here?"

There was a hint of hope in his voice. Jo knew what he must be thinking. He wanted to believe that Carmen was a double agent. She would turn her gun on her fellow Unet members and reveal her true loyalties.

Carmen couldn't look at Swann. "We needed a second person. For the sacrifice. One to represent authority. One to represent hedonism. I represented the hedonism angle, so we would only have to murder one person. It was the best way we could think of."

"They're insane," Kurt wheezed. He spat out a mouthful of blood. "Absolutely mad. I preached nothing but peaceful ideas to them. See how they've twisted my words?"

"You're having a moment, Father," Whitaker said. "You're scared. You'll get over it. Sometimes even the shepherd loses his way."

Kurt stared at him. "I haven't lost my way. You have, Samuel. I tried to save you from the world. But now you've chosen to doom yourselves."

Whitaker sighed. "I don't want to hit you again, Father. Please don't make me. For now, it's better if you don't talk."

Kurt winced as though remembering the blow that blackened his eye. He looked at the floor again. He was silent.

Being among her comrades made Carmen bolder. She looked straight at Swann now, squaring her shoulders.

"You were the best option," she said. "You fell right into our laps. We couldn't really say no, could we? I'm sorry, though. At first, I thought you were just some dumb young buck, but I started to like you. You were brave, Agent Swann. But this is the way it has to be."

Whitaker raised his eyebrows, smiling at Ford. "Not bad, huh, Detective Mama? This is a better torch-carrying group now, I'd say. Carmen and Father and me. We'll move on with our lives, and you'll never find us."

Jo shook her head. "You're wrong on both counts, kid. We *will* find you. And you might bring Kurt along, but he's not going to be your 'Father' ever again. You blew it."

"Can I pistol whip this lady?" Carmen asked.

"No, she's just scared and running her mouth," Whitaker replied. He gestured to Kurt. "You know, we thought he'd be pleasantly surprised. We set the whole thing up in secret. We wanted him to be proud of our bravery as we pushed our agenda to the next level."

"What happened to justify you beating him up like this?" Jo asked.

Carmen looked at Whitaker. "I want to know, too. I wasn't there."

"Do you doubt my choices?" Whitaker seethed.

"Not at all," said Carmen. "I just need you to bring me up to speed. We're in this together. We're going to get away, just as soon as these agents make up their minds. Until then, why don't you tell the story?"

Whitaker shrugged. "Not much of a story. While we were getting the snowmobiles gassed up, Father caught up to us. He wanted to know what was going on. Why we were suddenly running around like chickens with our heads cut off."

"The fires were supposed to be symbolic," Kurt mumbled, staring at the carpet. "Two pyres and two blank crosses to nail things to. Mementos of the world we were forsaking. Magazine clippings. Newspapers. Personal effects. It was going to be our way of solidifying our bond and becoming a proper family."

"We decided that wasn't enough, Father," Whitaker snapped, lunging toward Kurt. "Burning photographs and IDs? That's kid stuff! That's the stuff a thirteen-year-old does when he's feeling edgy. We wanted the real deal. We made the right call. Now you just need to catch up, old man."

"You're getting distracted," Candy barked. "Just tell the frickin' thing so we can move on."

"He tried to stop us!" Whitaker jammed the barrel of his gun into Kurt's cheek. Hard enough to make Kurt wince. "When we told him what was going on, he tried ripping me right off my snowmobile. That made me mad, so I hit him. Just a couple of times."

"More like four or five," Candy said with a snort.

"Whatever. Father's tough. It took a few, all right? Anyway, Ted and I tied him up real quick, then we came after you people." He twisted around abruptly, aiming his gun at McKinley.

McKinley quickly ducked, covering his head.

Whitaker roared with laughter. "Made you flinch. Come on. I'm not some idiot. I have trigger discipline. If I want you dead, you'll be dead. Until then…"

"You went and picked Father up after trying to catch us in the woods?" Carmen asked.

Whitaker nodded. "After losing Ted, we decided it was time to move to plan B and rendezvous here. We grabbed Father and headed into town. We knew we'd still beat you here since you were on foot. And that's that. You're caught up."

Carmen smiled. "Now we can turn the page and get to the next chapter. Agents, I'm giving you five more minutes to make your choice. Got that, Candy?"

Candy hit a button on her watch, then went back to aiming her gun at Phelps and Sheri. "Got it. Five minutes. What happens then?"

Carmen grinned and brandished her pistol.

NINETY-FOUR

A strange and foreshortened sense of peace fell over the station.

Carmen and Whitaker started chatting amongst themselves. Whitaker did have good trigger discipline, but Candy couldn't stop fidgeting with her gun. Her hands were all over it.

Candy stayed off to the side, covering the Sheriff and his wife. She found some bubblegum in her pocket and started chewing it. She kept blowing bubbles. Each time one popped, Sheri flinched in her chair.

Sheriff Phelps looked almost bored. His face was a gruff mask as he gave Candy a glaring side-eye. She ignored him. Finally, Phelps started kicking his foot at her. Trying to get her attention.

"What's your problem, Grandpa?" Candy shouted, stepping away from him. "Quit trying to kick me."

"He wants to say something," Jo said.

"So what?" Candy asked.

"He's not going to scream loud enough for anyone to hear," Jo said with a sigh. "Just take the rag off his mouth. And Sheri's, too."

"Just his," Whitaker called. "Let's see what the Sheriff has to say. Go do it, beanpole."

Ford and McKinley both looked his way. But Whitaker was staring at McKinley.

McKinley approached the old couple. He pulled the tape and rag from Phelps's mouth. Phelps coughed a few times, leaning over a bit to spit on the floor.

"About time," he growled. "Pretty rude of you all to do this to us. We use those rags to clean the dang bathroom with."

"Is that what you wanted to say?" Whitaker asked patiently.

"No." Phelps glared at Candy. "Young lady, would you kindly stop chewing that gum? I've got misophonia, and the sound makes me madder than all get-out."

Candy raised a petulant eyebrow. She blew her biggest bubble yet, letting it pop with a loud *snap*.

Phelps shuddered and looked away. He caught Jo's eye.

"These people," he said. "They hate the world and want to own it at the same time. I guess the older generations must have failed them somewhere along the way. But you know what? They're already a lost cause. I guess we can call it a wash and move on."

"That sounds good," Whitaker exclaimed. "We'll all just move on and live nice lives. Candy, has it been five minutes yet?"

"Not yet. Still got a couple left."

"Good. Spit that gum out. It's making me kind of mad, too."

Candy made a face. She spat the gum right onto the carpet.

Everyone went back to what they'd been doing before.

Jo wished Candy had quoted a precise figure. Exact minutes and seconds remaining on the countdown. That way, Jo could run a countdown in her head. She would know exactly how much time she had left. And when to stop praying for a miracle and start taking action.

Either way, she could feel a dark cloud hovering over her. Time was ticking away. Two minutes wasn't enough for much of anything. The only time two minutes felt long was when you were waiting for the microwave to finish heating up your food. In Jo's case, a nice low-calorie TV dinner. Something to get her through another lonely night.

She decided to watch Carmen again.

Carmen was still fidgeting. She was getting nervous. For a while, she had been playing with her gun's hammer. Running her thumb over the ridges. Now she had switched to the safety catch.

As Jo watched, Carmen pulled the catch with an audible *click*. The safety was engaged. A second later, she clicked it back. Readying the gun to fire. She kept on doing that, over and over.

Jo pulled her eyes away. But she kept on listening to those clicks. Keeping track of the status of Carmen's gun safety. On. Off. On. Off. On.

It was something. A base on which to build a plan.

Now she just had to come up with the rest.

NINETY-FIVE

As the five minutes came close to being over, the three cultists started getting nervous. They realized they would need to act on their threats. A shootout was coming.

Carmen kept messing with her safety catch. But she was the only one who kept her eyes on the captives. Candy and Whitaker kept looking away. Scanning the room anxiously. Looking for ways out or for things to hide behind.

However, they kept their fingers near their triggers. There wouldn't be enough time to disarm either of them, let alone both. Jo knew she needed something more. An extra edge.

A distraction.

The thought landed in her mind a second later. She reached slyly into her right pocket. With her left, she scratched her chin. If anyone looked at her, they'd pay more attention to the hand doing the scratching.

For a moment, she couldn't remember which pocket she put the car keys in. Or if she had them with her at all. Maybe she had left them in the car. Or set them down when she entered the station. Maybe they had fallen into the snow.

There was a soft jingling sound as her fingers fell on the set of keys. She had to stop herself from smiling. She looked around to see if anyone was watching her. But they were too busy worrying about themselves.

All but Ford. He looked down at her hand, then up into her eyes. She stared back at him. She could tell what he was thinking. He had no idea what she was doing. But he was going to back her up every step of the way.

Jo waited. Her fingers were on the key fob buttons. She couldn't remember which was which. There were three, arranged in a triangle. One was for locking the car. One for unlocking. A third for popping the trunk open.

None of those three mattered. She wanted the button on the back of the fob. The red one that would set the alarm off. She found it but didn't press it. First, she had to make sure some other pieces of the puzzle were in place.

"One minute left," Candy announced.

Jo took a step toward her. "Can I see?"

"What, you don't believe me?" Candy sneered.

"I just want to see the time," Jo said casually.

Candy looked at Whitaker. He nodded. Candy beckoned Jo over.

"Get your hand away from your gun," Whitaker snapped.

Jo nodded. She carefully tucked the keys into her hand and pulled it out of her pocket. As she walked toward Candy, she glanced around the room.

Whitaker and Carmen were standing on the opposite side. They had been very close together, but now they were drifting apart. Carmen was alone now, near Kurt.

Whitaker was still standing in his original spot. Swann was the closest one to him. But it was still a sizable gap. There was four or five feet between them. Swann would need to be quick as lightning. Jo knew he'd be capable of that normally. But tonight, he was running on fumes.

Time was almost up. Jo had to take the chance.

"Here you go," Candy said, sighing, showing the face of her watch. "Forty seconds left. See? You dummies better start thinking fast."

Jo pressed the red button.

The car's headlights started flashing first, lighting up the room with a strobing effect. The sound came a split second later. The blaring alarm.

NINETY-SIX

Whitaker and Candy both reacted the same way. The way anyone without extensive training would react. They immediately looked toward the window, squinting their eyes. The barrels of their guns dropped slightly. A reflex they were unaware of.

A reflex Jo could take advantage of.

She let the keys fall to the floor. She needed both her hands free. There wasn't enough time to unholster her gun, aim, and get a shot off. So instead of arming herself, she decided to even the playing field by disarming her enemy.

She swung her arms in opposite directions. The right hand came down on the butt of Candy's rifle. The left hand came up, gripping the barrel and ripping it toward the ceiling.

It was a lever effect. It caused Candy's gun to aim pretty much straight upward in a fraction of a second. Candy squeezed her trigger. Another reflex she probably wasn't aware of. A single shot went off. It blasted into the ceiling, causing a shower of dust.

The force of Jo's lever effect was still going. It ripped the gun from Candy's grip. The AR-15 fell. It hit the floor and bounced. Phelps's foot shot out, kicking it away.

On the other side of the room, another attack was unfolding.

As soon as Whitaker's gun dropped slightly, Swann sprang into action. He had been watching, paying close attention, and he was just as fast as Jo hoped he would be.

It was still too much of a distance. Whitaker was able to react. He lifted his MP5 and swung it around. He began to fire, spraying bullets in a fan across the room. Jo threw herself to the side to avoid them. She crashed into Candy and pushed the girl forward.

Phelps and Sheri ducked their heads to the side. They barely managed to dodge the hail of gunfire.

Swann ducked to the left. Staying ahead of Whitaker's swinging barrel. He surged forward, getting in close.

Jo and Candy stumbled away from the gunfire. Candy bounced off the wall. She nearly fell but righted herself. She saw her gun on the floor and made a move for it.

Jo was one step ahead. She shot her knee up, connecting with Candy's jaw. Candy made a muffled *oof* sound and fell straight down, splaying on the floor.

"*Carmen!*" Whitaker screamed.

Jo glanced over. Whitaker and Swann were engaged in a tug-of-war over the MP5. Whitaker's eyes were desperate. He was pulling with all his strength. It wasn't enough.

With a final yank, Swann grabbed the gun away. He hauled his right hand back and punched Whitaker in the face. That was all it took. He crumpled, his body folding like an accordion.

Carmen was the final problem. She was too far for anyone to reach and disarm her. She still had her pistol, along with a room full of targets. Any second now, she would start shooting.

Jo jumped over Candy's unconscious body. She dove into a somer-sault, grabbing the AR-15 on the way. She came up feeling dizzy. Her head spun as she looked around, trying to find her target.

If Carmen had started shooting immediately, she might have won the exchange. Instead, she decided to run. Still holding her pistol, she sprinted into the Sheriff's private office. She was out of sight in a flash.

Swann was unsteady on his feet. Fighting Whitaker had taken too much out of him.

McKinley was with Phelps and Sheri, helping them rip away the duct tape.

Jo checked the clip on the rifle. It was full. She stood up to give chase.

Ford suddenly rushed past. His gun was drawn, and he had a very angry look on his face.

"Get some cuffs on those jerks," he said. "And then catch up with me. I'll get Carmen."

NINETY-SEVEN

Ford darted through the door into the back office. He kept his sidearm ready, sweeping it in an arc. Covering the angle. But Carmen wasn't fighting. She wasn't making a stand. She was still running.

Her pistol was tucked into the waist of her pants. She was using both hands to wrench the window open. She tore the screen out and put her hands on the sill. Getting ready to vault through.

"Stop!" Ford shouted. "I don't want to have to shoot you!"

Carmen looked over her shoulder. There was fear in her eyes. But she had been willing to let herself burn for the sake of her beliefs. A bit of fear wasn't going to slow her down, and Ford knew it.

He aimed at the middle of her back. Then he switched to aiming at her legs. He could hit her with a disabling shot. Stop her right in her tracks. He could run up and rip the gun away from her. All remaining cultists would be neutralized.

But he never took the shot.

His finger shook on the trigger. Sweat poured down his face.

Carmen nodded at him. "Thanks for the candy."

She hopped through the window and ran away into the night. Her feet crunched in the snow. The sound faded away.

For a moment, Ford didn't think about Carmen at all. He was no longer in Lapse, Oregon. He was back home with his family. With his wife. And his daughter, Hazel. A little girl whose entire life was ahead of her.

All it took was one bad move, one mistake, one little accident...

It didn't take much to derail a life. To send someone down the wrong path.

He remembered the things Carmen had told him in the basement of that barn. He had every reason to believe they were lies now. But he didn't. He knew it was all the truth. Life had been unfair to Carmen Powell.

She had every chance in the world to shoot. She could have killed any of them. Ford, Jo, Swann, McKinley. The Sheriff and his wife.

Maybe Carmen was just a coward. Or maybe there was something there that was worth trying to save.

Ford cursed at himself. He ran and jumped through the window. Snow-covered ice greeted his feet, making him clumsily slip and fall with a jolt. Ice crackled under his body weight as he struggled back to his feet. He found Carmen's footprints and began following them at a run.

NINETY-EIGHT

Phelps came back out of his office with two sets of handcuffs.

"Here you are," he said, handing one to Jo. "I just saw that Ford fellow take a header out of my window. I suppose he'll need backup."

"That's my next step," Jo told him.

Candy was starting to wake up. The knee to the jaw had knocked a few things loose. She groaned in pain, spitting out blood and teeth fragments.

"You hurt me," she complained, sobbing.

"So what?" Jo said. "Put your hands behind your back, or I'll do it again."

Candy didn't hesitate. She placed both hands in the small of her back. Jo got the cuffs on. She didn't make them tight on purpose. But when they cinched a little too much, she didn't bother loosening them up.

McKinley was working on getting Kurt untied. The ropes were thick, and he was having trouble with the knots.

"Over here," Swann called.

Phelps tossed the other set of cuffs over. Swann caught them. He was currently sitting on Whitaker's stomach, who was awake and very angry.

"Get off me," Whitaker growled. "Right now. I'm unarmed, and you can't treat me this way. I know my rights."

"What rights? I thought you wanted to leave society behind," Swann growled back. "Remember when you cut my finger off? Thankfully, it's one I don't really need. And I can understand you wanted to send me a message."

Whitaker nodded. Jo could almost see him swallowing his anger. "I could have taken more than one finger, Agent Swann. I could have taken your whole hand. But I wasn't trying to do that much damage. I didn't want to. Remember that."

"Oh, I'll remember it for the rest of my life," Swann replied. "I thought you had a sense of morality. Not a normal sense, but at least your own ethical code. But being part of a cult that sanctioned your grandmother's murder? That's cold."

Whitaker shook his head. "Who's murder? What the hell are you talking about?"

Jo's own sense of righteous fury disappeared. She felt a deep sense of pity.

"Oh," McKinley said.

Swann looked at them. "He had no idea."

"No idea about what?" Whitaker roared.

"We'll tell you," Swann said. "But first..."

Whitaker showed his hands. Swann slapped the cuffs on him, then stood up and took a few steps away. Leaving Whitaker lying alone.

"Jo?" Swann said.

"It was Joey Malone," Jo said. "He visited the hotel your grandmother runs and killed her."

"It should have been the only clue I needed," Kurt said. "When I heard that Joseph had done it..."

"You didn't tell me," Whitaker cried.

"One of the many ways I've failed you," Kurt said breathlessly.

"Why did he do it?" Whitaker demanded.

"The sacrifice," McKinley replied, grunting as he yanked at Kurt's knots. "That's what he said when I caught him at the hotel. I guess he was impatient.""Joseph is dead," Kurt added.

McKinley nodded. "I shot him."

Whitaker's eyes filled with tears. "Good. I hope he suffered. I was going to see my grandmother before I left. I visited her all the time. I would go and stand outside the hotel, watching. There are so many times I almost let her see me. Now I wish I would have."

Jo knelt beside him. "Samuel..."

"Call me Sam," he said.

Jo smiled. "That's my brother's name."

Whitaker looked away from her.

"This has been one big mess," Jo went on. "But it'll be pretty clean once it gets to the courts. Even so, we could use someone on our side."

Whitaker nodded. "I'll do it. I'll tell you everything. If this Unet crap attracts people like Joey... I'm done with it all."

Jo tried to think of what to say. *Thank you* seemed like more than this young man deserved.

A realization struck her.

"I saw you outside the hotel when we arrived, didn't I?"

Whitaker nodded again.

"And that is when you began to think of your plan?"

"Yes," Whitaker admitted.

She heard a distant shout from outside. Ford.

"*Carmen! Get back here!*"

Jo jumped to her feet. "Gotta go. Swann, why don't you help McKinley with those ropes?"

NINETY-NINE

"It's all right, I've almost got it..." McKinley dug his fingernails into the rope strands. He pulled so hard that the veins on his neck bulged. The knot finally began to slip.

"Here, son." Phelps pulled a pocket knife off his belt. "Why don't you try this?"

McKinley let go of the rope, catching his breath. "You had that the whole time? And you didn't give it to me?"

Phelps grinned, his mustache twitching. "There's been a shortage of fun around here lately. Thought I'd have some. I also could have tried and used it on that bubblegum girl over there. But then I'd be out one life, plus about a third of my chest cavity from that rifle of hers."

McKinley unfolded the knife and got to work.

"Where's Sheri?" Swann asked.

"Up here," she called from the front. "Making some coffee."

Phelps shook his head. "No stopping that woman. Hopefully, it's decaf, at least."

McKinley finally got the last knot undone. Kurt's hands were freed. He rubbed his wrist, nodding at them all.

"Much obliged," he said. "I've never been tied up before. Never let myself be victimized."

"You tried to see the good side of a bunch of troubled kids," McKinley replied. "You tried to do something good."

Kurt scooted over to the wall. He leaned against it with a sigh. "And it blew up in my face. Yeah, I tried to do something good. Up until a few hours ago, I was feeling like a saint."

Swann sat down cross-legged in front of him. "This has been one crazy night, Kurt. How did it all start? How does it get to this point?"

"In a natural way," Kurt said. "One thing leading to the next. Places like my property tend to attract miscreants. One night not long ago, I decided to go for a stroll. I heard strange noises. Voices and music. I found a whole group of kids in one of my outbuildings, drinking and partying.

"They were all there. Candy. Carmen. Joseph. Samuel. And the rest. They were all friends. They united originally because they were all black sheep. Kids who skipped school, who disliked authority. Kids who thought they were too smart for all that crap. When I caught them that night, they expected me to turn them in. To call the cops, or at least their parents.

"I surprised them. I didn't get mad or yell. I didn't threaten them. I simply asked them what they were doing and why they were doing it. They apologized for using my property. I told them the building was falling down and I didn't care about it. That was how it started. We talked for a while. I explained some things to them."

"Religion?" Swann asked. "Spirituality?"

"Philosophy," said Kurt. "Everyone in the world wants peace. Those kids were no different. Instead of loud music and drinking, I gave them something better. I gave them a sense of eternity. They kept coming back, and I kept talking. I learned about all of them. They all had their reasons for wanting to leave their lives behind. I didn't judge them for doing it. My property became their new home. We developed our little code of honor. Our own faith." Kurt struck his head against the wall. "I was stupid. I thought the last thing those kids needed was an adult bossing them around. But that's what I should have done. I should have been stronger. This is the greatest tragedy of my life."

"Father, I'm sorry," Whitaker sobbed.

"I know you are," Kurt muttered. "Our path was meant to be one of righteousness. Unet was a structure for any unfortunate soul to cling to. The destruction of everything that holds us back from happiness. It was meant to be a spiritual revolution. A way to become free. Now all my kids are either dead or going to prison. And so am I."

ONE-HUNDRED

Jo charged into the back office. She approached the window. Freezing air blew through, depositing snowflakes across the Sheriff's desk. Jo climbed through, dropping to the ground.

She saw two sets of footprints leading into the trees. The bigger set, Ford's, overlaid the smaller tracks. Jo followed them both, keeping her weapon at the ready. It was a clear night. The moon provided plenty of illumination. But there were a lot of trees. Places where Carmen might be hiding, laying a trap.

Suddenly, Ford's footprints veered off to the left. Jo followed them cautiously.

"*Jo!*" Ford's voice hissed at her.

He beckoned to her from behind a tree. She jogged to a nearby oak and put her back to its trunk.

"Glad you caught up," said Ford.

"What's the situation?" Jo asked.

"She's somewhere that way." He pointed deeper into the forest. "I caught a few glimpses. I think she's stopped moving. She's hiding nearby."

Jo nodded. She stepped a bit to her left. Stuck her head out and scanned the landscape. There was very little to see. Most of the trees here were deciduous. They had no leaves. She could see between all the branches.

Then, there was motion. A flash of a flannel jacket. It dashed between two trees. A moment later, Jo saw it again. It was getting smaller, fading into the distance.

"She's moving again," Jo warned.

She and Ford resumed the chase. They ran toward Carmen, taking snaking paths. Staying about ten feet apart at all times. Carmen had been too afraid to shoot inside the station. By now, she might have gotten over her fear. If they got her cornered, she'd fight back.

"Spotted her again," Ford called between labored breaths. "She stopped. Behind that tree up there."

"There are a thousand trees, Ford," Jo answered.

He ignored her. "Carmen! This doesn't need to get any more violent. You can put your weapon down and come out. This is going to end with you in cuffs either way. Do you really want more people to get hurt?"

She didn't answer with words. Another quick burst of movement was their only warning. A muzzle flash burst in the darkness. The snapping sound of a gunshot echoed through the trees. It rolled away and then back toward them like thunder.

Jo hit the ground. Ford did the same. They lay still in the snow for a second. Then they both crawled for cover.

"Are you hit?" Jo asked.

"No," said Ford. "You?"

"I'm good. Now I see which tree she's hiding behind."

"Yeah. The big one with all the roots. I told you."

"You didn't say any of that. I'm going to take a look."

Jo had found a boulder to hide behind. She put one hand against its mossy surface. She pulled herself up, letting the top of her head poke into view over it. It took her a second to get her bearings and find the right tree.

As soon as she spotted it, there was another gunshot.

Jo dropped to the ground. The bullet hit the boulder and ricocheted, whizzing toward the stars.

"She's got good eyes," Jo said through gritted teeth. "And she's still behind the same tree. She's probably still watching me. Can you get eyes on her?"

Ford took a deep breath. He took a quick look, then darted his head back into cover. "Yeah. I see the tree."

"Good," Jo said. "Here's the plan. When I say 'go,' you start pumping lead into the tree. I'll run to my right. Get a better angle. Best case scenario, I get a good shot on her. Worst case, she moves to another tree. We can hit her on the run."

"All right," Ford said reluctantly. "I was hoping it wouldn't come to this... but I'm not going to let her hurt either of us. Ready?"

"Go!"

Jo jumped up and ran for it. Ford laid down suppressive fire, pumping his whole clip into the unfortunate tree. Shredding its trunk with bullets.

He ran out of ammo. The gunfire stopped. Jo positioned herself behind the closest tree. She didn't waste any time, immediately leaning out and aiming toward Carmen's hiding place.

The girl was in the open. Rushing for different cover.

Jo held her breath and fired twice. Carmen didn't slow down. Jo fired once more. This time, Carmen jerked around clockwise. She pirouetted once, stumbled a bit, then half jumped, and half fell into her next hiding spot.

"You got her!" Ford called out.

"Only once," Jo shouted back. "She might be at her most dangerous now. Watch out."

ONE-HUNDRED ONE

Jo and Ford moved in a leapfrogging fashion, running from tree to tree. While one of them was on the move, the other covered them. In this staggered way, they drew closer to where Carmen had gone to the ground.

Jo was afraid the shooting would start again at any second. They were moving targets. Easy for Carmen to spot. On the contrary, Jo and Ford might never spot her. If she was lying low, holding her breath, she'd be pretty much invisible.

When they had closed within ten feet of the target, they heard a whimpering sound. It was Carmen crying in pain.

"It's over," Ford yelled. "You're hurt. This is where it ends."

"Stop following me!" Carmen screeched. "I still have my gun!"

"Be smart about this, Carmen," Jo replied. "You aren't running anymore. Where are you hit?"

Carmen sniffled a few times before answering. "The shoulder. I can't feel my arm. It's all cold."

"You're just in shock, kid," Ford assured her. "You'll be just fine as long as you let us help you. We can get you some medical attention."

"You're going to put me in jail!" Carmen whined.

"That's not up to us. All we can do is make sure you don't bleed to death," Ford added. "Are you going to let us help you?"

A tense moment passed. Jo gripped her pistol firmly. Ready to shoot the first thing that moved.

Something flashed across her vision. She nearly shot it. But it was just the magazine from Carmen's gun. It landed soundlessly in the thick snow. A moment later, it was followed by the gun itself. Empty and harmless.

"Good," Ford cried out with relief. "We're coming around now."

They found Carmen shoved up against the gnarled roots of a tree. She was gripping her wounded shoulder. Applying pressure. Her pretty face was streaked with tears.

"Don't hurt me anymore," she pleaded.

"Of course not." Ford holstered his sidearm. He pulled his belt off, letting his pants sag. "I'm going to put a tourniquet in your armpit. It'll help control the bleeding until we can get you somewhere safe. Just try and relax."

She screamed in pain as Ford lifted her arm. He quickly wound the belt around her shoulder, pulling it tight gradually to avoid any jerking motions.

"Thanks for surrendering," Ford said. "If it came down to us having to kill you... I'd see your face every time I looked at my daughter."

***

Carmen didn't say anything on the way back to the station. She let Ford carry her without complaint. This time, she didn't act exhausted and comatose. She stayed alert, her head swiveling like an owl's.

They entered the station by the front door. The smell of coffee filled the place. Everyone but Candy and Whitaker had cups in their hands. McKinley was at the pot, getting a refill.

"You made it back," Swann said.

Ford set Carmen down and eased her into a chair. Phelps brought out another pair of cuffs and put it on her.

"I'm almost sorry about this," Phelps said. "I appreciate all the tasty grub you've served me at the diner. But I guess that's all in the past."

"It's over for me," Carmen said dully. She kept staring at Swann, hoping for some kind of forgiveness. But he ignored her completely.

"It's not over," Ford said, crouching beside her. "You're still breathing. And trust me, those orange jumpsuits are pretty comfortable. Everyone in prison will know you're in for trying to kill FBI agents. You'll command immediate respect."

"Is that supposed to make me feel better?" Carmen snapped.

Ford shrugged. "Dunno. But it was worth a try. You weren't really going to let yourself burn at the stake, were you?"

"Of course I was," Carmen said defiantly.

"That's crazy."

"The *world* is crazy."

"That's true," said Ford. "But you're crazy too."

Carmen smiled. "What's done is done. All the roads are closed. There's only one left, and I have to go down it. And now I'm taking a vow of silence. Let the world do what it wants with me."

She stopped talking. And Jo had a good feeling that her lips were sealed forever. Nothing Carmen said now could possibly hurt her more than her actions already had. But nothing she said could help her, either.

Why say anything at all?

ONE-HUNDRED TWO

Everything happened quickly after that. Time moved in a blur.

Phelps called the state police while Sheri tended to Carmen's gunshot wound. In less than thirty minutes, the parking lot was swarming with cop cars. Their flashing blue-and-red lights turned the night into a feverish rave.

People came out of their houses to see what was happening. They came down the street in pajamas and winter coats to gawk. Jo thought it was the most excitement the town of Lapse had had since the beginning of time. It took a few angry shouts through a megaphone from a state trooper to finally send the onlookers back to their beds.

A medic tended to Swann's injured hand. Carmen was immediately hauled away to the nearest hospital. Candy and Samuel Whitaker were put in the backs of different cars. While two officers sat with Whitaker and took down his initial testimony, Candy was alone and scared.

Ford thought about going to console her but didn't. His fatherly instincts didn't extend quite that far.

The FBI agents did what they could to pass the torch to the state police. They told their stories in condensed form. They demanded that Kurt be treated well. They also recommended that Kurt be brought to a high-security location. Given his FBI training, he posed a bigger flight risk than his misguided apprentices.

"We all know Kurt's in trouble," Ford said as he and the agents stepped into the parking lot. "But how deep is it?"

"He'll be helped by the fact that he didn't know what the kids were planning," Jo replied. "But he was still basically a cult leader. Who knows where he got all those weapons from?"

"I talked to him while you and Ford were chasing Carmen," said McKinley. "He claims all those weapons were black market. He was buying them and keeping them safe, so no one else could use them for 'misdeeds.'"

Ford laughed in disbelief. But Swann looked convinced. "Kurt Black seems like a pretty unique guy. I can almost believe that story."

***

"That's quite something you've just told me, Agent Pullinger," Grantham said through the phone.

They were back in Jo's room at the Lapse Lodge. Gathered around a box of donuts procured from the local grocery store. The sun was coming up now, and the power was back on. The town was on its way back to normalcy.

"It was a sleepless night," Jo said. "But we learned some things. Like the fact that Kurt Black was *not* leading the cult."

"A technicality," Grantham said.

"Not really, sir. He didn't authorize the sacrifice. That means you owe us all dinner."

"Fine. We'll go out for steak once you're all back in town. Speaking of that, you still have business to finish. Agent Swann is required in Boise."

"No rest for the wicked," Swann replied. "I'll be there."

"You all will," said Grantham. "I've arranged a flight from Boise to Seattle for the rest of you."

"But what about my hand, sir?" Swann asked. "It's been patched up, but I need to get a doctor to look at it. I can't just report in and get to work like nothing happened."

"You are correct, Agent Swann," Grantham conceded. "I'll call the SAC in Boise and request you get some medical leave."

"Thank you, sir," Swann said.

Jo took a big bite out of a glazed donut. "Sir, I think you can cancel my reservation. I was going to let Ford drive the others to Boise."

"That's fine with me," Grantham replied. "But what are you going to do?"

"I was thinking I would actually take that vacation, seeing as this whole road trip turned into a fiasco."

"That it did. Your request for vacation has been granted, Agent Pullinger. Please do not keep me updated. I expect you back in Seattle in five days."

"Four, sir," Jo corrected him.

"Four?"

"That's when my family gets back from their trip. I want to pick them up from the airport."

EPILOGUE

Jo allowed Ford to drive her as far as the next big town. There she found a rental agency and her own ride back to Seattle.

The others saw her off in the rental agency's parking lot. It was easy saying goodbye to Ford and McKinley. After all, she knew she'd be seeing them again soon.

It was harder with Swann.

"Well, this is it," he said awkwardly.

"It is," Jo replied.

"We probably won't see each other again," Swann added sadly.

"Who knows?" said Jo. "Boise and Seattle are relatively close. Our paths could cross in the future."

"Yeah. Maybe." Swann was cheered up by the thought. "Are we friends, Jo? I feel like we might be. But it's not like we've been able to spend much quality time together. I just admire you so much. And I feel like..."

"We're friends," Jo confirmed. "What's more, we were partners."

"We were," Swann added.

"We were. And now it's time to go our separate ways. I think you'll do well in Boise."

Swann groaned. "I hope so. Things can only get better from here, right?"

He was about to walk away. Jo spread her arms wide. Swann grinned and stepped up to her. They hugged.

And then they separated. Jo got into her rental and waved as she drove away. As soon as she was out of sight, she picked a random town in western Oregon and set her GPS to route her there.

Who knows what kind of adventures I might find along the way? she thought.

***

Jo kept her eye on the time while she drove. She was aware of the time difference between where she was and the beachside town her family was staying.

When enough time passed, she gave them a call.

As usual, it was Chrissy who answered. "Auntie Jo! I just found a really cool seashell. I'm going to bring it back, and my mom's gonna make you a whole necklace."

"Better than anything in a souvenir shop," Jo said, laughing. "Still having a good time?'

"The best time! Oh, the waves are coming in!"

Her last words trailed off as Chrissy sprinted for the water. The phone was passed along to her father.

"There she goes," Sam said. "You there, Jo?"

"Of course. You sound... content."

Sam sighed. "It's been amazing. The only thing I can complain about is the sunburn on my pasty Pacific Northwest skin."

"*I* haven't had a problem," Kim added from the background.

"That's because I know how to apply sunscreen to someone's back," Sam answered in mock irritation. "Anyway, we all wish you were here, Jo. Especially Chrissy. Just expect her to talk your ear off when we get back home."

"There's nothing I'd like more."

"You're still planning on picking us up from the airport, right?" Sam asked.

"I'll be there. I'm making my way back to Seattle now."

"Cool. How did things go in Boise?"

Jo smiled to herself. "I'll tell you about that another time. Just enjoy the beach."

The call ended, and Jo was left to sift through her thoughts.

This case might have been the most dangerous she had faced since moving to Seattle, but she felt clean of it already. It was all in the past, and it no longer haunted her. It took her a moment to figure out why.

It was because it happened far away from home. Her loved ones had never been at risk. The case hadn't bled into her personal life. It had all happened in a snowy town she had never heard of. And would never return to.

Maybe, in the future, it would be smart to take more cases away from the city. She was sure Grantham would find some for her if she asked.

Then again, now wasn't the time to think about these things. She was on vacation, too.

It was time to push all decisions into the future. And focus on the road.

BIO

THOMAS FINCHAM holds a graduate degree in Economics. His travels throughout the world have given him an appreciation for other cultures and beliefs. He has lived in Africa, Asia, and North America. An avid reader of mysteries and thrillers, he decided to give writing a try. Several novels later, he can honestly say he has found his calling. He is married with two kids, and he lives in a hundred-year-old house. He is the author of **LEE CALLAWAY** series, the **HYDER ALI** series, the **MARTIN RHODES** series, and the **ECHO ROSE** series.

Made in the USA
Columbia, SC
28 August 2024

41256402R00189